Deadly Mission

Dr. Sublett faced them across the OR table much as she had faced them across the fallen tree at their first meeting. Just as she had then, she kept the rifle leveled.

"Now listen carefully. What I'm about to say is of utmost importance and time is running out. I have a proposition for you, Mr. Rosst, that would be most foolish of you to try to turn down. While I keep your family hostage here, I shall send you on a mission. If you fulfill it—and with your reputation for cleverness I believe you won't fail—I shall in turn provide you all with impeccable documents of identification and insure your safe passage to England immediately afterward. I believe England is where you want to go?"

A tense silence ticked along. Then Larch said, "What sort of mission?"

"Not a simple one, but this is no longer a simple world. I want you to kill Jacot Mosk."

CADUCEUS WILD
Ward Moore
with Robert Bradford

A Futorian Book

PINNACLE BOOKS   LOS ANGELES

CADUCEUS WILD

Copyright © 1978 by Ward Moore

An original Pinnacle Books edition, published for the first time anywhere.

ISBN: 0-523-40246-5

First printing, February 1978

Cover illustration by Howard Darden

Printed in the United States of America

PINNACLE BOOKS, INC.
One Century Piaza
2029 Century Park East
Los Angeles, California 90067

Thanks to Jean Ariss, novelist, critic, friend,
for her help in the original weaving of this tale.

Cur'd yesterday of my disease, I died last night of my physician.
—Matthew Prior

In the Third Reich, I decide who is a Jew.
—Hermann Goering

A good number of our ailments are, frankly, iatrogenic.
—Anonymous twentieth-century M.D.

AUTHOR'S NOTE

Although this is a new book, recently written, it is not the first *Caduceus Wild* with which my name has been associated.

The original *Caduceus Wild* appeared in *Science Fiction Stories*, edited by Robert A. W. Lowndes, as a four-part serial in the issues January through April, 1959, under the by-line of Ward Moore and Robert Bradford, and was a collaboration by novelist Jean Ariss, Robert Bradford, and myself.

Since then, this world has changed and so have some of our expectations about future worlds. At the same time, many of our anxieties and forebodings have remained.

For this reason, an effort has been made to build the new novel upon the ideological armature of the original, and to use, wherever possible, material conceived for the original work.

Ward Moore

CADUCEUS WILD

Larch

Struggling up over the last rise, the small, clattering train with only two passengers left aboard exhaled a gray, diesel miasma into the clear, still air of the wilderness as it halted at the final station.

"This has gotta be it," said the boy, jumping down into the midafternoon sunlight. "End of the line. But where's Shelby?"

The man alighted on the station platform only a little less actively. He was forty-two, passing for thirty-five, with a well-built, cared-for body and only a light dusting of silver through his dark brown hair and darker brown beard. "Cool it, Jode," he cautioned his ten-year-old companion. "No names, remember? Forget I just called you by yours, and let's both avoid mentioning hers; too many people know it. While we're at Orthohaven we keep a low profile, as they used to say back in the twentieth century."

"Okay, Larch—whoops! Sure is hard to remember. But where's my sister?"

"She wasn't supposed to meet the train. We've got a hike through the woods ahead of us to get to where she'll be waiting. You up to it?"

"Let's go!" Jode yelled. He tugged at his backpack to adjust it, raced to the side of the platform, and jumped off beside a small sign with an arrow pointing out a trail through the redwoods.

Larch shrugged into his own pack and began to stride in the same direction.

"Just a minute . . . *sir*."

The stocky young woman had emerged from the tiny shack of a station in absolute silence, a feat made possible by the thick, flat crepe soles of her improbably white oxfords.

Larch groaned and made the expected, ritual complaint. "Oh, no. Not here too? You people are incredible. Whoever heard of a medcheck in the middle of the forest primeval?"

The nurse smiled with a bright lack of sincerity. She held out a stubby, scrubbed-looking pink hand. "Goodhealth. And now your chart, please. And also your son's chart, if you're carrying it for him."

"My nephew," Larch corrected, and belatedly returned the formula greeting. "Goodhealth."

Jode, who had returned from the woods path, dropped his jaw as if about to speak, then closed his mouth and looked with close attention at Larch, apparently determined not to miss any cues in the drama about to be played out.

4

From a pocket of his heavy jacket Larch removed two plastic-bound folders about the size of passports but with many leaves bound thickly into their spines. One, however, was noticeably thicker than the other, marking the difference between an adult's chart and a child's. He handed them over. "This way," the nurse ordered, leading them toward the open door behind her.

The tiny station was spare and functional, divided at its center by a scrupulously clean, white-topped counter behind which the woman now stepped, keeping Jode and Larch standing on the opposite side, putting the proper official distance between them and herself as she examined their documents.

The far end of the counter was obviously the railroad department. A sheaf of schedules, a reel of tickets, a locked steel cashbox. The near end, where they were being received, was something else. Behind the nurse loomed a battery of equipment: three shelves full of bottled and packaged pharmaceuticals; a glass case of small medical instruments including suture equipment, suction bulbs and levine tubes, syringes, ophthalmoscopes, otoscopes and other spotlights, probes and expanders for all orifices, clippers, scalpels, forceps. And on the wall a pair of sphygmomanometers, one mercury, one aneroid.

"You're Jimmy Archer, eh?" Nurse looking at Jode critically. "All your shots seem to be up to date. No recent illnesses, no injuries." Jode said nothing.

She transferred her attention to the second folder, turned toward Larch. Reading laboriously, slowly, brow creased: "Fred Koyne. Thirty-five.

5

Master plasterer. Three ribs fractured in construction accident five years ago. Treated, healed, cleared. Vasectomy on required date. Innoculations maintained, current clearance. Organs consigned at clinical death to Ama Transplant Bank System, etcetera, etcetera. Mmmm."

To preserve his outward calm, Larch concentrated on the official caduceus badge in black enamel which she wore on the wingtip of her uniform collar, thought: *Why not a rendering of an endoscope as a more appropriate symbol for the World Medarchy? It keeps the Doctor so preoccupied with peering into a Patient's insides that the Patient might, with luck, be able to right a few wrongs in the outside world without the Doctor suspecting.*

The stocky nurse in white was still taking her sweet time over Larch's records, her forehead holding the frown of concentration.

I should be feeling more tense than this, Larch realized. *This woman could clobber us, right here, at the very beginning of our dash to freedom. She could find something "wrong" with one of us, real or imaginary, and cost us days, weeks of delay.* Their chances depended solely on her mood and inclination. There was no doubt that she had the power. Since there was no other official at the station, and only one desk, she obviously served as station chief and ranking medical police officer for the whole Orthohaven area.

Had Shelby been wrong, perhaps, in choosing this place as a rendezvous and temporary hideout? It was inaccessible to Patients except by way of the funky train they had just debarked from, running on its anachronism of a railroad, a museum piece,

6

built generations after railroading had become obsolete. But to Doctors and others certificated to own cars and airhoppers it was a matter of an hour's drive or a quarter-hour's hop from the city. Only Doctors could expect to have their presence go unquestioned, however. For Orthohaven was a vacation retreat for the cream of medical society. A few members of the Ama, law-making body of the continental government, and members, wives and families (adoptive) of the CGP (Cloned Generation of Physicians) owned property here, as well as a few other renowned specializing practitioners. Somewhere hidden away in the densely forested mountains was the Summer Whitehouse, holiday home of Owen Carvey, Surgeon General of America, the office being an amalgam of three former positions of some power: President of the United States, President of Mexico, and Prime Minister of Canada. In the vernacular of another age, Carvey would thus have been top dog; in 2055, inevitably, he was Top Doc.

It was this very quality of rarification among the regular residents, of course, which had led Shelby to choose Orthohaven. Who would think of looking here for a party of Abnormals about to flee the continent?

No law in the Ama's civil and criminal code actually forbade an ordinary person from visiting Orthohaven, but since there were no public recreational facilities, there was no point. No one used the passenger accommodations on the thrice-weekly train except an occasional cook or maid whose job was with some resident family, or a retainer and his wife homeward bound after a visit in the city.

7

For even with a devastatingly shrunken world population, there was never a lack of domestic help at Orthohaven or at any other Doctor-owned country estate anywhere else. Even a half-century after the dropping of the last bacterial bomb, the cities of the world were avoided by everyone who could possibly get employment—or any other kind of living arrangement—elsewhere. It was in the metropolitan centers, of course, where the pandemics had culled most ruthlessly, paring down the earth's billions, once such a threat in themselves, by more than sixty percent. All past history now, but memories were long, and human beings by nature fearful that history might, somehow, repeat itself.

Upon this very fear rested the whole interwoven fabric of world government: the Medarchy. Supreme authority vested in a select few. For at the time of the exploding of the aerosol germ bombs in the last stages of the war, the ascendancy of physicians went unquestioned. Doctors had to be in complete charge of survivors in order to prevent further epidemics, dietary mistakes, and total chaos. Doctors' orders thus became the only legal and legitimate orders. Unchallenged.

Unchallenged, that is, except in secret (so far) by a scattered but growing world underground movement of which Larch Rosst was a part, along with his fiancee, Shelby Harmon.

Larch had spent long hours just before boarding the train risking his neck to find and return to Shelby's care her brother Jode, who despite his young age had been arrested for questioning and "treatment" by the medical police, or Medcops.

"Hey, Uncle Fred," Jode said now, "how about us getting on the road?"

"Steady, nephew. We have to wait for this lady to be through with us."

Seeming not to hear, the nurse continued to study Larch's forged chart, turning the leaves slowly. At last she snapped the folder shut. "It seems to be in order," she said reluctantly.

Reluctantly because she suspected something amiss among the carefully falsified data? Or because boredom must loom large in such a job as hers and she preferred to detain as long as possible what few Patients passed through the dinky train terminal at Orthohaven? More likely the latter, Larch decided.

She could hardly be called an attractive girl. Too big-boned and thick-figured for her short stature. Did any man—could any man—love this woman with the single-minded, dedicated passion he himself felt for Shelby Harmon? Certainly not with the insane, all-but-uncontrollable, young man's devotion he had lavished upon his first love, Kira, who had died a martyr very early in the underground cause. Yet who was he to say? In the unscientific business of love, these illogical possibilities abound. It seemed likely, however, the stocky nurse had put all her resources into her job, in order to have risen to a substantial post at her age (which he judged to be about the same as Shelby's). He had by now noticed that she was a full lieutenant in the nurses' corps of the Medcops, her rank announced on the collar-tip opposite the one with the black caduceus.

Their examiner had briskly popped a thermometer into Jode's mouth and at the soft sound of the bleep briskly removed and read it. Her failure to note anything further on Jode's chart indicated—

fortunately for them—that he was running no fever.

"And in whose house in Orthohaven will you be plastering, Fred Koyne?"

"Wha—? Ah." The fact that she chose that moment to insert the thermometer, covered anew with a plastic shield, into his own mouth gave him a moment to phrase his answer. At the sound of the bleep, he said, "No plastering for me this week, Lieutenant. We're just on a visit to my brother. He's a gardener at Dr. Freehausen's estate."

It was perfectly true there was a gardener named Phil Koyne on the Freehausen estate. Larch knew Phil Koyne's personal history forward and backward, just in case the questioning became more rigorous.

The real Koyne was a memory defective, having undergone "modification" in compliance with a court sentence. Presumably no layman knew exactly what the treatment entailed, except that it was permanent, irreversible, and a replacement for the crude lobotomies and psychotropic drugs of the previous century. Several years before, Koyne had been arrested and convicted of a burglary involving manslaughter. While his ability as a gardener remained unimpaired, by now he couldn't recall if he had a brother named Fred or not. And in any case the story was not immediately checkable. On principle, because it was a vacation home, there was no telephone line to the estate of the mildly eccentric but famous hemotologist Dr. Freehausen.

But all Larch's homework now proved unnecessary. After a quick job on Larch with the mercury sphyg (the Iatrarchy was hell on checking BP for everyone over twenty-one), the white-garbed,

10

crepe-shod female lieutenant lifted a thin upper lip in what in another woman might have signified a wistful smile. "Well, have a good visit to your brother."

Larch was quick to recognize her benediction as highly unusual compared with the acerbic commands and irritated comments usually doled out to Patients by officers in the Medcops, including especially checking nurses. Most of the past century's courtesies had long since dropped away. She had not once called him "Mr." nor uttered a "please." (Please open wide. Just relax now, please. Please remit.) True, she had called him "sir" when she first came out of her office to intercept them, but that had been understood by all concerned to be largely sarcastic. The fact they had detrained from the local shuttle, and their clothing—old-style bluejeans, hiking boots, and windbreakers—plainly marked Larch and Jode as ordinary Patients entirely unconnected either as family or friends with the medical regime, or that part of it which inhabited Orthohaven.

Larch nodded noncommitally at their interrogator and the pair trudged away from the little building bearing the sign, ORTHOHAVEN, *District of California, Elev.* 1563 *m.*, Larch keenly aware that the nurse was watching them out of sight. *She could still call us back for some infringement or afterthought*, he decided. *Hey, you, I forgot to give you a pill, an injection for typhus, urinalysis, prophylaxis, tracheotomy, barium enema, duodenal biopsy, psychoanalysis, hemogram, radiation therapy, leuko-phoresis—whatever.*

How he hated them all! Yet as a reasonable man he had long since learned how to hate ideologies

11

as opposed to individuals, and how to focus that hate into productive activity. For by his own definition he was a political objector. And by *their* definition an incurable Ab (official name for people like himself and Shelby, whose anomaly might be physical, psychological, or even congenital), since anyone objecting to the Iatrarchy was clearly classifiable as a psychological deviate, or Abnormal.

The word "Iatrarchy" itself had taken on a specialized meaning in the new medical culture. It now designated the North American quarter of the four main geographically arranged sections of the World Medarchy, the American Doctors having opted for a purist rendering of two Greek roots meaning "government by doctor" rather than the Latin-Greek mongrel word which might be misinterpreted as meaning government by the science of medicine. Which might in turn leave room for biochemists, metabolic physiologists and godknowswhat other borderline professionals to begin giving orders too.

Each section had, in fact, its own pet idiosyncrasies. In continental Eurasia the Medburo had been named by the Slavics but organized by the Teutonics with impressive efficiency. There Doctors were easier to distinguish from Patients at a glance; the former wore uniforms and were assigned rank, from the lowliest Schütze, or first-year medical student, to the Haupt Chirurg himself. Surnames were largely dispensed with, to help erase any bothersome sense of the personal between physician and supplicant. (*I have this pain when I cough, Herr Doktor Oberst.*)

Unabashed hero worship was a feature of the South American Regimiento Medicamentoso.

12

There equestrian statues of El Cirujano had sprung up like crocuses in public squares, and around his dashing image much folklore had accumulated. No one was sure, after a few years, if El Cirujano, seen always at a distance waving from balconies or from behind the obscuring explosion-proof glass of his Daimler, was one man or several. But no one ever asked.

A not dissimilar situation existed in Africa, except that there the mysterious and invulnerable Madaktari was given to sudden appearances among his people. He would materialize among a chain gang repairing a railroad on some far-flung veldt, or appear wearing only a loincloth and sitting in a marketplace exhorting chance listeners about habits of health.

On all four major continents, however, society was equally rigidly stratified into the two acceptable layers, Doctors and Patients, the governors and the governed.

"Oh, just a minute. You there, come back." Larch, now far down the woods trail, immediately froze. Jode, still taking his cues from his rescuer, imitated the action. *So it's happened*, Larch thought. *She's smarter than I suspected. Not simply bored, she's uncovered some chink in the armor, blast her. Trouble with me is, my worst reveries are always realized.*

At least I won't give her the satisfaction of walking back to the front of the station, Larch decided. He stood his ground, as did his small shadow, Jode, and to Larch's considerable surprise the nurse bustled down to where they waited on the woods path. "Forgot to find out how long you'll be staying in Orthohaven. Need it for my records here."

Was that really all she had in mind? "Four or five days, maybe a week."

"Don't forget to allow enough time to check in with me again on the way back. Before train time."

We'll never come back here if I can avoid it, Larch thought. He said, "Will do. Thanks for the reminder." Was this really part of her official routine, or had she already signaled the Medcops when he and Jode had their backs turned, possibly with a communication device concealed in the pocket of that impossibly white uniform? Was she only stalling them now until help came? Help for herself and the Iatrarchy, that is. No help for them. They'd be finished off one way or another, especially if word had already spread about Jode's rescue from the facility. A serious offense, kidnapping from a government institution, far worse than a prison break in the old days. Maybe under the circumstances her signal had gone direct to the Subcutes (Surgical Bacterial Custodial Technicians, the elite corps of the police, assigned to emergency cases).

Once again that harelike slight lifting of the upper lip that was not quite a smile. "Is Jimmy a son of your brother?"

Surely this proved the worst. She was going to make conversation that would hold them there the necessary few minutes. Larch moved nearer to Jode and laid an arm around his shoulders. "No, he's our late sister's boy, Phil's and mine." Here he lowered his eyes and swallowed in an apparently painful way. (No accident that Larch as a young student had been torn between architecture and theater. Trouble with the latter would have been there wasn't much around these days, except for the

14

ubiquitous OR theater. Wasn't much call for architects either, unless they were content to do donkey-work drafting, endlessly cranking out plans for the block- and bulb-shaped medical facilities that dotted the half-empty and deteriorating cities like mushrooms on rotted logs.) "The boy's mother was—" *Inspiration here,* and a forgiveable borrowing from his own real life. "—a nurse like you, Lieutenant, only not in the medical police, just on the staff at one of the facilities. She—uh—contracted a bronchial infection—terrible cough, quite obvious—and on her way back to the Facility for official medication one night after her shift she was caught by a gang of Mercifuls and . . ."

Larch let the story trail off meaningfully. He felt Jode watching him with rueful but open admiration. How did one manage to instill in a child of the underground the old-fashioned negative virtues? (Don't ever tell a lie.) But Jode should be used to these glib and outrageous improvisations. On other occasions he had been passed off as Larch's son, stepson, pupil, cousin. Still, Larch's histrionic recitals never failed to draw an appreciative look from Jode.

This one had the unexpected effect of touching off a larger response than he'd figured on in the unpredictable lieutenant. This time the rabbit in her disappeared in favor of the bitch. The lips drew back in a definite snarl. "Why, those filthy swine," she growled. "What right have *they* to take the law into their own hands? Abs—all of them. Ought to be rounded up to the last one and thanatized in the *old* way. Not painlessly the way we do it now, make them *feel* it. Myself, I've always been for law and order and doing things the right way. But

15

there's nothing makes me madder than to hear a story like that one—about your poor sister."

"Yes, well, uh, I—" So he'd overdone it a bit, evoked an overload of sympathy. Now she'd want to hear more, and he wasn't up to an encore. "I don't like to speak of it too much. You can understand, in front of the boy?" He glanced tentatively at Jode and discovered a delighted grin which was—if such transposition is possible—not on his lips but in his unflinching green eyes, eyes like Shelby's. He could only hope the nurse didn't see it. Feeling doubly threatened, he decided to take a chance that she was not, after all, waiting to have them arrested. "So if you're through with us, I guess we'd better be getting on our way."

He took a step down the path. So did Jode. She didn't try to stop them again. You really *are* a bitch, he thought. Why can't you see that your outfit and the renegade Mercifuls are only two sides of the same damned coin? A moment ago you'd have liked nothing better than to discover some incipient ailment in one of us that would allow you to dispatch us to the nearest facility.

"You know the way?" she called. "To Dr. Freehausen's estate?"

"Well enough. We can find it."

Obviously she didn't believe it. "Take this trail for about two kilometers till it forks, take a left and go till you come to the dry falls. Can't miss it. A right there and about a kilo more'll bring you right to the driveway."

"Thanks. Goodhealth."

"Goodhealth."

This time she went back up the trail and withdrew into her tiny station, probably to wait out her loneliness until another train arrived in two days' time.

They tramped the path in silence for a few minutes, Jode in the lead, setting a good pace. For all his having been reared by his sister Shelby in the poverty of the underground, with nutrition—particularly the supply of fresh vegetables and fruits—always a concern, he was a sturdy child on the threshold of becoming a handsome adult. His highly expressive face with those clear green eyes that could emit signals of adoration or wry humor was not only a match for Shelby's but also for that of their dead father, Gerrod Harmon, who in life had been Larch's friend.

The trail wound through an impressive stand of California redwoods, very massive at the trunk and tall enough to blot up the sun, which gave the ground cover of the forest a moist warmth under thick shade. Higher in these coastal mountains jack pine and ponderosa thrived in the same way. But these forests were strangely quiet, oddly free of the multiple rustlings of small mammals and the flurry and chirping of birds, the clatter and whirr of insects. True, certain species were said to be coming back, but no one knew—no single expert really knew—exactly to what degree the germ aerosols had damaged the ecological balance. It was one of the blindnesses of the Iatrarchy, its insistence that no money, energy or time be expended in what it officially considered peripheral considerations. Everywhere in the world "the people first" had been the motto during the last days of the war and the years of aftermath, a defensible position, certainly, in those earlier times.

The same thinking was responsible for the

anachronisms in other areas of the society which prevailed at mid-21st century. The curiously outmoded means of production and transportation, for instance. The biocide assault had left factories, superhighways, air facilities, and communications systems undamaged, but with very few knowledgeable people left to run these factories and maintain the vehicles and the systems.

This seemed not to concern the medics much, then or now. They concentrated on taking care of their own, and in all fairness had performed a miracle of self-perpetuation. The cloning of human beings, for example, a perfected technique at the new *fin de siècle,* was used exclusively to "save" the talents and skills of hundreds of medical specialists whose original bodies had succumbed (or were succumbing) to the bacterial ravages. Another perhaps defensible action at the time, performed in the name of Public Health. For cloning the best minds among engineers, astronomers, space technicians, geologists, agronomists, artists, business executives, architects—not to consider plumbers, carpenters, shopkeepers, artisans—would not lead so directly to benefiting the whole (or what was left of the) human race, would it?

Thus, in abandoning all science and technology but their own, the medics had been correct. Who could argue that? There was at least sufficient truth in their position to give pause to any opposition argument through all these years. Until the Abs began to organize.

Larch had met Shelby as a result of this organizational activity a decade ago when he was invited to the home of Gerrod Harmon, the only Ab so far who had actually had the temerity to make his views public. In a fearless gesture he had declared his own candidacy for Surgeon General of America. At the time Dr. Harmon himself ranked high in government as a member of the Ama, and personal physician to the then SG. But his radical views were against him from the start, and it was the candidacy itself which caused Harmon and all his family to be declared Abs by the authorities. Although the Iatrarchy had been careful to preserve, at least nominally, the civil rights of the free election and the secret ballot, it was midway through the campaign that Harmon's controversial name and distinguished face had begun appearing on the familiar posters which proliferated on the walls of public buildings:

> WANTED
> For Treatment
> The patriotic cooperation of all Patients is sought in discovering the whereabouts of this Abnormal. Notify your local office of the Medical Police.

By that time Harmon was in hiding in a remote cabin in these very mountains, not far from Orthohaven. Knowing he would eventually be caught, he spent his time busily writing down all he knew of corruption and crime at the top of the Iatrarchy.

Publication of the story through underground channels (using the system of *samizdat* which became so efficient in late 20th century Russia) had not been accomplished before Dr. Harmon was arrested and thanatized after a "trial" presided over by the man who had "won" the election, Owen Carvey.

But the writing had been finished. Larch carried the manuscript with him at this very minute, transposed to microfilm and concealed in a razor box in his backpack. Even Jode didn't know this, but he had been told that if anything "happened" to Larch while they were together, he (Jode) was to grab Larch's pack and deliver it to his sister Shelby if it were humanly possible.

Not that carrying the film was as dangerous as it might have been in some past era when luggage was searched on the least suspicion by zealots at the borders of nations and the terminals of public carriers. Less imaginative perhaps, though far more thorough in other respects, the investigators for the Iatrarchy often passed over luggage, pockets and mailings but looked unfailingly into bodies and minds. And it was true enough that a Patient whose thoughts were judged worth scanning with the aid of chemicals and read-out machines didn't have much chance of keeping anything from the authorities. Larch hoped that in his own case it wouldn't come to that. And it hadn't, yet.

In that time ten years back, though, the manuscript had not yet taken form. Larch had entered Gerrod Harmon's hideaway home and been struck as forcefully by Harmon's family as by his demonstrated courage and his plans for the book. The single room of the lodge was slightly untidy, but in a comfortable way, with a melting warmth coming from the large fireplace, hassocks and pillows scattered about on a room-sized rag rug, and books and papers everywhere.

When Harmon led the visitor through the door,

the doctor's fourteen-year-old daughter Shelby came to greet them, courteously shaking hands with Larch before throwing herself ecstatically into her father's embrace. "How's the baby, honey?"

Larch thought Gerrod meant the inquiry for the girl herself, but she answered, "Jode's doing fine. I think he's getting another tooth. Marty and I took him for a walk this afternoon."

Gerrod stiffened visibly at this seemingly innocuous news. "But I told you not to—were you careful? Did you meet anyone on the trails?"

"Not anyone, Daddy. Marty carried Jode most of the way. We thought we saw a squirrel but it got away too fast—and I only know what they look like from pictures in books. Marty thought it was, though."

This Shelby had a girl's voice but a woman's burgeoning figure and strong features. Reflections from the firelight played in her gauzy dark hair and the clear depths of the green eyes. She was neither shy nor forward. Her gestures were confident, her smile serene. She was—quite simply—beautiful.

"My daughter has certainly had responsibility thrust on her," Gerrod had remarked later to Larch. "Alice—that's my wife; you never met her—died in this very room six months ago of an endometrial cancer she'd developed without our suspecting it during her pregnancy with Jode."

Harmon shrugged helplessly. "A cluster of ironies here: no one these days dies of cancer, it's ninety-eight percent curable; it wasn't possible in our situation to apply for surgical help, they would have wiped us all out immediately; and finally, I'm a doctor—or once was—and wasn't able to help her. Not just because my field was epidemiology

21

and not gynecology, but because I had no access in the end to anything that would have helped. Sedatives, morphine.

"Shelby's been great with her little brother, though. And we have Marty staying with us some of the time. She's a nurse who was on my staff years ago when I was employed—God forgive me—at one of the facilities."

About a year after Larch's visit to the Harmons (the first visit followed by many more), Dr. Harmon was fortunately able to send both his children to safety before his arrest.

His last message, to the children and to his friends in the underground, was found later, scrawled in charcoal on the stones of the fireplace in the ransacked lodge, done probably in the moments Harmon spent waiting for the surrounding Subcutes to take him. "This too shall pass away—but only if we insist on it." There was no doubt in any of their minds that Gerrod had meant not their grief at his death, which was to be considered unimportant, but the Iatrarchy itself, and its worldwide extension, the Medarchy.

They had threaded the shady trail so long in silence that Larch now began to wonder if something was bothering the usually ebullient and talkative Jode, still forging on ahead at the same even, quick pace. He was about to speak when Jode, not slowing down, called over his shoulder, "Things still look okay for us, wouldn't you say, Larch? I mean, if that big mamma back there had spotted anything wrong with our charts, we'd already be on our way back to the Facility."

"Well, I've always leveled with you, Jode, and always intend to, no matter what happens. And if you really want my opinion, I'm not going to heave any sighs of relief till we're actually on the plane out of the country. And by the way, we're at it again, using real names. I'm your Uncle Fred. Better keep calling me that just to keep in practice, huh?"

"Sure thing, Unk."

"And you're on your way to visit your good old Uncle Phil."

"Right."

"And you have never even heard of anyone named Shelby Harmon."

"Never in a million years. But all this saying we're somebody we're not doesn't do any good, does it, under interrogation? Because they use those things where they, like, look into your brain and see what you're thinking?"

"I was just musing about that business myself a few minutes ago. Yes, it's far more sophisticated than the old so-called lie-detector and the drugs like sodium pentothal. You'd have found out this morning what it's like, I guess, if we hadn't got you out of that facility just in time."

"Wow! I sure would've. They'd already talked about 'interrogating the child' before you walked into the cubicle in that funny white suit with the pants too short. I was really scared. Besides, can you figure what it's like being called a 'child' by a bunch of dummies who you know are so much dumber than your own dad that if he were alive now he wouldn't even bother to speak to them, even when they're in his own profession?"

"Yeah, I can appreciate that, Jimmy my boy. You're no child, and that's for sure. You've had to lead the life of a quick-witted and very clever adult for most of your conscious years. You're wrong, though, about your dad. He would have been willing to talk with the flunkies in the Iatrarchy or anyone else. He was a very articulate man and he never gave up on the notion than an exchange of spoken ideas brings understanding—eventually. That's why he tried to run for office, not with any hope of winning, just to give himself a platform from which to deliver his views, which did not happen to coincide with the views of those in power. Who knows, if he'd been allowed to do what he set out to do, how many people might have gained the courage to agree with him, even some in the Iatrarchy itself? Not everyone born to this age is unreasonable. At least I'm not able to believe that. Most are just caught up in the status quo, as happens in every age."

They reached the fork in the trail. "We go left here," Jode asked, "like Miss Thing said?"

"No, take a right. We don't want to end up anywhere near the Freehausen estate or poor Phil Koyne, though I'm sure Koyne's harmless enough."

"Then where *are* we going?"

"Follow me and you'll see, nephew. It's a far piece, farther than Freehausen's place, maybe. But we'll get there before dark or my name ain't Frederick P. Koyne."

Jode grinned appreciatively at the joke, an old one between them now, and Larch, having sensed Jode's accumulating weariness, probably before he was aware of it himself, took the lead this time, settling into a slightly easier gait. No need to knock themselves out at this stage of the journey; they'd need plenty of energy for whatever might come, though he admitted to himself that, had he been alone, he might have jogged down this path, even run, for at the end of it Shelby waited for them.

Run several kilometers without a breather at forty-two years old? Sure. He was in good shape after having avoided hundreds of regular full physical checkups required by law over the years. (Perhaps because of this avoidance?) The fictitious Fred Koyne was only thirty-five, anyway, and not once in the several weeks he'd been using these particular spurious documents had his age been questioned by any checking nurse. That ought to prove something.

Under different circumstances, his real age could have presented a major problem. Even had they not been Abs, he would have been unable, at forty-two, to marry Shelby under Iatrarchy regulations. She was only twenty-four. Marriage and the propagation of carefully planned and officially permitted children was an institution dear to the hearts of the Iatrarchists. But like all else, only on their own terms.

For an interminable and convoluted list of reasons, some of them opaque, others perhaps medically, geneologically, or sociologically sound, only certain Patients were permitted to mate legally with certain other Patients. Literally a clean bill of mental and physical health was prerequisite (as it was in fact simply for continuing one's very life as a citizen of the state), and also a difference of not more than five years in the ages of the applicants. From here the list nosedived into a quagmire of restrictions involving racial characteristics, body proportions, bone structures, blood types, brain types, dental configurations, intelligence quotients (now called the Sapington Scores after a psychometrist credited with perfecting the testing methods), childhood environmental considerations, forebears for five generations, and on and on.

Those applicants without the stamina to hang in for the several months required to accumulate and collate all the information often gave up the idea of marriage. Others—like Larch and Shelby—with insurmountable "wrong" answers to key questions simply did what has been done in nearly all human societies since society began. They enjoyed their love without sanction of authority.

Permission to bear children was even more restrictive, however, and extra-wedlock pregnancies were aborted without appeal. Ideal reproductive years were considered to be between twenty and thirty-five for males, between eighteen and twenty-eight for females. And once a Patient had reached the cut-off age, married or single, he or she automatically received a vasectomy or tubal ligation (usually on the relevant birthday) as part of his or her regular medical regimen.

One might imagine, then, that otherwise healthy couples already sterilized as over-age for parenthood might be allowed to seek waiver of the connubial requirements and receive official sanction of a marriage for companionship, sexual or otherwise. Not so. Once the laws were on the books there was no changing them or circumventing them. The Iatrarchy was nothing if not "fair" to all. ("If we made an exception for you, we'd have to make one for everybody, now wouldn't we?") Several times arguments had raged in Ama sessions over the marriage laws, some speakers claiming that any amendment to this or any other statute would be a crack in the dike and a detriment to Public Health, others admitting to not understanding the reasoning involved in the laws themselves. And yet the reasoning was ridiculously simple: scrupulous and detailed regulation of every phase of living was, in Iatrarchy belief, the only way to retain a firm, paternalistic hold over the bodies and minds of all Patients.

Anything, at any time, even the ostensible freedoms of speech, press and individual movement within one's own country, might without warning have to be curtailed if it happened to encroach upon the area of Public Health. And since only the Doctors could decide when an encroachment had occurred, or was about to occur, there was little chance of any kind of political breakthrough by legal means. Witness the experience of Gerrod Harmon.

There had been times in Larch Rosst's life when he deeply regretted having become an unemployed architect instead of a doctor like his friend Gerrod. For at least Harmon had had an insider's knowledge of what had gone rotten in the state, and exactly how the rot was being perpetuated.

In this respect most of the members of the Ab resistance were handicapped, for only a few were Doctors. Several hundred years ago, all you needed to start a revolution was numbers and muskets. Now you needed knowledge, *their* kind of knowledge. A lack of it kept you under their thumbs. Who can argue with a physician who tells you you have a diseased liver? A diseased psyche? The ability to cure (or assist nature in curing) had always depended upon a specific kind of knowledge and probably always would. Hence the practice of

27

medicine, like the church, required a secret brotherhood of the initiated committed to withholding its lore from the layman who could only put it to misuse.

Though he had more than qualified in the tests by means of which government universities selected students for their medical schools, Larch as a young man had rejected the chance out of personal revulsion for what the profession of medicine had become. So had many equally qualified others. There was no pressure on these defecting students, no overt pressure. They were allowed to go their ways, electing to warp their otherwise superior minds with arts disciplines of little or no practical value to the society.

But they had been watched as incipient Abnormals. He knew that now, and often wondered why he had not suspected it much earlier.

Occasionally it even seemed to him, as an amateur student of history with plenty of leisure for reading in a small architectural office visited by very few clients, that time had actually come full circle. Now it was learning such as his own which was not taken seriously, whereas in the eighteenth century the doctor himself had been a figure of fun. Barber-chirurgeon with his leeches, cups and basins, salves and purges. Called Quack, from quicksilver, specific for syphilis. Dose them, bleed them, and watch them die. Next came the fad for Jenner's cowpox, followed by the subtle advance of the physician from valet to authority, Figaro to Lord Lister, servant to master.

And the arrival of Science with the initial capital. If Science could invent a breechloading rifle to kill a man a mile away, then Science could save his life. If Science could wipe out virtually all the animal life in whole cities with an aerosol bomb exploded two kilometers in the air overhead, didn't that establish its right to rule the lives of those few animals who were somehow spared? If a physician could perform a Cesarian section on an incapacitated womb, didn't this give him implicit authority to decide which wombs should bear, whose seed was fit for procreation? (Brother Mendel, innocent monk, your cherished generations of peas have produced poisonous fruit.)

But only for the good of mankind, of course. Only to make Patients healthier, happier, longer-lived. If in the process a physician became venerated, what harm? Patients recovered more quickly when they had faith in their savior. So who took fright or even noticed when the kindly, wise, overworked healer turned despot?

"Hey, Uncle Fred," came the voice suddenly from behind him, "haven't we been hiking an awfully long time? Looks like it's almost beginning to get dark."

Jode was right. The sunlight, straining now through the shade of pinewoods, had faded a bit, dimmed. They had passed, without comment, a fenced clearing carefully laid out in a nine-hole golf course which formed some Doctor's backyard, his house barely visible above a hedge in the distance, and some other resident's private hopper field. Otherwise the landscape had been all forested. Larch checked his wrist. "About two hours. Want to rest a minute?"

"Naw. I'm not tired."

Wrong again, Larch thought. *Should have said, I'm feeling a bit wiped out, let's take a break.* Put the burden on himself. Then Jode might have agreed to stop. In any case it wasn't too much farther. "The place we're headed for is right around a few more turns in the trail if the map in my head is right."

"You got a map in your head?"

"I memorized a map of Orthohaven when I first knew we were coming here. Thought it might come in handy."

And sure enough, ten more minutes and they had arrived at a barrier of tall iron pickets, one of which bore a metal plaque: PRIVATE PROPERTY. Here the trail, undefeated, changed direction to parallel the fence, which in turn gave way to a masonry wall, then a gate. And another sign:

GALENTRY
Private Residence
Of Luke Algis, M.D.
(Visitors must phone
from gate for admit-
tance.)

Larch now had another qualm which he hoped for Jode's sake did not show on his face. Was Shelby really waiting for them on the other side of this gate? Or was it all a mistake, or worse, a trap? Their planning had necessarily been quite hasty. Today's early-morning raid on Shelby's underground school back in the city, staged for the purpose of kidnapping both Jode and his teacher-sister, had happened to occur when Shelby was taking a half-day off, leaving a substitute instructor in charge. (So the other side could plan badly too and often did; it was a small comfort, but a real one.)

Larch had first heard of the incident an hour later when he received a clear, and curiously lengthy, code message through regular underground channels from Shelby: "They grabbed Jode from school. He's being held at Facility 167-3, Cubicle 904a. Get him back any way you can. Soonest. Luke will help. Am frantic but holding up. Bring him and film to me at Galentry, Orthohaven. Plans now viable to begin our final phase from there. Pray! Love you both. S."

The reference to a final phase meant she must have arranged tying of the last few loose ends of their plan to reach safety (at least for a cooling-off period, while they remained high-priority fugitives) by leaving America for the only country on earth left free of iatrarchal rule—England. Considered backward by the rest of the world, the United Kingdom occupied much the same position as had neutral Switzerland during the old wars. A thorn in the flesh of progress, but not troublesome enough to attract reprisal.

And Luke Algis, to whose Orthohaven home Shelby had taken flight and whose anonymous assistance at the Facility had helped Larch free Jode, was a member of a secret group of disaffected physicians called the HAs (for Hippocrates Anonymous), who while continuing to work for the Iatrarchy held privately to what they considered fundamentalist medical ethics. Because of their beliefs they were occasionally willing to help the Abs, particularly the organized Abs of the underground.

So those parts of the message had sounded valid, at least on the surface. It also should have been

31

reassuring to Larch that the tone and phrasing had sounded like Shelby's, except he well knew how easy it had become for technicians who could enter a Patient's mind to duplicate precisely the style of the output of that mind.

Larch's hesitation at the gate had become increasingly obvious to his companion. "You got a key for this, Unk, or what?"

"No key. I suppose we just—uh—do what the sign says and hope for the best."

Jode stared up the smooth face of the masonry fence. "Or we might try climbing over?"

"Not a chance. All these properties have some kind of early-warning system. A few even use dogs."

Jode's interest flashed into excitement. *"Dogs!* You mean real honest-to-god *dog* dogs like in the old times?"

"Sure thing. There were some dogs hardy enough to survive the bacterials, mostly mongrels, interestingly enough. A few people well situated enough to feed them took them in, I suppose, and began selling the litters to others wealthy enough to buy and feed them. Doctors, that is. I understand there are enough dogs by now that they're not just a curiosity any more. They're being used for guarding property and so on."

As if to corroborate Larch's remarks, a throaty growl rose from the opposite side of the gate. There was a flash of movement barely visible through the narrow cracks between the metal plates.

"Hey!" Jode said delightedly, ignoring—or perhaps not realizing—that the growl had been anything but friendly.

That settled everything, Larch thought. Their

presence had already been detected and announced. He reached quickly for the intercom equipment set into a niche in the wall beside the gate. The transmitter-receiver was black and nostalgically shaped like that of an obsolete telephone. "Fred Koyne and Jimmy Archer," Larch said to the waiting hum of the connection. "Here to visit Landra Mackin."

"Than-queue," responded the mechanical voice. "Our scanners are confirming your presence and checking the names of those expected here. If all is in order, at the sound of the buzzer the gate lock will open."

A peeved snuffling sounded from under the gate, another low growl. The animal was evidently largely ornamental after all, since the doctor had an electronic observation system. But from the sounds being made, the dog had not been informed of this; he was taking his watchdog job seriously.

"They used to keep dogs for other duties too, in the old days," Larch told Jode as they waited. "The police used them, fairly or unfairly, to catch suspects and sniff out illegal drugs and other contraband. Blind people were led around by them." A thought came that caused him to produce what Shelby called his cynical smile. "No need for that in our new perfect society, of course, since no one is unlucky enough to remain blind for long. He's either immediately cured or immediately thanatized. Could anyone ask for more?"

A prolonged buzzing cut across Larch's last words. An inside bolt slid and clicked home, the iron portals swung inward, disclosing a neat lawn, a wide path covered with whitish crushed rock, and a cluster of log buildings in the near distance.

Whipsawing and cavorting around their legs was

a fuzzy gray body, low-slung, disproportionately large-headed—a mutt. At one end of the body a tail waved frantically, from the other hung a lax pink tongue. They had been accepted.

Jode threw off his backpack and rolled on the grass with the animal, accepting a sloppy shellacking of his face and neck. Larch watched with the air of someone witnessing a miracle. Jode, who had until now probably never seen a dog outside a zoo. Jode, who had never owned a pet of any kind. Larch made a mental note that as soon as possible, when they got to England (*if* they got to England), no matter how hard it might be to find a dog, no matter what a dog might cost there . . .

"What a pair of idiots you two are!" she called. "That's only a dog. *I'm* over here." She was running toward them across the lawn from one of the cottages, the movement of her body fluid among the long shadows of early evening.

Jode scrambled up. "Shel—I mean, Landra!" They both ran to meet her halfway.

Before they had closed the gap, he saw that she was crying, long black hair blowing wild across her wet face as she threw her arms around them both. The dog, drunk with their collectively exuded joy, spun circles around them, going first one direction, then the other.

At last Larch lifted the wet face to his, examined it closely. "You've been feeling all right?"

"Frightfully worried. Fine physically. And now that you're both here safe, you, Fred, can help me worry about something else that's bad for us all: I won't be able to appear in public from now on. I'm beginning to show."

She stood back so that he could see, and it was

true. Despite the full and flowing lines of an emerald-hued kaftan, her slender figure showed a substantial bulge just below the waist, the contours of the curled, unconscious body of his child, seven months in utero. Caught up in their separate concerns back in the city, reluctant to meet for fear of possibly giving each other away to the police with the pressure to find them on full, they had not seen each other for almost a week. In those few days the change had come.

"Beautiful," he said, and drew her back to him in order to kiss her again. "How did you get past Lieutenant Checking Nurse at the train station?"

"Luke flew me up here this noon in his hopper, but he was on his lunch break and had to get right back to the Facility. It was one more terrible risk for him on our behalf, of course. We owe him a lot."

"The remarkable thing about the pregnancy showing, though, is that it's taken so long. You're built just right for such concealment, I guess, and if you bundle up in something bulky, and we leave the country very soon . . ." He leaned to plant his lips this time on her waist, at the apex of the swelling. She laughed, shivered slightly.

"Luke is letting us have one of his guest cottages for as long as we need it, but Jeff Rawter is arranging for a plane that should get us to International Airport in West Metropolis, no questions asked. You remember Jeff?"

"Gastro-enterologist," Larch recited. "HA member like Luke. Comes to the meetings and talks a lot. Has a house here in Orthohaven."

"The same. He's going to contact us here about the plan, what time and so on. He might be able to arrange for us to be picked up as early as tomorrow."

They had been walking back in the direction from which Shelby had come. Walking slowly, holding hands. Jode and the dog, on the contrary, were racing back and forth over the neatly clipped grass, ranging as far as the high fence at the edge of the forest, returning to base with the walkers, racing forth again.

Larch and Shelby reached the cottage, stepped onto the self-consciously rustic porch reminiscent of vacations in the Catskills a century earlier, and entered. The interior bore the same stamp of determined rusticity but was not unpleasant. The long rays of the brilliant evening fell on chintz, brick, and exposed redwood beams, suggesting warmth and well-being. "Will Luke come here tonight then?"

"Not till the end of the week, I think. After we're safely out of here. I suspect our presence might compromise him. As it is, he can always pretend to the authorities, if necessary, that we're squatters, that he never heard of us."

"Not with that smart-talking entry gate he can't. Or it would be difficult, anyway. But who *is* here? Surely not just us?"

"No," she told him. "There's a handyman or watchman or some such. Named Strong Bayet. I don't know what Bayet's been told, but I expect not much except to expect visitors named Landra Mackin, Jimmy Archer, and the inimitable Fred Koyne. So we'll just have to go on using those names in front of him for as long as we're at Galentry. And Bayet has a granddaughter Angelique. Odd kind of girl. I'm a little uncomfortable around

36

her for reasons I'll explain later. But right now I have food ready. You must be starved and I know Jode is."

She stepped to the porch and called her brother into the cottage, not demurring when the dog was invited in too. "Wash your hands before you eat. The bathroom is upstairs. And get the backs clean. And use soap. I shall examine the towel afterward, as usual."

Jode sighed. "Just like home, huh? We're in a house—any house—with Shel—I mean Landra—for two seconds and it's just like home."

"I think so too, Jimmy," Larch agreed. "But for perhaps slightly different reasons. And since this is the only home the three of us have right now, let's do as she says, how about it?"

Later, with Jode fed and out on the lawn again with his friend, Larch and Shelby lingered in the tiny kitchen over the coffee-and-sandwich supper. (Real coffee, grown in the District of Mexico; real bread, from wheat flour, but the sandwich filling made of a vegetable mixture guaranteed by the government to be adequately nutritious—nothing at all being guaranteed about taste.)

"This girl, this granddaughter of Bayet's," she told him, "is a Caducean."

"Caducean? What's that?"

"Church of the Caduceus. Fanatical far rightists very gung-ho for the status quo, and she's just the age for fanaticism—sixteen. I have the feeling Bayet himself either knows or suspects that we're Abs on the run and doesn't much care. Algis must trust him or he wouldn't be here. The girl is another story."

"Yes, it could be bad news, but it's good news that we'll be leaving tomorrow."

"That still leaves plenty of time for Angelique to report to the Medcops anything she might see or overhear that she considers suspicious. So let's be extra careful. She's already observed that I'm pregnant, of course, and asked me about it. I told her I was the wife of a Facility Doctor, friend of Dr. Algis. And I came up here to meet my brother—which is true, except in this case the brother is supposed to be you—and his ward."

"What a tangled web we weave." Larch groaned as he remembered. "Migod! I shouldn't have kissed you out there on the lawn in plain sight."

Shelby smiled. "In plain sight of Dog only. The Bayets went out this afternoon for groceries."

"Don't forget Luke's a neurosurgeon. Can Dog possibly be an experimental transplant case with a human brain under all that shaggy hair?"

"Ho-ho. But it isn't funny, you know. Crazy things happen in the healthfare state or we wouldn't be here right now."

Jode came into the kitchen through the rear door of the cottage, slamming the screen. "Did you tell her yet," he demanded of Larch, "about how you got me out of the Facility?"

"Thought you might like to tell her yourself. Better yet, we can all tell what we know, fit the pieces together."

"Yeah," Jode agreed. "Landra first. It started with her, kind of."

"That may be, but my part in it was very small compared to both of yours. I took the morning off from school—fortunately as it turns out—and was down at the Ab printers on the wharf picking up

38

our bogus passports, and along with the passports the printer handed me a code note saying there'd been a raid at the school and my brother had been picked up, so I wasn't to go back there at all. I was to get a message to 'Fred' quick and then come here. That's the last I heard about any of it."

"Well," Jode took up the story, "all five of us—Joanie, Buddy, Vince, Hy Cohen and me—were in the middle of a geophysics lesson at the school—that sub you got isn't nearly as good a teacher as you, though, Landra—when the door busted open and three big guys were standing there. But not dressed in uniform or anything. Still, we all knew something was wrong. The teach snapped the book shut and we just sat there with our mouths open, and finally one of the big guys said, 'Goodhealth. We're looking for a woman teacher named Shelby Harmon and a boy named Jode Harmon. Are they here?'

"Since the sub was a man it was pretty plain even to those Medcops, who are plenty dumb, that Shel wasn't there. Which left Buddy, Vince, Hy and me. I could see the little wheels spinning in those cops' heads, trying to begin to figure which of us might be me.

"But both of you have always said that when it's dead sure they've got the goods on you, the best move is to admit to whatever they want so as to save the rest of the people who might happen to be with you. Else they might take the whole bunch of us.

"I was plenty scared, scared as I've ever been in my life, but I stood up from the table and said, 'I'm one of them.' They said, 'Where's your big sister, boy?' But I said I didn't know, which was the truth."

"You were very brave, honey," Shelby said, "brave and smart. We're proud of you. What happened then?"

Jode shrugged. "Oh, then two of them grabbed me and the third one opened the door and we all went outside the building where there was a Medcop hopper waiting in the middle of the street, with all the traffic stopped by other Medcops.

"In about five minutes we put down on the roof of one of the facilities—I never did find out which one—and they took me in an elevator to a special room they have where they check Patients in. And some more people came and they began all that paperwork and taping stuff that they do when they book people, or whatever it's called. They were plenty upset when they found I didn't have my chart on me but I said my sister probably had it, which is perfectly legal, isn't it? And they admitted it was. But they spent an awful lot of time writing things down and talking about which doc was supposed to be called to 'interrogate the child,' like I was saying earlier on our way here, Fred.

"Finally another more important guy in a white coat came in, the doc they'd decided should be called, I guess, and he glared at me and said, 'Is this the boy, then?' And one of the others said yes, they were almost sure of it.

"Well, he went into a blue fit over that and hollered at them that 'almost sure' wasn't really sure and then they all went a few rounds about that till the doc said, 'It won't excuse *your* inefficiency, but *I'll* know in a few minutes. Take him to the cubicle for prepping and I'll see him right after that in the examination room.

"So a couple of nurses put me where he said, and

took all my clothes. I fought them hard but they got it done. Then they fastened a paper thing around me but the fastenings were in the back where I couldn't reach them to get it off. One of them gave me a pill. I held it under my tongue and tried to spit it out when her back was turned, but the other one saw me doing it and they brought another pill just like it and held my nose and mouth shut this time till I had to swallow it. Finally they just went away and left me in this little tiny room. I was surprised at that.

"I sat there on the bed, trying to figure what I should do with maybe only a few seconds before they came back. There weren't any windows and only the one door into the hall, and they were probably right outside. I was scareder than ever. And I felt low, I mean really low, because of you. I knew there'd be no way, after that doc worked me over, that I could keep from telling all about the Ab school and how it meets around different places, and about Shel going to have the baby, and the underground press in Larch's apartment, and how we were maybe going to England—everything.

"I'd really worked up a sweat by then, when all of a sudden the door opened and instead of those nurses it was Larch—I mean Uncle Fred. He was pushing an empty wheelchair and he was all dressed up in a white shirt and pants that didn't fit too good, and white shoes, like one of those guys that empties bedpans and stuff."

"Orderly," Shelby supplied.

"Guess so. Anyhow, it wasn't one of those it was good old Unk and was I glad to see him! I didn't take time to say so, though, not then. I got the idea what he wanted right off and I quick jumped off the

41

bed and into the chair and we pulled the blanket off the bed and stuck it over my lap and started down the corridor and into the nearest elevator. Then up and down some more halls going like crazy.

"Once a big old nurse stopped us and said where the hell did we think we were going. So Unk said to OR-5 for routine minor surgery. She got mad as anything and said to him, 'Well, how the hell long have *you* been working here? Don't you know that OR-5 is three floors up and in E-wing instead of this wing, which is G?' Or something like that. So we had to get into another elevator and pretend to go up, but we didn't really, just waited inside holding the button till that old nurse disappeared down the hall. Then we merely wheeled into this vacant room where Unk already had some regular clothes stashed that would fit us. We both changed and walked, real cool, down some stairs to the basement and out to a parking lot and found a cab."

Shelby said only, "Oh. Oh, what an experience!" But again there were tears in her eyes.

"Unk was the greatest," Jode added. "You're really lucky, Sis, to be married to such a smart operator."

"Lay off, pal," said Larch. "We did it together."

"We're not married yet," said Shelby. "The government won't let us be married. But once we get out of here—"

The sharp rapping at the front door visibly startled all three of them. Shelby recovered instantly. "Wait here," she ordered the other two, and went to answer.

Larch tensed at the sound of a deep male voice. Surely not the Medcops already? *Let it not be trouble just this once*, he prayed to a god he had purposely never defined but utterly believed in. *It's damnably selfish, but let me have this one night with Shelby, and let Jode have a few hours to be just a boy playing with a dog . . .*

"—want you to meet my brother Fred," Shelby said, coming cheerfully back into the kitchen trailed by two strangers, "and his ward Jimmy. Fred, this is—"

Larch rose abruptly to find himself shaking hands with—who had Shelby said it was? He was more tired than he had imagined. Even the coffee hadn't managed to dispel the accumulation of fog in his brain. This big, paunchy, gray-haired fellow would be Strong Bayet, of course. And the sharp-featured blonde young woman in a high-necked long dress would be Angelique. The blue gingham dress had a quaintness about it. Lace on a white piqué collar and the collar neatly secured at the throat by a black onyx brooch overlaid with a slender silver caduceus.

Bayet finished shaking hands and plumped down the small bag he'd been holding under his left arm. "Goodhealth. Pleased to know you," he said, but on a slightly sardonic note. *So maybe he knows who we really are,* thought Larch. *And so what? In order to do anything, living the way we do, we have to go on trusting strangers occasionally, hoping that some law of averages will operate to make at least some of that trust merited.*

"Thanks for bringing our groceries along with your own, Mr. Bayet," Shelby said. "How much do I owe you?"

Bayet's eyes remained on Larch as he spoke to Shelby. "Eight units thirty-six, ma'am. No rush about paying."

43

"Better do it while it's on our minds," Shelby dug into a slit pocket in a side seam of the kaftan. "Do you have to go all the way to town to shop?"

"Naw. Usually we just go to the country store down below the train station. It's an easy trip in the Doc's bug."

"What kind of bug?" Jode wanted to know.

"Golf cart, 'lectric golf cart. We do errands in it."

It now seemed that Bayet wasn't the only person in the room whose attention was riveted on Larch. He felt Angelique's eyes, knew she was staring with the invincible arrogance of a young woman who has discovered that she is attractive. "What did you say your name is?" she demanded suddenly.

"Koyne. Fred Koyne." Had she seen some poster, heard some rumor? Although Jode and he had not happened to see it, the store might be very near the station; Angelique might recently have exchanged gossip with the checking nurse, talked about strangers in the area.

But her next question jarred him almost as much as if she had accused him on the spot of being a fugitive, exposed him under his real name. "Are you saved, Mr. Koyne?"

"Why—uh—I don't think I—"

"Knock that stuff off, Angie," her grandfather intervened. "Religion's all right in its place, but—"

"But this *is* the place. Life is religion and religion is life, Grandpop," the girl shot back at him, slipping easily into a conversation they had obviously exchanged many times. "Anyway, I was only wondering if Mr. Koyne might like to come to our services tonight."

Tired though he was, Larch had now been

44

shocked back into a certain ration of aplomb. "Where are the services?" he inquired with a polite interest that seemed real enough. "I'm told you belong to the Church of the Caduceus. I'd certainly not mind finding out more about it."

Shelby, putting packets and cans from the bag into kitchen cupboards, shot him an opaque look.

Angelique tenderly smoothed down her straight blonde hair, using both hands at once. Then she reached to her throat to finger the winged brooch, Mercury's staff. "We don't have a chapel yet. We meet at one another's houses. But the spirit is there, wherever we are."

"Do you have many members, up here in the woods?"

"So far we're just a small chapel, about ten, but there are over a hundred chapels on the continent, and some of the city chapels have more than five hundred. But our membership figures are only temporary. Before we're through spreading the word we expect to have enrolled—"

"Angie, hadn't we better be running along?" her grandfather persisted. "It's already suppertime."

"—every Patient in the whole world." Her eyes flashed with missionary fire. "Some of you will be slower to see the light than others, but that's the way the spirit works in us. As for myself, I knew right away, at the first meeting I went to, that—"

"Angie?" Bayet had stalked into the other room and was calling from the front door.

"Right away, Grandpop. Anyway, Mr. Koyne, I'll stop by here on my way to meeting tonight, to see if you decide to attend. Landra too, if she changes her mind, though I already asked her earlier and she said no. If you don't attend, that's all

45

right too. It only means that your time for joining hasn't come yet. Well, it was nice meeting you. Goodhealth." With a whirl of gingham, she was gone.

"Nice girl," he said into his coffee cup when Shelby returned from seeing them off.

"Very nice," she answered vaguely, her head already bent into the refrigerator where she was storing the last of the groceries.

"Old-fashioned kind of kid."

Shelby straightened, came back and sat across the table from him again. "She's appropriately turned out. That church is the old-fashioned kind of religion. Intransigent. Fundamentalist. Dogmatic. Follow us or burn. There are no paths to salvation but this one."

"What do you suppose it means, the government suddenly giving a spiritual movement its head when they've been so inimical to established religion all this time?"

"Somebody in the Ama, or maybe in the World Association, has figured out how to take up the slack. With an official spiritual outlet added to the Iatrarchy's material appeals, the Dis-ease State could become absolutely invincible, if it's not already."

"There always has been the need. Don't you remember your father saying that in the early days one of the Ama's difficulties was with the Patients who literally began worshiping medicine as a diety, with altars and all the trappings of sanctity?"

"My history lessons from Dad go back even further. He used to say that the medical state is anything but a new type of government. Primitive

46

tribes, for instance. The shaman was the real boss, and he ruled by fear just like the Ama does now. Do as I say or you will die, for I know all the secrets of life. Swallow this potion, take this pill. Destroy the individual in the name of safety for the group. You've been chosen by lot to die a scapegoat and save the crops so the tribe won't starve; sorry, we're going to have to thanatize you in the name of Public Health, to keep your disease from spreading to others. Shaman or Surgeon General, it's still the same ballgame. Did you know that among some of the ancient Native American tribes their whole body of knowledge and system of teaching was called, simply, 'the medicine'?"

"Yes, I do remember now. And this was one of his favorite topics. By the way, you certainly do him justice. Jode must be right when he says you're a good teacher."

Looking at her as he was looking now, with respect and admiration, Larch recalled other times during the ten years he had known her when he had looked at her in the same way, first as Shelby Harmon the child, then as Shelby the woman. And he wondered if it might be possible that these occasions taken together might have outnumbered even the many, many times he had looked at her with desire.

It was something to wonder about.

"I love you," he told her.

"And I you," she answered, and added, as if she had read his thoughts precisely, "in more than one way, but the several ways we have of holding another person in high regard are all part of the same whole."

When the summer darkness had settled over the mountains, they went to bed in one of the two small bedrooms on the second floor of the cottage. Across the landing, Jode had finally fallen asleep after reluctantly parting with Dog outside.

Angelique had not returned, as promised, to try to persuade Larch again about the church meeting. "She must be hot on the trail of some better prospect for conversion than I seemed to be," Larch decided.

He had spent the half-hour before retiring examining the upstairs windows to discover which of them opened most easily, looking out of them to figure jumping distances to the ground, and generally planning what they would do if visited by Medcops or Subcutes in the night.

"You're right about not being able to feel secure even for a moment, especially after this latest episode at the Facility," Shelby said. "We have no idea how much they know about us this time. There are too many unanswered questions. How did they find the school, for instance? Why didn't they arrest everyone there instead of just Jode?"

"Maybe they thought they could come back and round up the others any time," Larch speculated. "Or believed that once they had you and Jode the others would panic and turn themselves in. Don't forget what we've learned from their past behavior: police reasoning under the Iatrarchy is all geared to the complacent notion that nobody really *wants* to cross them, that any good 'normal' Patient will always cooperate. And in the past they've been about ninety percent right. That's why their retribution is relatively sophisticated and so is their intelligence apparatus, but in application they make a lot of misjudgments."

"Which we can't count on taking advantage of," Shelby pointed out, "because we never know when they might sharpen up, possibly with the help of an informer."

It was a fact that the strength of the Iatrarchy was also one of its weaknesses. Unlike authoritarian governments in the past, it was so confident of its own essential "rightness" that it offered no rewards to informers. Its supremacy depended on the absolute acquiescence of the Patients, acquiescence based on the assumption that the government was purely benevolent, that those who opposed it were hurting themselves.

And Patients did betray other Patients. This happened for reasons which would have been unbelievable in other times—a bronchial cough or a broken ankle. Subversive political activity, however, doesn't show up like a festering boil or a fever; political notions were either beyond most Patients or boring to them. They simply did not want to be wakened from their unconscious contentment. Hence a political Ab might operate for years virtually unnoticed. The underground organization counted on this strange immunity, made use of it. But then the organization itself had grown large, making it no longer possible for every member to know every other well. And the time had inevitably come when the informers to be feared most were those possibly enlisted in their own ranks.

The night with Shelby, for which Larch had prayed, was granted, however. It was because they had spent so few full nights together that he considered it no less than a miracle. They had always lived separately in order to substantiate the "single" designation on the medcharts they used. And there had always been the night meetings of the underground, the paper to put out, Jode's needs to think of, and—most detrimental of all to any kind of private life—the running from the authorities, the constant shifting of identifications and residences in order that their existences might never become too crystallized on official records.

Toward morning he woke. Suddenly. Had there been some strange noise, either inside the cottage or nearby in the otherwise perfectly still night?

Larch pulled on his jeans and tiptoed barefoot through the shadows cast by a three-quarter moon, looked again out of windows, went downstairs to stand on the porch and peer down the white gravel path, glittering now with a hoarfrost of moonbeams. Even the Bayets' cottage three buildings away, identifiable by the moon-limned shape of the golf cart parked at the door, was absolutely dark and quiet.

He returned to bed, resuming the same position in which he had slept, his body curled around the slender but gravid form of Shelby, who cuddled closer but did not waken. But deep sleep was no longer possible now, and he fell into the familiar, half-conscious nightmare-fantasy he'd endured many times since he and Shelby Harmon had pledged themselves to each other.

Born of his not unreasonable fear of somehow losing her as he had lost Kira, the unwelcome mental drama always began with Larch's having been sentenced by the Medicourt to "modification," the goal being to cure him of his desire for a woman whose statistics could never be brought into harmony with his own.

In the dream he was presumably in a treatment room of a facility, surrounded by white-coats, about to undergo some series of injections which would cure him of all the loin-yearning for, all devotion to, even all memory of Shelby. Absolutely painless (a Patient couldn't even feel the touch of the injector syringe), absolutely impersonal, presided over by an ultra-competent technician employed by a wise and compassionate society.

Even comfort and reassurance, of a kind, poured soothingly upon him throughout the ordeal, supplied by a nurse assigned to this duty: You understand, don't you, Larch Rosst, what we're doing? (Smile.) You'll be a new man tomorrow when you wake up. (Smile.) All right now, relax. Doesn't hurt a bit, does it? All right now, once more . . . zzz . . . and once more again . . . zz . . . why, you're going right off to sleep. Just make yourself comfortable. My, how you must have been suffering . . . zzz . . . such an unfortunate aberration . . . zzz . . . such ridiculous ideas for a man your age . . . zz . . . after this you'll be an asset to society instead of . . .

. .And then later, not being able to remember why he had been fighting this, not even able to recall what it was he had been fighting. Catching a glimpse of Shelby one day, crossing a street half a block away, and feeling some buried part of his dulled mind give a slight twitch, fleetingly gone. She perhaps looking back for a moment over her shoulder and then smiling in a polite, puzzled way. He returning the same kind of smile. Each thinking: *Isn't that person someone I once knew? No,*

51

probably not, and what difference anyway? And then continuing their separate ways.

A rank, chill sweat always sprang out on his skin after one of these nightmares. It did little good to remind himself that such a thing could never happen in reality. If he and Shelby were caught by the Subcutes now, with information about them both including right names, correct ages, and a full report on Jode's removal from the Facility, they would undoubtedly have no "chance" for "modification," only thanatization after interrogation. They had discussed these possibilities often enough, and agreed to the obvious: better to be dead than not to love you; better to be dead then never to be with you, not even to remember you.

From the waking dream he slid once more into dreamless sleep, and woke finally to a sense of sun-high lateness and the sound of voices in earnest, low conversation downstairs. Shelby had risen from beside him and gone down. Hers was one of the voices. But the other was not Jode's. A deep, authoritative voice, something slightly familiar about it.

He hurried into his clothing and made ready to go down, but the ingrained habit of the long-time fugitive made him pause for a moment on the upper landing and listen for some clue about what he might be getting into. He had already discounted the possibility that the visitor was an official sent to pick them up. Shelby's voice was friendly and confident and he had heard her laugh. The overall tone of the dialogue below seemed serious, however.

". . . Because your father started the illegal schools, because he hid rather than surrender his family and himself, because he produced a time-bomb of a book exposing everything including the names of those benighted physicians who helped develop the germ aerosols in the first place, the manuscript of which they still haven't found—all these factors alone would make you vulnerable, especially since you carried on with his work. And then your teaming up with Rosst, probably the most-wanted Ab since the arrest of your dad, and protecting your brother Jode who in spite of his age is a hot prospect on their interrogation list—what with everything you three have outlived your usefulness to the underground at this stage. Your staying would only make things worse for the rest of us."

"Yes, of course. You don't have to spell it out for me, Jeff. I live with this knowledge every minute. And we're *glad* to be going, if we can make it. I only meant that, with our numbers still so relatively thin, it'll be a blow to some of you to be losing the editor of the Ab paper at the same time you lose a pretty fair teacher (if I do say so myself) and a star pupil who's a prospective crack underground agent. Let us at least keep our illusions of irreplaceability. It's good for the ego."

"A pretty teacher indeed," the male voice bantered. "Fair as any I've seen. Yes, you'll all be sadly missed."

Only Jeff Rawter, Larch decided, come to tell them about the arrangements for their leaving Orthohaven. Why he had chosen to call in person instead of telephoning, which would seem less risky, was puzzling, but Jeff must have his reasons. And it was certainly in character. The gastro-enterologist had consistently been more open than the other HA members about his sympathy for the underground, even to the extent of attending meetings and giving advice as well as assistance and funds. This when most HA people preferred no personal contact at all with the untouchable Abs, even as they sympathized. HA members particularly wanted to steer clear of being told plans and names, and this applied even to Luke Algis, who had been a friend of Gerrod Harmon's. Jeff, leaning far in the other direction, seemed to enjoy meeting Abs and talking with them about what was going on in the group.

While Larch admired Rawter for what had to be a great deal of courage (if Dr. Rawter were ever suspected and interrogated, he would hang himself at once with all he knew and would spill), he had never really warmed to him personally. For one thing, in Larch's opinion, the short, husky, blond-bearded physician talked too much. (But didn't all Doctors? It was traditional, an occupational disease. Probably had a rule about it in the Guide to Successful Care and Feeding of Patients: Keep talking at all times to the Patient, it puts him at ease; tell him what a fine job his physician is doing for him, how well he's doing himself, how often to take the medication, how much better he'll feel afterward. By no means, however, make the mistake of really telling him anything about his case, or anything else of any importance.)

Larch descended the steps two at a time, as if he were just bouncing down from bed, full of vigor, without even having considered pausing on the landing. "Goodhealth, Jeff. Landra didn't tell me you were expected. But then you live nearby, don't you?"

"In the summer I do. I have a house down the road a ways. What's this 'goodhealth' stuff? You're among friends now."

"Landra and I figure that in our situation we can't be too careful. She calls me Fred, we call my ward Jimmy. And we try not to mention the things that don't really have to be discussed."

This implied criticism of Jeff's recent fulsome discussion was lost on the physician, who undoubtedly didn't even suspect that Larch had been eavesdropping. "You're not worried about listening devices, are you? And here, of all places? I tell you, that's not the way the Iatrarchy thinks. They don't *need* to listen. They arrest first, collect evidence later, from the arrestee himself. All their police-equipment money goes into gimcracks for the Subcutes, like those tracking cyborgs and so-called tachyonic weapons. And if they happen to disintegrate the suspect with a zipgun during the excitement of the capture, well, it saves court costs later."

"You make me gladder than ever to be getting out of the country for a while."

"What I came to talk with you two about. Everything's all set, but there's been a small hitch in the plans."

"What kind of hitch," Larch inquired, "and how small is 'small'?"

Rawter waved away all thought of worry. "As you may know, there's an airstrip up here in the mountains, its whereabouts known to only a few of us."

"I know," Larch told him. "It was on the map I studied so we'd know our way around Orthohaven."

"Good. I've arranged for a private jet to pick you up at the strip. Only trouble is, the plane can't get there until tomorrow morning. I'd hoped it would be this afternoon, but—"

"How far is the airstrip?" Shelby said. "Can we walk there?"

"It's too far to walk and I've a better plan laid out. First you come to my place. It's about eight kilometers. Not to my house, it might attract too much attention, but to the summerhouse on my golf course. A driver will meet you there and take you the rest of the way. He'll also have new charts for you, to match your passports. They tell me you didn't have time, Shelby, to get the charts too before you left town so suddenly."

How much he knows, Larch thought. *He's thorough and he obviously has the confidence of everyone in the underground. And why not? He's part of the underground himself. And he's doing all this to help us, so what am I so nervous about?* "When do we actually meet the plane?"

"Just before noon tomorrow. That'll give you another night here in the cottage, a good rest, then an early rising and you're off. The jet will take you direct to International Airport in West Metropolis where you get the regular morning flight to London."

"Only trouble is, it gives us that much longer as sitting ducks here," Larch complained. "By the way, who knows we're here, that you know of, besides Luke Algis and you and the Bayets? And while we're at it, who *are* the Bayets and can we trust them?"

Rawter smiled his bedside-manner smile of reassurance, showing no teeth. "Those of us you just named are the only living mortals who are *sure* you're here. It's not outside the realm of possibility, however, that eventually the Medcops might stumble upon something or someone that might direct their attention to Orthohaven in their search for you. I shouldn't think we'd have to worry about a thing like that happening for several days, maybe weeks, given the track record of the police in such instances."

"They found the school," Shelby reminded him.

"So they did. Let's hope that uses up their quota of success for this month. But you wanted to know about the Bayets—"

"Whatever you can tell us about their reliability," Larch said.

"I know that Strong's as sound as his name would imply. Angie is something else altogether, an unstable adolescent with a crush on the new gospel-bringer, the Reverend Medical Love."

"Are you speaking metaphorically, or is that a real person?" Shelby inquired.

"Not only is he depressingly real, so help me, he bears the name his parents gave him. Mr. and Mrs. Love, it seems, suffered such a serious case of iatrophilia that their son was destined to found the Church of the Caduceus. And with a name like that, who could avoid his destiny? Around here we've been more or less following the church's progress mostly on account of Angie and her missionary work. She tried to convert you yet? You didn't succumb to her irresistible arguments and not-so-spiritual charms, did you?"

"Not entirely," Larch answered, "though the charms shouldn't be underestimated."

"Well, the word is out that the church is on the way to becoming the new spiritual arm of the government, a kind of Second Estate."

"So that makes Angelique an employee of the

government, in a way," Shelby said, "which is just what we fear."

"You're both overestimating the Bayets," Jeff said. "Angie probably doesn't know who you really are, and her grandpop has been close-mouthed in the past about Ab activities at Orthohaven. Don't worry, friends."

Shelby said, "Oh, Jeff, I don't mean to be snide, especially when you're risking everything to help us, but your casual 'don't worry' is an iatrarchist formula if ever there was one."

Jeff smiled, a bit tightly. "I *am* a Doctor after all. I find myself saying that to Patients up to fifty times a day and, believe me, it *does* help."

"Helps the Patient, you mean? I'll bet that was the first order the Doctors issued after the first bomb fell. Don't worry. Go immediately to your homes and wait. You may notice a slight headache followed by blurred vision, difficulty in breathing and swallowing, weakness, a bit of abdominal pain, and increasing pulmonary edema. But *don't worry*. Very shortly you will be in deep coma and your troubles are over. Slow death always takes a while."

Jeff sighed. "You're in a strange mood today. And you're wrong about the slow death. It so happens that the bacteria used in most of the aerosols was a special strain of *serratia marsencens* which acted very rapidly. In fact it was practically foudroyant."

"Yes, pardon my error. Hours instead of days?"

"Exactly. And what could a fatally infected Patient gain by adding anxiety to the other symptoms? The trouble with you people in the underground is you always overstate. Not all the so-called cruelties dispensed by physicians are cruelties and the reassurance of a professional is a case in point. You know as well as I that anxiety can be utterly destructive. That's why I'm not altogether against this business of 'modification' that most political Abs take such a strong stand against. Oh, I agree that the Iatrarchy goes much too far with it, and that some of the anxiety illnesses are iatrogenic. If the state is going to thanatize a deformed child or an elderly parent, then naturally the survivors, especially the sentimentalists, are going to grieve. Or a man can worry himself into that kind of illness by being cuckolded or becoming afraid of losing his job. But once the suffering, discontent, anxiety or whatever one calls it has appeared, it must be dealt with, because it affects Public Health. It can spread as surely as typhus. Carriers must be taken out of circulation. It's the only ultimately humane course. How else would the Iatrarchy have eliminated crime except by removing the element of malcontentment from society? But that's an argument for another day, eh?"

"Yes, and I certainly hope to be on hand to argue with you about it, Jeff," Shelby said.

When Jeff Rawter left, they walked as far as the gate where he had left his car. It was almost as if this was a normal act taking place in normal times, a couple of people in leisured surroundings strolling with a friend to his car.

The electric motor whispered to a start. "If you're at my place by ten-thirty tomorrow, there'll still be plenty of time to connect with the plane. I won't be there, so I'll say good luck now." They shook hands. "If there's any change in plans, I'll telephone you here."

Before driving off, he cocked his blond head out

the window of the little car and looked again at Shelby. "Landra, dear, I can set it up for an exam on your obvious condition with an obstet neighbor of mine. He's here in the woods, probably could see you this afternoon. You really should, you know."

Shelby shook her head. "It'd be just one more person knowing we're here, one more iota of risk."

As they walked back Shelby bemoaned the news Jeff had brought. "We've been granted twenty-four more hours of life under the Iatrarchy. It should be like nothing to us, yet right now, to me it seems doubtful if I can live through such an eternity."

"The convict's hardest time to serve is just before the sentence ends," Larch reminded her, "or so it used to be when cons were cons and not Patients being Treated. I suppose it could be different now. Anyone serving time for extended treatment probably gets time-collapsing drugs."

"I hope we never find out. Since Jode's the only one of us—besides Dad—who's ever been arrested, I'd kind of like to keep it that way."

"Where is Jode, by the way?"

"With Dog, of course. And I have mixed feelings about where they've gone. Last night, when you were checking escape routes, Jode was listening, I guess. Anyway, this morning he immediately asked me if he could go for a walk in the woods from the small back gate you found in the fence. I said yes, but to be back in half an hour."

"You can't say no all the time, not to a ten-year-old boy."

"I'd go on saying things will be better in England, but right now I'm not sure England exists."

"I know what you mean. In fact, I'm almost sure it doesn't exist."

The depression caused by the delay still clung around him later, lunching on the porch with Shelby, neither of them eating much, and still later, when they spent the afternoon at the Galentry swimming pool, a natural rock basin at the rear of the property.

Of course there was no such place as England, not outside of literature and people's imaginations. How could there be a spot left in the world where he and Shelby could live openly together, marry with impunity, make a home for Jode? Where they would be treated as individuals and not as faceless parts in the mechanism of the state?

Cheerio there, Mr. and Mrs. Harmon-Rosst. I hear you're just over from America? Rest easy, no extradition here, you know. Somehow we get away with it. We see so few Americans, though. Are things there as shocking as they say? We never let our situation deteriorate to that point over here. Wouldn't tolerate it. Strongest people in the world for the rights of individuals. Wind may enter, rain may enter, but the King . . . and after the Harley Street Massacres—they weren't really massacres, you know; a few medical chaps got a bit cut up, no fatalities—we had no more trouble on that score.

"Free and safe," Larch muttered. "Not likely. Not likely for us."

Shelby in a flame-colored sack tunic that de-emphasized her pregnancy but enhanced her rich coloring and long, perfect legs. "What are you muttering about?"

"Our lives, our chances—everything. I was thinking about England."

"When we get to England," Jode declared, "I won't have to pretend to be a Patient any more. I'll

61

be an Ab like Dad was, and Unk Fred and you, Landra."

"You can't be an Ab in England. It's meaningless because everyone's an Ab there," Shelby told him. "And I even rather wish that after today you'd forget that word. It's been a good, useful term for us in America. And its etymology is interesting because it began as a goverment designation for abnormal, became a hate-word meaning anyone who disagrees with Them, and has finally come to stand for those who reject absolutism, who are willing to risk everything for freedom. However, now that we're going to a place where liberty has never really been lost, it might call too much attention to us if we called one another that, and maybe even cast doubt on us when we need to make friends."

"Yeah, that figures," Jode agreed. "I'm not so dumb that I think everybody's going to like us there, any more than *everybody* hated us here. You already told me that. But I can hardly wait to be eighteen so I can come back here and wipe them all out. I'm gonna start with those three dumb Medcops that came to the school, then I'll find the Subcutes who killed Dad, and then I'll—"

Shelby rose to a sitting posture from the towel where she'd been lying since swimming in the rock pool. She grabbed the boy squatting by her side, pressed a firm hand over his mouth. "Oh, Jode, Jode stop it," she ordered. "You know better than to talk like that. We've been over this so many, many times."

Larch felt himself being drawn into their altercation. "Would it help any to know, nephew, that I feel exactly the same? But I'm older, so I can feel the same and feel different at the same time. What happens is that over the years you figure out that if you go around killing and cutting up your enemies, you're only sacrificing your own ideals to theirs. Then you start thinking about channeling your gut-hate—and it's real enough, I don't deny—into something a little more acceptable to your own way of thinking, but more efficient too, like trying to change people's opinions by persuasion."

"Too slow," said Jode gloomily, wriggling out of his sister's grasp.

"Ah, yes," agreed Shelby. "In all the years our organization has been at work we have accomplished very little. An illegal school involving a dozen volunteer teachers and a hundred or so children, a secret press that circulates an illegal paper, a network of hideouts through the country similar to the Underground Railway of the abolitionists (the Abs of another time), and a few 'friends in high places' upon whom we may or may not be able to count in a crunch."

"Could be worse," Jode said thoughtfully. "Could be that we had none of this stuff at all."

A sudden threshing sound in the brush above the pool. Someone arriving in a hurry. Medcops? They were obliged to think of them, even here. Subcutes? Then a shower of pebbles loosened by the feet of the intruder, who was descending to the basin where they were without bothering with the path. A flash of gray. Restored peace of mind for them all. One friend, at least, whose loyalty was beyond doubt even though he belonged to another. Dog.

Their only other interruption through the long day came that evening from the Bayets. First a brief visit from Angelique, blonde hair carefully brushed, another gingham frock, pink this time, the caduceus brooch carefully in place. "Goodhealth. The meeting of our church was postponed till tonight. If you'd like to come——?"

"Goodhealth, Angie," Larch greeted her. "But I'll pass it up this time."

"In that case, Mr. Koyne, so will I. That is, if you all would like some company for a little while, I'll bring my grandfather over. He gets so lonely out here with no one but me to talk to most of the year." Here she lowered her voice conspiratorially. "Actually, he'd be much happier in an Age Adjustment Center. He's eligible, you know, but he refuses to listen to reason, and for three more years he still has his option."

Despite all he knew and had heard of requirements made by the Iatrarchy upon Patients (not Doctors) past sixty, Larch felt mild shock. He spoke before he thought. "But that's absurd, as you yourself can plainly see. Your grandfather is a robust, healthy——"

"Not really. I live with him, so who could know better? He coughs at night sometimes. And I see him failing year by year, forgetting where he puts things, getting all tired out just driving to town, and doing the jobs he always did before without getting tired at all. At his regular checkups they always say he's doing okay, for his age. But one of these days I know I'm going to have to take things into my own hands and——"

Larch felt an unexpected surge of sympathy for Strong Bayet. He sighed. "Yes, yes. Well, bring your grandfather over. We've no plans for the evening." A social lie. Their plans had been to go to bed as early as feasible so as to be rested for the demands of the morning, including the eight kilos on foot to the summerhouse at the Rawter golf course, with who knew what exigencies en route. Reminding himself of this, Larch added, "Or at least *I* have no special plans. But I'm going to send my sister to bed early. As you know a prospective mother needs lots of rest."

"Oh, I do understand, Mr. Koyne. Really I do."

"My ward also. He's spent a very active day."

So a little later, with both a grateful Shelby and Jode asleep upstairs, Larch found himself stretched in one of the comfortable chintz-covered chairs, listening to the Bayets fighting over him.

"How much longer will you folks be staying?" Strong asked. "Like to have you over for a little poker some night. That is, if you like to play."

"Or he still might agree to going to one of the meetings," said the indefatigable proselytizer. "The Reverend Love is coming all the way up to Orthohaven next week just to address our chapel."

"Sorry, but we'll probably be leaving tomorrow. We're all going back to the city together. On the train." (Did the blasted train run again tomorrow? He should have checked before committing himself so definitely.)

"A pity," mourned the grandfather. "I'd hoped—" It was true that Bayet looked his age, which would have to be at least sixty if he was eligible for the "benefits" the Iatrarchy bestowed upon retired Patients. He had wide, soft, stubbly jowls and the leathery hands and sinewy arms of a man who has done hard work for a lifetime. Denim pants hung loose on his thighs, but the plaid shirt was tight over heavy shoulders. Looked his age, certainly, but did not seem "old" unless one considered the sixties old. The Iatrarchy did.

"Never mind, Grandpop, before long Doc Algis will send some other interesting people around. He always does. Never did figure why he sends so many guests here when he's hardly ever around himself. How long has your sister known Doc Algis, anyway?"

Larch was about to launch one of his ultra-convincing extempores when Strong Bayet cut in, "Never you mind, Angie. None of your business." And to Larch, "Consarn this girl anyway. Talks too much. Ought hear her at home nagging me how to run my life. Forgets I was running it myself for more than forty years before she was even thought of."

Though her grandfather spoke with obvious good nature, Angie cut in with an equally genuine ill-will. "I have already mentioned to Mr. Koyne that you're too stubborn to do what's best for you, Grandpop. Mr. Koyne agreed with me that you're making a big mistake by not deciding to go to the Adjustment Center."

Larch realized the unwisdom of making any anti-establishment remarks in front of the Bayets, as well as the foolhardiness of entering into a family squabble which didn't directly concern him. But he was unable to let the girl's utter falsehood pass. "Hold on there, Miss Bayet. You misunderstood if you think that. Quite the contrary. I believe your grandfather should hang in as long as he can. As long as he feels he can live his own life—even if he's ninety and still feeling fit—then he should be allowed to. For myself, when They decide my time

66

has come, They'll have to take me kicking and screaming all the way."

A bit dismayed at what she obviously considered his treachery, Angie leveled a righteous look at Larch and said, "But the Doctors know best, surely you're not arguing with that? There simply wouldn't be any Age Adjustment Centers if it hadn't already been proven that older people are happier there. Why, there's all kinds of social life, and Gramps is always complaining there's no company around here. And sports, and useful things to do. And no worry about personal affairs because they just take over and provide you with everything you need."

"And They always know, do They, Angie, exactly what an older person needs? A person like your grandfather, for instance?"

"Why of course they do, Mr. Koyne. People of all ages must take advantage of all the wonderful things Science can do for us. Why, we learned in school that if it hadn't been for the Doctors, we'd all be dead by now."

"And does that mean that the Doctors will be able to go on forever, always being able to determine what's best for us?" *You'd better shut up,* Larch warned himself. *You've probably gone too far already.*

But Angie seemed airily unconcerned, and at the same time firmly convinced any challenge could be headed off with yet another spate of platitudes. "Of course they'll know. That's why we have Scientists and Doctors. They *know.* I can't see how anyone could even think of setting himself up against them. Oh, I've heard there have been people crazy enough to go around questioning things. But that's the point, they're *crazy*. Abnormals. And anyway, that's no problem now because all the really dangerous Abs that organize and talk against the government have already been rounded up and 'modified.'"

"Really? Where did you learn that?"

"School. At church too. Religion isn't just a suit of clothes to be taken out and worn on Sundays," she preached to him. "It has to enter into all of living in order to be any good. We're taught to be aware every minute of what's going on in our homes, among our friends, in our government, even in the world, and to be Witnesses for Right. That's what Reverend Love says on the teleron. If we see something going a little wrong, we can become an instrument to notify the authorities what that wrong thing is so it can be set right. It makes us that much more valuable to our society."

Larch felt the expected inner chill, the droplets of sweat beginning to ooze down his back under his shirt. Here was the thing he had spent his life struggling against. Each time he confronted it, he was forced to realize anew how strong were the enemy's entrenchments. This was a sixteen-year-old, only a few years older than Jode. Little Red Ridinghood.

He was reasonably sure it had not yet occurred to her that the man in the same room with her and grandfather was one of the wolves. They were still in the grandmother-what-big-eyes-you-have stage. However, realization might come any time, even later on recollection. (Hey! I wonder if Mr. Koyne isn't an Ab himself. Better report him, just to be on the safe side.)

How much longer until she reported her grandfather's cough, and what she considered his addleheadedness? "I always figured religion to be a lot like whiskey," Strong said now, "not fit to take until it's aged some."

Angie sighed in exasperation at this but refused to be baited.

"What does a mere Patient like you know about whiskey?" Larch asked.

"Oh, Doc Algis isn't above sharing some of the good things of life, a fine man to work for. The Doctors were smart, regulating the sale of alcohol so they're the only ones can buy it. Know a good thing when they see it."

"Grandpop, you shouldn't talk like that. It's irresponsible. *You*'re irresponsible."

"Maybe," Strong allowed. "And maybe one of these days I'll agree to chucking it all, so I can start living easy and taking lessons how to run around with a stick after a little ball."

"He means golf," Angie explained, sighing again.

"And maybe I won't mind having my BP taken every day instead of six times a month, and weaving a few baskets and learning to knit and crochet, or whatever the hell the psychs decide us old crocks are most useful to the society for."

"You'd be happy for a change, Grandpop."

"Happy? Naw. Happy I wouldn't be. I've known happiness, and it was nothing like that. My happiness was when your grandma was alive and I was a landscape gardener at one of the facilities. And before my only son joined the Medcops and then died with his wife in a hopper accident on his vacation, leaving me to raise Angie all alone."

For some reason this seemed to agitate Angie more than ever. "All right, then, you've raised me. Your duty is done. I'm able to get on better on my

69

own now. I know Doc Algis would sign a permit for me to get an apartment down in the city even though I'm not eighteen yet. If you'd only cooperate, Grandpop. I don't know why you're so stubborn, what you're so afraid of."

"Afraid of? That's easy, honey. When I got to the Center I'd start being afraid every day that this would be the day they decided that old Bayet's circulatory system was too far gone for him to be any good to himself or anyone else and it'd be best to order up the thanatizers—or whatever they call them—before the stroke or heart attack laid him out anyhow and he began to take more time and care than he did when he was ambulatory."

Angie jumped to her feet and said, "Oh, you're impossible, Grandpop! Just impossible! I'm going home. I'm sorry I brought you over here tonight. How can you expect to carry on a decent conversation with anyone when you have only this *one topic?*"

She boiled out of the room in a steam-puff of pink gingham, leaving the front door of the cottage ajar. But a moment later she stuck her head back in and said, "I apologize for my grandfather, Mr. Koyne. I keep forgetting that every time he meets a stranger he begins talking like an Ab. Goodhealth." Then she closed the door with a small but emphatic slam, and they heard her running down the path.

For some reason the word "Ab" seemed to hang in the air between Larch and his visitor. Larch decided he could erase the stigma by use of an old tactic, paste the label on someone else before it gets stuck on yourself. "You're not, are you?" he asked Bayet.

"An Ab, you mean?" Strong Bayet laughed.

"Hell, no, I'm just a Patient. Good as any, better than some. Have my chart handy at all times, follow Doctors' orders, cooperate down to the ground. Sure I give Angie a bad time, but you know and I know—and you can bet *she* knows—that one of these days before long I'll give in. She's right, too. With all Doctors do for people, I can't understand anyone wanting to run away from them." He looked quizzically at Larch. "Those who do try to run away are just letting their feelings get ahead of their minds. Like Angie says, the Doctors are here to help us. They've saved my life a couple of times. When I had pneumonia and again when I had something like hepatitis that they could never quite figure what it was exactly. At least I lived, and was under Doctors' care at the same time."

Larch thought of responding: Coincidence does happen. But reconsidered, sure that it would be the remark Bayet expected of him, and further aware that it would be off the point as a clear reflection of his own position. For he had never felt comfortable among those Abs who criticized categorically the professional competence of physicians. The objection, he felt, should be to the doubtful use to which that competence was occasionally put, and the fungoid growth of Doctor Power over matters having nothing to do with the practice of medicine.

With his granddaughter gone, however, Bayet evidently felt compelled to take up the torch where she had cast it down in pique, and if Larch failed to argue with him, mere listening would also be acceptable. "Doctors spend years learning what to do. Maybe saving lives is putting it pretty strong, but they can make things a lot easier all around."

By euthanasia, for example, Larch thought.

"I recollect a friend of mine, little older than me, his first wife died of the bacteria, though it was a considerable time after the war—took them quite a while to get it all stamped out. Thought he'd never get over it, miserablest human being I ever saw. So grief-struck it's a fact you couldn't even pour him a drink before he'd already begun crying into it."

"Too bad," said Larch encouragingly. "Happens that way sometimes." After all, this was why he had agreed to this evening's encounter, so he could provide a little company for a lonely man. He only hoped Strong's reminiscences wouldn't take them too far into the night hours.

"Well, finally he ran clean out of grief and tried again. Real nice woman, his second wife. Didn't nag, laughed at his jokes. But then she died too. Looked like we were set for another round of trying to comfort him, but then one of his other friends—not me—must of mentioned this guy's trouble to the Doctors, because all at once the Medcops picked him up for treatment. At the facility they put him on an anti-depressant program, they called it. Worked fine. No loss of memory, he just began to be happy and satisfied."

Hideous, Larch thought, remembering Kira's death, his own wild refusal of all comfort for months, for years. Does any state no matter how benevolent have a right to interfere with such a private emotion as grief?

"Treatment was permanent too," Strong went on. "Last time I saw my friend he was sitting around relaxed, still feeling happy and satisfied. He was in an Age Adjustment Center by then. I visited him there. It's where I got some of my notions what those places are like, and they're not really so bad as I let on to Angie. Lots of flowers, trees, someone like me, they'd probably let help take care of the landscaping. I wouldn't mind. Wouldn't be like it was my own place, but at least it wouldn't be lonely."

Though the feeling of being drawn into argument did not subside, Larch, with no clear reason or evidence, began to feel now that Bayet was less of a threat than he had imagined earlier. Why not play his game, in a limited sense, on the theory that he was exactly what he seemed, a solitary man, hungry for company? "Yeah, the Doctors do what they can. We can hardly ask for more than that, can we? They decide whether you're fit for your chosen occupation and arbitrarily assign you one more 'suitable' if your aptitudes by the Sapington Scores don't test the way they were supposed to. They judge if you're fit to marry, and if so what genes are compatible with what other genes. Meanwhile, no expense is spared in the endless business of adjusting all bodies and all minds to a society which might not be to their taste if they were left alone. Performing 'indicated' operations, quieting the disaffected with psycho-pharmacology, forcing the rare dissident to testify against himself under hypnotic drugs and ultrasensitive equipment, killing off those who've outlived their social usefulness or who are in pain from some cause the Doctor finds difficult to diagnose."

Strong Bayet might be an uncultured man, but he was not a stupid one. Larch had not thought he was. Bayet cleared his throat now and said politely, "It may surprise you to know this, but I've heard all those things said before. Anyone who lives long as I have hears everything after a while. I've even lived

73

long enough to know the trouble with your argument: it's all in black and white, like those first TV sets a hundred years ago that people used before we had teleron. In the real world—and that's what we're talking about—things just aren't that way. They come in all colors and all shades of those colors. Doctors, for instance. There's bound to be good and bad Doctors, along with a few good ones forced on account of the law into doing what some people might consider bad acts. And in between are all sorts of borderline cases that only God can judge, if you believe in Him.

"And speaking of God, I've noticed that the Church of the Caduceus makes the same mistake as you. To church members God is the Big Doctor up there, all-good and all-powerful. And if God is all-doctor, then it follows by their kind of reasoning that all Doctors are God. Well, I for one don't believe that for a minute, any more than I believe all Doctors are the devil incarnate. That's *your* church and it's just as far in the dark as Angie's."

Larch started to answer but the older man, hot on the trail of his own ideas and plainly delighted at last to have someone to convince, went on excitedly. "Now I'm a Patient because it suits me. If it doesn't suit somebody else, I don't say they ought to fall in line anyhow like a bunch of iron filings across a magnet. So the doc who checks your Sapington Scores tells you you're smart enough to be an engineer. But you already got this notion you want to be a farmer. But they won't let you because by their lights you'll be more valuable to society if you do as they say. All right, *I* say why not go somewhere and farm and pretend you never heard of engineering? So they won't let you marry? Hell with it. Men and women been managing to get in bed together without marrying since before marrying was invented. They say you can't have any kids? Same thing. They can't cut you into a eunuch if you stay out of their way. At least, I ain't heard they got long-distance surgery yet."

Larch smiled. "Whose side are you really on, Bayet? That's an Ab position if I ever heard one. A soft-Ab position, sure, but a bona fide anti-establishment stance."

"Wrong, sir, and you know it. People like you and Doc Algis and old Doc Rawter who I saw coming out of your cottage this ayem—you all aren't running away from the Iatrarchy so as to have a chance to live as you please. You are *fighting* the Iatrarchy in the name of benefiting everybody whether they like it or not, same as the Doctors are trying to sustain the Iatrarchy in the name of benefiting everybody. Your kind aren't satisfied to slip off and hide out and just get along to suit yourself. And even those of you who do go away just go while the heat's on or to solve some immediate temporary problem maybe, like having an illegal baby, or to get regrouped for a new onslaught. Then afterward you're right back in there. Can't stay away."

So it looked as if Bayet knew everything about them, practically the story of their lives. Just as well, then, that he had decided to put a limited trust in Algis's caretaker. "Resistance to tyrants is obedience to God," Larch quoted quickly, using up his chance to get a word in.

"So I've heard tell. But who's doing the resisting? Only a few Abs here and there. Things aren't changed that way, never have been. I mean really changed. Change happens when conditions are ripe for it, not when a few people decide the hour has come and holler, 'To the barricades, comrades!' Here, have one of these. Home-made. The best."

From the breast pocket of his overalls, Bayet had removed an aluminum cigarette case, inside of which was a row of neatly rolled cigarettes. "Real tobacco, eh?" Larch marveled. "There's just no end of the surprises you can spring, Mr. Bayet. I thought that for fifty years tobacco had been prohibited to Patients, limited to use by Doctors on grounds the latter are the only ones who can be trusted to exercise moderation."

"Raise my own," Bayet said proudly, as he lit both their cigarettes from an old-fashioned match he had also produced from his pocket. "California always had a good climate for tobacco. Now where were we in this argument?"

"At the barricades," Larch remembered. "You had just reiterated the old fallacy that change happens only when conditions are ripe. Now how do you imagine, Mr. Bayet, that these conditions happen to get 'ripe'? Not without fertilizer, certainly. And if that makes it sound as if the Ab movement just spilled out of the manure spreader, then so be it."

Bayet put out a comfortable rumble of mirth that was almost a laugh. "Your notions are all wrong, son, but I can't help wishing you luck with whatever foolishness you're up to."

"Thanks. I wish you luck too. Maybe you're old enough and smart enough to avoid the worst aspects of the system for the rest of your life. It rather looks to me as if you can. But have you thought about the ones who'll come after you, your granddaughter Angie, and our Jimmy? It'll be worse for them than it's been for you."

"Worse? Why worse?"

"Surely you've noticed that benevolent despotisms are all benevolent at first, and then all despotic toward the end? When the physicians took over, it was because they were desperately needed. But you can't run a whole society with just Doctors and nurses and laboratories. So they had to get cops. But Medcops are only good for checking out cranks and bringing them in for treatment. What about the really hard cases, the psychs, the resisters? For those they had to develop the Subcutes. Right up the old medical alley, that was. They'd been looking for some use for all the accumulated knowledge about combining man and machine for specialized efficiency. All the sophisticated etiology of weaponry too. Why waste that?

'Keep the Patients in Line'—that has been a secondary consideration after 'Get Them Well Again,' but now it became the primary consideration, almost the only consideration. The schools were geared to it, and there went the concept of liberal education. The government was geared to it; good-bye democracy. And of course the hospitals—medical facilities—were geared to it. But with all available technicians drafted into cybernetics and weaponry, who was left to think about space travel, the earth sciences which had already developed new energy sources now no longer necessary because of curtailed population, marine biology which was solving the mysteries of the seas at last but now who cared? Not to mention a few dozen other things rightly or wrongly abandoned as not necessary to Public Health at the time.

"Oh, they were willing to let a few harmless ones have their way. I happen to know for a fact that a young man whose tests all showed he could be a technician or even an MD, but whose heart was set on architecture, could be allowed to toss his life away. If a few were spared to their own foolishness, it would only enhance the aura of benevolence."

Strong Bayet flicked ash from the slow-burning, hand-made cigarette toward the empty fireplace. "Like I said," he pointed out, "not all black and white."

"But not real colors either. Mostly shades of gray that darken ominously as time goes by. Like the government position on informing. No real rewards for it, no real encouragement except the strong appeal to a Patient's loyalty. And that appeal works best in the very place it should never operate in a free society. The home. Children are encouraged to betray parents 'for their own good.'" Was he hitting Bayet personally now? Would Angie eventually appeal to the authorities to have Bayet committed? "'Did your folks have their shots this month, dear? No? They don't like shots? Thank you, dear, we'll check on that.' If every child can be led to inform, then every intimacy of every home can be recorded in dossiers."

But Bayet remained impassive. "All I know is I get along fine my own way. I carry my chart. I don't try to figure out what they write down on it about me every time they change the code. I can't do anything about it, so why break my head over it? I go to my regular checkups, I take the medicine they give out and tell myself it makes me feel better."

"Haven't you tangled with them yet, then, about what Angie talks about?"

"You bet. Last thing they told me was they think my personality is destabilizing due to age. See Doc Soandso, the psych man, they say. So I see Doc Soandso—what the hell, they're paying the bills, not me, and that's something people like you forget, how much it used to cost to see a doc but now it's free—and he gives me the old runaround: 'Ever dream of crowds, Mr. Bayet? Must be interesting working for Dr. Algis, but haven't you been wanting to move to town? Lead a less lonely life? Be with people your own age? We've had very satisfactory results with indrawn Patients once they become part of a peer group. And while Orthohaven has the finest collection of medical men on the continent, they don't practice there. They're on vacation—ha-ha. There's no facility there, no public clinic like we have here in the city, and it's such a long way for you to drive.'

"But I'm an oldhand at dealing with them. I feed them the line about how good it feels to chop wood or hoe your own garden. How I never have insomnia because the nights are so quiet. After a while they get all mellow and they say, 'Well, now, maybe you're right after all. For a while. Just remember you're not getting any younger, Mr. Bayet—ha-ha. Don't know what would happen, though, if everyone your age wanted to live your way.'

"And it doesn't cost anything for them to say that because they know very well that not everyone my age does want to live my way. In fact hardly anyone. Most people like to be doctored and nursed, told what to do and what not to do. Saves a lot of thinking. Like the army used to be, when we had armies in the world. And that's another thing you can't deny, that the Medarchy rid this old earth of war and the situations that lead to it. No more unfit administrators, no more alcoholic statesmen, or dictators with crippled arms and damaged psyches, or unstable ambisexual conquerors like Julius Caesar. No more conquerors at all with the psychs controlling all symptoms of aggression in the incipient stage. And not just in America. All over. Used to be an Iron Curtain between here and Asia. But between our Doctors and theirs, it got knocked right down. Same way with the African problems. All that nationalism melted right away as soon as the racists on both sides got thinned out. Granted, mass death by bacterial warfare is a harsh way to solve population problems. But it wasn't the Doctors who planned it that way; it was the generals. They're gone now, so it won't happen again."

"You can always buy security at the cost of lives and liberty," Larch argued. "And you've got a warped way of looking at where to put the blame. If it wasn't Science—including most importantly Medical Science—who thought up those bacterial bombs and produced them, then who did?"

"A few Doctors went wrong, that doesn't mean the whole science of medicine is wrong. Medicine is still the one profession that combines science and humanity. Your own game isn't even humanity, Mr. Koyne. It's politics. Bringing back politics may blow the whole thing wide open again, with poverty, wars, unhealthy living conditions, preoccupation with money-getting—everything we had before and didn't want."

"A chance we have to take. Anything's better

80

than living forever in a paternalistic world-state. All these sincere, dedicated types who can do no wrong have to be at least father figures, if not gods, as Angie believes. Adults outgrow the need for fathers, and give *voluntary* allegiance to gods."

"A quibble," declared Bayet. "Casuistry."

"Why you old phoney," Larch accused him, "you come into this house drawling like a peasant and end up articulating like Daniel Webster. How do you explain that?"

Strong gave his comfortable, rumbling laugh. "I've read a few books," he admitted somewhat apologetically. "Those Doctors are too busy to read anything but their journals and take in any news but what their own Authorized Public Enlightenment Service dishes up on the teleron. They never saw the need to burn libraries because they never discovered how dangerous books can be."

"And you claim not to be an Ab—"

"I'm not an Ab. In my opinion, Ab stands for Abscess. An abscess on the body politic."

"All I can say is, if you ever change your mind, the Abs could sure use you on their side."

"If I ever change my mind," Bayet promised, "I'll just go have my head examined again."

They shook hands warmly when Strong at last rose to leave. Larch followed his guest out onto the porch. Having lived the life of a fugitive for so long, he was keenly aware of the risk of appearing on a porch silhouetted before a lighted window. But this time the risk seemed worth the luxury of having met and talked with Strong.

"When you get back from wherever you're bound," Bayet said, "look me up in the Adjustment

Center. Hope I won't be so adjusted by then that I won't recognize you."

"I'll count," Larch said, "on your not being. We'll talk more then."

"Ain't no use to keep trying, son. Put it down that I'm too set in my ways to ever change now."

She was waiting for him on the dark landing at the top of the stairs. Her white nightgown was of some soft, closely gathered fabric that drifted over her body like a cloud. He had never seen her look more desirable.

"Larch," she said, speaking his real name softly, cautiously, her voice muffled by his throat against her lips as she stood in his embrace, "I have a feeling we should get out of here tonight. Not wait till morning. You can put it down to the vaporings and malaise of a pregnant woman if you like. I won't be insulted. But I think we ought to go. Now. As quickly and as quietly as we can."

Shelby

They left everything but bare necessities that would fit into the backpacks, working hastily by the smoky flutter of a candle-end Shelby had found in a utility drawer in the kitchen. She had a tiny pang of regret over leaving most of her personal belongings, including the clothing she had planned to take with her to England. But her judgment told her the space in her pack should be used for food, in case something went wrong with their plan to meet the plane, and they were forced into hiding in the mountains.

"I'm convinced you're right," Larch reassured her. "I should have thought of leaving myself, even though it'll be hell finding our way on these woods trails without a light, and worse hell when the moon comes up and anyone looking for us will be able to spot any living movement. But however far we get tonight will be that much closer to the goal in the morning."

"It's not rational, you understand, my asking this. I was all right up until the time I went to bed tonight and lay there thinking about the day's delay. Not Jeff's fault I'm sure, but what really got to me was what you told him about its making sitting ducks out of us for that much longer. Well, we don't need to be sitting, we can be moving ducks. Just in case things aren't what they seem."

"Say no more, darling. We're just about ready, aren't we?"

She loved him. She could almost not recall a time when she had not loved him. As an adolescent she had looked at the man her father was bringing into their secret home and known this was not just another underground comrade invited into their circle of firelight for purposes of sharing an illegal drink of whiskey and a discussion of plans.

He had scarcely noticed her that first time, had surely seen her as the child she still—partly—was. But her own imagination had raced in passionate abandon into a possible future; she had thought, without surprise: *There* he *is. My waiting, my looking is over before it's really begun. How shall I make him notice me, make him know what I know?*

From the beginning she had not fooled herself about his being "older." A forbidden—by Iatrarchy standards—eighteen years older, she learned later. But she had been brought up to value other standards than those of the government. Also, he had already been in love, a girl in the underground who had resigned her job as med technician as a matter of conscience. And had received retribution at the hands of the Subcutes a year later when they finally tracked her down. Larch had told her the story of Kira—a difficult story for him to tell, even then—after Shelby and he became friends.

The friendship too had been surprising. Her intuition had warned her that she might, for a time, have to endure some kind of avuncular relationship with Larch. It had not been like that. From the first he had treated her as an equal, asked her opinion on things, respected her intelligence in much the same way her father had. And on her seventeenth birthday, when they met again after her father's death, and when she was returning from the necessary period of exile to work in the same underground unit as Larch Rosst (assignment to this particular unit having required quite a bit of manipulation on her part), he had pulled her joyfully to him, in the presence of a roomful of others, and kissed her. First in greeting, as an old friend. And again with a new and different message.

Larch's fondness for Jode had set the seal of rightness on their alliance, for Shelby's single other personal attachment was to the brother she had taken care of since his birth to their fatally ill mother.

The years had been difficult, fraught with alarms, filled with demanding and perilous labor for them both, marred by long partings and painfully brief meetings, but never short on mutual love. Until finally it seemed that those seven or so years of trial had runneled together, and channeled, and broadened out, bringing them—almost, not quite—to a quiet pool of peace upon which they could float for a time in relative ease, enjoying freedom, and a real home, and each other, and Jode's development toward adulthood.

But that time was not yet. Evidently they still had to earn their way, meter by meter, moment by moment. For here they were, embarked on yet another dangerous excursion, the precipitance of which was of her own responsibility.

What had made her so insistent? Her unease had begun as she had said. Lying in the small upstairs room, window open on the night scent of pinewoods, her attention pleasantly buoyed by the rumble of voices in friendly argument downstairs (a situation poignantly reminiscent of her childhood when she had lain in similar bedrooms half listening to the conversation of her father and his friends), she had for no apparent reason been rocked by a sense of wrongness. Had tried at first to talk herself out of it. The plans they had lain still seemed sound as she reviewed them: first as much sleep as possible, then early rising and readying for the hike to Rawter's golf course, meeting the person there who was to supply their new charts, the quick ride to the secret airstrip where the jet would be waiting, and the equally quick flight north to the commercial airport.

But reassuring herself didn't help. The sense of wrongness persisted, became even stronger. She knew—as surely as in adolescence she had known that Larch was for her and she for him—that every minute they remained in the cottage would enhance their chance of capture.

When they had put on jeans and jackets, Shelby's several sizes too large and properly concealing, they went together into Jode's room and woke him. "We've decided to leave a little earlier than we'd planned," she told him. "Get dressed quickly and don't make any noise."

A child of extremity, already a veteran of other such midnight wakenings, Jode slid from under the blankets and into his clothing without protest. "Your job," Larch explained, "will be to keep Dog from making a fuss when we go out the gate. He knows us, but he knows you best. You can do it."

"Sure I can," Jode agreed. "Are we bringing anything along to eat?"

"Already thought of," his sister assured him, sliding the straps of her pack over her shoulders.

She blew out the remnant of candle and they descended the stairs in a silent file, Larch in the lead, and let themselves out into imperfect darkness. The white crushed rock of the path glittered, a mild night wind swept over the clearing where the lawn and buildings lay and lost itself in the surrounding trees. There was no light in the Bayet cottage.

As they approached the gate, Dog slouched out of his kennel and sniffed at them questioningly. Jode knelt down and hugged him. "Good-bye, old pal. Goodhealth and all that. Thanks for the hospitality and stuff." Dog whimpered a little, then waved his tail. Larch pressed the button that freed the gate lock from the inside. But the animal, reassured by the boy's arms around him, sounded no alarm.

"I suggest we walk as fast as we can down the road for an hour or so, until the moon begins to rise," Larch said. "We can put quite a bit of the distance to Jeff's place behind us by then, maybe. Then at moonrise, we can take cover and wait."

"Wait for what?" Jode wondered.

"For dawn if necessary. Or at least wait until we're sure we're not being watched or followed. There'll be plenty of waiting involved in this trip anyway, since we're not due at the summerhouse until eleven tomorrow."

"If they send Subcutes after us, they can see in pitch-dark anyhow," Jode said.

"Then we'll have to outwit them by other means. They're more machine than human, and we'd have to start thinking in their terms. But let's not borrow trouble. We haven't seen any Subcutes yet. Let's hope nothing happens except a brisk night walk through the woods."

"I'd like just a little something to happen," Jode disagreed. "Nothing really serious, only exciting."

"You're an incorrigible adventurer," Shelby told him. "I would have thought your fun-and-games with the whitecoats at the facility was enough to last you for some time."

They walked in silence for a while, Shelby beginning to feel foolish at her nameless alarm, Jode darting at shadows, cavorting, play-acting, Larch seeming relaxed but watchful.

But they were only about a kilometer from Galentry when the tiny whine began to sound in the distance, growing louder. A motor straining up the mountain. Clash of gears on a diesel vehicle, coming fast now, moving up the very road they walked alongside. It had to be, since it was the only road in the immediate vicinity.

"We'd better head for the bushes," Larch said. "No matter who it is, it's better for us not to be seen."

He took Shelby's arm helpfully, but she said,

"Not necessary. I can make it. Pregnancy is not an illness."

They lowered themselves into the scraggly chaparral that fringed the roadbed. Not much protection, but the only cover available. Without another word they took their places, lying flat, close together, looking out at the road and waiting.

With excruciating slowness the noise continued. What had seemed a moment before to be considerable speed now became a labored rumbling up the steep grades, a chugging around curves.

"Some boozing sawbones coming home late," Larch whispered. "The road leads to several other gates before it ends at Algis's place."

But the vehicle did not seem to be halting at any property below them. It came on inexorably, and in a few minutes they could discern a glow of headlights very near.

Then the car flashed past, but not too rapidly for them to miss the lighted, revolving emblem mounted on its roof. A black caduceus that seemed to writhe reptilian fashion. Archetypal barber pole. Fluttering stave of Hermes in the person of Caducifer, guide of the shades. "Medcops," Larch breathed. "How right you were, Shel. And heading right for the Galentry gate."

"Couldn't they be just making nightly rounds? Like they do in the city?" But she knew better. Police forces were carefully allocated to areas considered to need the most watching. Orthohaven was not one of these places.

"They've been sent up here by someone," Larch said.

"Or called up here?" Shelby was thinking of course of Angie. She hadn't been able to find suffi-

91

cient excuses for Angie's constant questions and challenging manner. And she had overheard some of the girl's conversation with Larch earlier in the evening, before Angie stomped off in anger. Purportedly anger with her grandfather, but she could have staged the display of pique as an excuse to run straight home to the telephone. Even the grandfather, still visiting with Larch, would not have known. (Or Strong Bayet himself might have put in a call when he arrived home somewhat later?)

Larch was already on his feet, pulling Shelby up. "Let them raid the cottage and sift through the garbage looking for clues. It'll keep them busy for a while. They're nothing if not thorough. By the time they call for reinforcements and begin beating the brush around Galentry, we'll be long gone. Only trouble is, we can't stay on the road now. We'll have to cut straight through the woods."

"Is there a trail?" said Jode.

"No trail, but I have a compass. Actually it's shorter to go cross-country to Rawter's property than it is by the road, but it'll take considerably longer. We'll spend a lot of time stumbling around in the dark, I'm afraid."

Jode said practically, "How will we see the compass?"

"Good question. It's self-illuminating, as I recall. If that fails, I suppose we'll have to risk lighting a few old-fashioned matches."

Half an hour later they were feeling their way from treetrunk to treetrunk in darkness that had become almost total. For the rising moon could neither help nor hinder their progress in the dense shadows massed under an unusually thick stand of pines.

They had started off hand-in-hand, Jode between Shelby and Larch, but that method had only contributed to their slowness, excruciating enough on account of the darkness alone. They had discussed the wisdom of halting where they were, to wait for dawn. After all, there was no problem of their being late to meet the driver at the golf course. Hours still remained before the time of rendezvous. But Larch had rejected the idea of stopping while they were still so close to Galentry, from which point they must assume the Medcops might even now be broadening their search in a radius of ambitious proportions.

Shelby, determined not to retard or complicate the painful journey even more, inched her way with special care, aware as always lately of the quickening new life her body had contained for seven months, six of them blessed by the immunity of secrecy.

She had undergone no medical examination since conceiving. Regular physical checkups she avoided anyway, as all Abs had to, with a variety of circumventions worked out over the years. Now, however, as a traveler, she was vulnerable to the chance or casual checkup such as Larch and Jode had faced at the Orthohaven train station. Particularly vulnerable, since the current forged medchart she carried, in the name of Landra Mackin, did not list her true condition. That is, Landra Mackin was not pregnant; Shelby Harmon was. (Even as Fred Koyne had been vasectomized, while Larch Rosst had not.)

And there was a further worry, one which Shelby was determined to spare Larch unless it became impossible to avoid. Several days before, when she'd been teaching a math class at the school, she had felt a slight visceral cramp. She thought nothing of it until, about ten minutes later, it was followed by another, slightly stronger, and definintely a labor pain. When a third occurred at approximately the same interval, fear had enfolded her. School was over for the day by that time. She returned at once to the apartment she and Jode shared and lay down.

Nothing more happened. False labor. Well, it happened to pregnant women. She had read all the forbidden books. (Under the Iatrarchy Patients were forbidden all literature dealing with physiology.) It happened not uncommonly in the seventh month, as could real labor leading on to parturition. A child could be born alive and healthy in the seventh month too, if care were taken. Shelby would have no access to the official kind of care, no incubating apparatus to assist an underdeveloped tiny body, but she was prepared to do all she could if it came to that. There were reliable midwives among the underground, serving in utmost secrecy. A premature child of the underground was even fortunate, spared the Damoclean sword under which its counterpart born in a facility was forced to lie: the chance of an arbitrary obstetrical decision to terminate a life judged not quite fit to endure.

Under the demands of her forced flight and the worry over the safety of her missing young brother, however, Shelby had allowed her concern with this possibility to drift out of mind. Until just after her arrival at Orthohaven when one of the mild, indeterminate contractions had clutched at her again.

And again. And still again, this time fifteen minutes apart.

Once more she lay absolutely motionless, this time on the chintz-covered daybed in the main downstairs room at the cottage. A fourth seizure came along ten minutes after the last, but then an hour went by with no further signal.

Difficulty with a pregnancy was a possibility she had never been quite 'able to excise from the picture, given the circumstances of her own mother's death. Though she had never allowed herself to dwell on it, she had been aware at the time of exactly how Alice died, in horrendous pain for which no palliative was available. In the last days of his wife's life, Gerrod Harmon had even tried to burglarize a pharmacy at a facility—privately operated drugstores no longer existed—but a hidden, silent alarm had been tripped. Harmon, forewarned by the same sixth sense which now served his daughter, had escaped only seconds before the Medcops descended.

Premature birth would be a far different kind of difficulty, to be sure. And yet in their present circumstances, which seemed almost to be deteriorating by the hour, it might also mean immediate and certain death for both herself and the baby.

Several times, at Larch's insistence, they rested, huddled together in the immense dark through which only an occasional thin flicker of moonlight came. The compass showed that their course remained true. "How much farther?" Jode asked over and over. It was the question uppermost in all their minds. Eight kilometers if they had gone by the road, a distance now both less and more. Finally Larch answered, "We've been making better time than it seems, I believe. I figure we'll be almost at the golf course just before sunrise. We'll find a safe spot near there and really rest. We'll have earned it."

But when the first dishwatery light of breaking day finally reached them, they seemed to be still threading their way among the same anonymous treetrunks, feeling for footing over the thick mat of fallen forest debris which concealed treacherous protruding roots and rock outcrops.

"Could the compass be screwed up?" Jode demanded.

"Compasses don't lie," Larch assured him. "At least not often and not under socalled 'normal' circumstances like this. Give me just thirty more minutes as official pathfinder of this expedition, and if some of that emerald turf on Jeff Rawter's private golf club doesn't start to show, I'll turn my badge over to you, Jode."

During their night walk, they had neither seen nor heard any sign of Medcops either tracking them or waiting in ambush, and had long since stopped whispering. And with the daylight came new hope. It really seemed possible now to Shelby that the difficult part of the journey was behind them, that they might indeed be transported without further incident to the landing field carrying medcharts to match the passports hidden deep in her pack. At least part of this near-euphoria was due to the fact that she now felt so well. Light of foot, though she had walked for hours, possessed of energy reserves not yet tapped, suffused with a feeling of being insulated from ill fortune. She would not know, she thought (as she had thought before in recent weeks), that she was pregnant if it were not for the occasional sudden nudge from within, the restless, impatient movement of fetal torso and limbs which reassured her that the baby lived. She smiled to herself.

Up ahead Larch was waving them back, or telling them to stop, it wasn't clear which. He returned to her side. "We're here. This is it."

"It doesn't look as if we're anywhere," said Jode.

"We mustn't go any nearer now, but you can see it through the trees."

Shelby looked too through the trees and saw the abrupt change of landscape, the forest ending at the inevitable high fence, this one meshed steel, and the brown carpet of groundcover giving way at the same time to a gently rolling golf green. On the far side of all this was, apparently, Jeff Rawter's vacation home.

For a moment she was able to look at this massive building through Larch's architect's eye, saw it as bluff, ugly, domineering, costly. A Doctor's house. A man who would build or buy such a residence must be afflicted with a towering arrogance, self-assured beyond lingering doubt. And yet the man who dwelt here was at the same time an HA member, sympathetic over a long period to the Ab cause, willing to run certain risks on their behalf even though his views didn't exactly coincide with their own. People, including Doctors, are no more consistent in their own singular and various tastes than they are in their habits, she thought. What a madness that this curious ideal, consistency, nonexistent in a natural state even in the same individual, was such a highly rated commodity in the Iatrarchy, the enforced norm.

"Shall we climb this one, like you said we

couldn't climb the one at Galentry?" Jode asked, peering at the top of the fence, which rose at least three meters above them.

"No, let's not go in," Larch said.

"We came all the way here to *not* go in?"

"I mean, not now. There's no car waiting for us there yet. Couldn't be at this hour. We'll circle the links, adjacent to the fence, but keeping just out of sight in the woods. That way we'll get to a place I know about at the back of the property. We'll be out of sight there, but we'll have a good view of anything that goes on. It's a big pile of rocks, a kind of butte."

"Will Jeff know we're here?" Jode said.

"No one will know, if we keep quiet and out of sight. So far as I know, Jeff still thinks we'll be leaving Galentry about now and walking over here by the road. In any case, he said he wouldn't be here."

"Oh, Larch, but what if he telephones? I mean, calls the cottage with some new change in plans, and the Medcops answer if they have some posted there?" Shelby said. "Or what if no one answers? What'll he think has happened to us?"

"If no one answers, I suppose he'll think we left earlier than planned. And if a stranger answers, I hope he's been working with the underground long enough to know to finesse a wrong number or something."

"But the Bayets, what'll they make of it?"

"I suppose they'll think what they please, but they'll have been instructed to protect Algis, or Strong will. They've undoubtedly been told that if a raid occurs when Luke has Ab guests, they're to say they know nothing but that the visitors were supposed to be Algis's guests. Then Luke will say he didn't know anyone was there, it was just someone who wandered in and lied about having been invited, and Strong believed them. Could happen to anyone."

"Can you really discount the danger that Angie might spill everything to any Medcop who questioned her? After all, her father was a Medcop, Strong told me, his late son. And even without the image of her father as hero, to Angie cops are sacred, consecrated to the work of the Great Physician in the Sky."

"I have no illusions about Angie," Larch admitted. "And I haven't forgotten that she may be the one who summoned the law. But there's nothing we can do now except hope that when we weren't found there, it'll all quiet down. The Medcops aren't notable for discussing their business with the press, especially their failures.

They had walked only a few minutes through the fringe of woods along the golf course when the landscape changed abruptly, became massively rocky, with no more trees. And there was the butte, as Larch had promised, a steeply rising granite face with an occasional patch of brush clinging along its lines of cleavage.

"Great place to do some climbing," Jode said.

"So we shall," said Larch, "if Shelby's up to it."

"Of course Shelby's up to it," Shelby said, and she thought: *After coming all the way through a trackless woods in the middle of night, I will not fall now, not let myself hurt the baby or bring on labor.*

"If memory serves, this place is called Cooper's Butte. The trick will be to climb to the top of the pile, using the easiest footholds we can find. After we're over the rim, there are depressions and hiding places, but first we have to get up there as quickly and as unobtrusively as we can. Right now we're out of cover and will be godawfully visible as we go up."

"Nothing to it," Jode declared, running up the slope of loose rock at the base of the butte, then beginning to monkey his way from boulder to boulder, each step taking him higher.

Shelby went more slowly, testing footholds and handholds with great care. Just below her, Larch moved among the rocks easily, swinging from promontory to promontory as he followed in Shelby's steps, watching her, plainly waiting to catch her if she fell or slid.

Already on top now, Jode shouted his enthusiasm and had to be admonished by both Shelby and Larch.

But enthusiasm was called for, Shelby thought when she also arrived at the top of the butte. The sun was well up in the sky now, the day was beautifully clear and cool-warm, typical summer weather in the mountains. They could see for several kilometers in every direction, the forest they had emerged from, the full extent of the golf course stretching at their feet, the grounds and fenced backyard of the Rawter summer mansion. And in a small grove of acacia trees on the course, placed about midway, where players might choose to rest briefly, a small kiosk partly enclosed with what looked from this distance like woven matting. The summerhouse.

Its air of innocence was enhanced by a carefully tended bed of pansies surrounding the foundation.

It certainly didn't look like a place of rendezvous for three fugitives from the government and their contact from the underground.

From this vantage could even be seen the way they were to enter the property. Someone—Jeff, in preparation for their visit?—had cut a crawl-hole in the steel on the side of the fence adjacent to the summerhouse.

All three stood staring at the panorama until Larch again reminded them of how visible they would be to anyone who might happen to glance up at the top of Cooper's Butte.

They turned to face the wide, shallow depression, like a pie plate, that formed the butte top. Here brush grew thickly, boulders stacked haphazardly among it, forming possible hiding places.

Rather suddenly, Jode was already in the depression, having scooted and slid and eased himself down from the rim. Shelby started to do the same, but found herself held in the grip of overcaution until Larch held her hand from above, steadying her.

But he was in the wrong position. Or she was already off balance. Or perhaps the rock slide would have happened anyway. He managed with a sideward thrust to cast her free of his own weight so that she was crouched, still clinging to the side of the incline as he plummeted to the bottom.

He landed on the floor of the small pit in a frightening position, sprawled on his back.

Because Shelby was frozen in shock, it was Jode who yelled, "Larch! Larch!" and came running to kneel over him.

Agonizing moments then, as he fought visibly to

regain the breath to speak and Shelby eased herself down to where he lay.

Finally he swore softly, and even managed an ironic smile. "Better I than you, all the same. But I took some impact on my right knee on the way down. It's maybe sprained, maybe even broken."

Shelby bound the knee tightly, using strips torn from the extra shirt she'd brought in her pack. She rolled his trouserleg back down over the bulky dressing. "There'll be a lot of pain."

"Already a lot of pain," he admitted. "The numbness is fading out, the pain is fading in. At least we won't have more walking. We can hide here just as we planned, and when we actually see the man with the car coming to pick us up we can signal. It'll be safer that way."

"Or we could send Jode down for him so the driver can help us get you down from here," Shelby suggested.

"No, I'm sure—almost sure—I'll be able to bear some weight on it now you've bound it up. Let's just go on as if it hadn't happened. Eat something. Crawl into the brush and rest as long as we can."

She drew her confidence from him. Though her euphoria had evaporated with the anxiety of the accident, they were still reasonably safe, and nearly ten kilometers from Galentry in a direction the Medcops would have no particular interest in looking. As for Larch's injury, it shouldn't be too long before they could get medical attention for it, of the kind that required no loss of freedom as payment.

She dumped small parcels from her pack and set out vacuum containers of a cold beverage that contained all the elements of milk without actually being milk. (Cattle and goats had suffered virtual extinction in the war; for some reason the bacteria had been even more lethal to ruminants than to dogs and humans.) The parcels contained a food concentrate guaranteed by the Doctors to sustain life, of a kind most Patients made the mainstay of diet. She and Jode had always preferred "real" food when it was available. However, even though agriculture was an approved activity under the Iatrarchy, perishable foods and grains were still scarce in stores, and very expensive. Fish were coming back, though slowly. Meat was something else. Most Patients had never tasted it.

They settled themselves, Larch with his injured leg stretched straight and slightly elevated. Jode ate hungrily when Shelby handed him his share of the brown, crumbling staple that looked vaguely like the brick chewing tobacco of a previous era. (The time was not yet when the aesthetics of edibles would concern the Doctors.)

Later, when his sister mildly suggested that Jode rest lying flat on the ground, as she and Larch were already doing, he said he *had* rested, and couldn't he go back to the rim of the butte top to see if there was anything they'd missed before?

"Let him," Larch said. "He can be a lookout. We might need one."

They had only just relaxed again when the lookout came running back. "Wow! Oh, wow! You'll never guess what's down there, on the golf course, just walking along."

Both Larch and Shelby looked at him in alarm. "Don't play games, honey," Shelby said, "just tell us."

"A cat! Doc Rawter must have a cat of his own. I've never even seen a cat up close."

"First a dog," Shelby said, "now a cat. Well, Jode, at least you're having some diversion on this trip."

"Could I go down and try and get it to come over to me at the fence? It's all white, except for where it's gray, and I'll bet it's friendly. Cats are supposed to be."

"No," Shelby told him. "I'm sorry, but no."

"It's not a good idea," Larch said. "We've had fair luck so far, if you can call being looked for by Medcops and me falling down a cliff luck. But you shouldn't push luck. Better not go out of the way to attract attention while we're waiting."

Shelby said, "Maybe the cat'll wander up this way. Even when they're kept as pets they range pretty far, or so I've heard."

"How could he get out through the fence?" Jode said disgustedly.

Shelby told him, "Sometimes a cat will find a way. Squeeze under the wire somewhere, or come out that hole we're going to use to get in. Don't count on it, though. Cats are usually friendly, but they go their own ways."

Jode returned to his post, and in the lean shadow of the rocks they even managed to sleep a little as the sun moved toward the meridian, bringing warmth.

Shelby could have gone on sleeping for hours, she thought, waking to a rumbling noise that seemed to be coming from above them. An airhopper, but not very near, not yet in sight. She turned to wake Larch but he was already sitting up, looking at his watch. "It's ten-thirty already, only half an hour till the car's due. Could they be sending a hopper for us instead?"

The churning drone increased and the aircraft itself came into view. Airhoppers of the mid-twenty-first century represented not much advance over the helicopters of the mid-twentieth. After all, the latter had been highly maneuverable, easily landed in small places, and not so complicated that a non-expert in aerodynamics (like a Doctor, with his mind on more important affairs) couldn't operate them. Why try to improve on a perfectly serviceable invention when there were so many other technical projects better deserving of attention? Like treating ailments. And saving lives. And terminating those lives deemed not worth the salvage effort. And keeping the Patients adjusted so they don't go around asking questions and stirring things up.

When the thing came into full view and began to reduce its altitude, Larch was the first to apprehend the new peril.

"Get back out of sight under the rocks on the far side away from the golf course. Take along the packs and anything else we may have left in view—papers from the lunch, anything."

Shelby withdrew quickly to the shelter, pulling Jode along with her. "Why didn't we guess earlier that it might not be friendly?"

"It's black, black all over," said Jode.

"Black and no markings of any kind," Larch confirmed. "It's the kind of hopper the Subcutes use."

"Oh, Larch, they have those—tachyonic guns or whatever they are. The kind that disintegrate everything."

"They're not really tachyonic. They only call

them that for the intimidation value. Tachyonic application wasn't that far advanced before the war ended that kind of research. But they're bad enough. Our only hope is to hide here so invisibly that they won't use weapons because they won't see anything worth shooting."

Jode said, "What if they hover over the butte?"

"Exactly why we have to lie low, if we can. Then we might still have a chance if they search only by air and then leave."

But the black craft showed no inclination to leave. It did indeed hover over the butte and also scouted the edge of the woods, flying very low. There was no sign of personnel visible inside the craft, which was without windows except for a few slits in the underbody. Subcutes "saw" with their equipment, some of it apparently built into their vehicles, some into their own brains. Or at least so it was widely believed. No member of the underground had ever been able to discover exactly how Subcute equipment worked, or the full extent of what could be done with it, though it was known to be incredibly thorough, absolutely invincible. Subcute forces had always been maintained in strictest secrecy and sent out only after criminals (Abs) considered most dangerous to the social order. Thus no quarry had ever been left alive to describe their methods. The Medcops handled ordinary cases.

"I suppose we must have been upgraded," Shelby said gloomily as the hopper passed once more over the butte and then began making helical sweeps deeper and deeper into the forest in the direction from which they had arrived. "Up to now we've been worth only a few Medcops. What are they doing now, do you think?"

"They must know we're expected here in about twenty minutes and they're trying to spot us as we arrive," Larch said. "Would have, too, if we'd kept to the original schedule."

"But that must mean—" Shelby began. "That someone has betrayed us even more efficiently than we thought before."

"Then it couldn't be Angie. She didn't know we were coming here at all, let alone when."

"Both the Bayets knew Jeff was at the cottage yesterday morning. The old man even mentioned it to me. And it would be an obvious move for us, from there to here. As for the time—I don't know. Don't forget that several other people had to know about the rendezvous. The man who is—or was—to pick us up, for one. Jeff himself, for another."

"Are you thinking that Jeff—?"

"No, I'm not thinking Jeff would betray us. He may fumble a few things, and he may talk too much, but I believe he has too much of himself invested in the underground to sell it out. I don't think Strong Bayet would betray us either. But isn't that the fundamental value of any espionage operation? An informer can function *only* because he's not suspected."

"Their motor sounds different now," Shelby said.

Peering out from their awning of rock, Larch said, "Looks like they're lowering to set down. On the golf course."

"Are we going to stay here?"

"Can you think of anything better to do?"

"Oh, Larch, I'm all out of ideas. I didn't expect this. I really thought everything might go right from now on, that we'd get to the airstrip, board the plane, maybe even make it to the regular airport and safety."

"We still might. Whoever informed the Subcutes that we'd be here at close to eleven o'clock may have known only that much and not that we were going from here to the airstrip. Strong, for instance—if it was Strong—he probably knows only what he observed: that Algis gave us sanctuary, that Rawter planned to help us on from this point." Larch was thoughtful for a moment. "If that black hopper really is setting down, at least it'll give us one advantage. We can go over to the rim of the butte and if we keep quiet and out of sight, we'll be able to see what they're doing down there."

Half-crawling, moving with utmost care up the slope so as to start no more rockslides, they made their way to the lookout point. Jode, who had been quiet for a long time (out of fear, Shelby wondered, resignation?), stuck close to them.

The craft had already settled and its rotors turned more slowly, stopped. Almost immediately a vertical slit widened in the black fuselage. Figures appeared and one by one dropped to the ground. One, two, three, four. Then no more. The slit remained open while the four Subcutes moved to surround the summerhouse.

All were suited in unidentifiable gray material with a faintly metallic glister under the sun. Not unlike the chain mail jerkins of the Middle Ages, Shelby thought. The same fabric covered heads and faces. Not as in a conventional mask, however. There were no eyeholes, no breathing space for nose and mouth. Just an unbroken, seamless head sheath.

Uniform in build as well as garb, they were man-shaped, certainly, neither large nor small, neither overweight nor underweight, neither tall nor short. They even walked alike, with smoothly mechanical aplomb. If they were equipped with weapons, this was not obvious. They carried nothing. Shelby noticed that at the end of each right arm, where a hand should be, metal of a darker color extruded for about ten centimeters. Some kind of special gauntlet, perhaps. It was difficult to see clearly at such a distance.

"Are they human?" Jode whispered.

"Don't talk, Jode, sounds carry," Shelby answered, moving only her lips, not even whispering. "They probably have electronically augmented hearing too."

Moving from the four points of the compass, they closed in on the straw-covered kiosk. Finally one of them spoke. The voice was impersonal, monotonal, uninflected. The sound was audible to those on the butte, but not the words. Yet no words were necessary. It was obviously an order to anyone in the summerhouse to surrender.

They waited. The Subcutes also waited.

After some forty-five seconds, which seemed like many more to the watchers, some signal, this time inaudible, caused the four to regroup on the same side of the hut.

The hut? The summerhouse? The kiosk?

But there was no such building.

There had been no flash, no bang, no mushroom cloudlet. Not even a faint glow. And yet the place where Jeff Rawter's summerhouse had stood was now bare ground. Even the pansies were gone.

Shelby drew in her breath sharply, then let it out with a soundless sob.

The curious quartet wasted no time. It was already on the way back to the black hopper, walking with the same stolid, smooth confidence shown on the advance.

Job finished. Chalk up one for us. No more fooling around.

One by one they raised themselves through the slit, which closed after the last. The rotors whirred.

"But how—? How—?" Jode whispered.

"I don't know, Jode," Larch admitted. "It must be some kind of emanation, released from somewhere on their bodies. I just don't know."

"What if they'd looked up here? Could they have made us disappear the same way?"

Larch sighed. "They might have had to adjust the range of the weapons first. That destruction you just witnessed was done at very short range. You'll notice nothing was destroyed but the building. That clump of trees only a little distance away is still okay."

"Impressive in a hideous way," Shelby said. "But what are we supposed to think? Did they believe we were inside the summerhouse and they got us? Or aren't they sure? And how could they have discovered the truth, with no evidence left?"

"We could have been inside," Jode exclaimed in awed tones. "We *could* have been."

"And if they think we were in there," Larch said, "will they stop looking for us now? *That* would be helpful."

"But we can't count on it," Shelby reminded him. "And what should we do now? It's already past eleven. We can't go on waiting at a summerhouse that no longer exists for a car we're reasonably certain won't arrive."

"We could walk to the airstrip," Larch suggested. "It's only a little farther from here than this place is from Galentry."

"You can't walk, Larch. Your knee—"

"I'm going to give it one hell of a try, though. If it turns out you're right, then you and Jode will go on without me."

The words struck through Shelby like an electric shock. "Absolutely not," she said quickly. "We are not going to separate for any reason."

"This is no time for sentimentality, Shel."

"I agree. And the worst sentimentality of all is self-sacrifice."

"Who's talking about self-sacrifice? If I can't walk the distance, I'll find some other way of getting there. Separating might help our chances by dividing our pursuers, if there are going to be pursuers, and we're not sure there won't be."

"Empty rhetoric," she accused him. "You know you can't find 'some other way' of getting to the airstrip without contacting Jeff Rawter. And he's certainly not at Orthohaven now. You know both he and Luke make it a point not to be on the scene when they're trying to help Abs, and you can hardly blame them. No, we'll just stay together no matter what. You can lean on me, if you need to. Or we'll improvise some kind of crutch."

"Nonsense. See? Already I'm standing up," he boasted. "If I can stand, I can walk."

"How much pain?" she wanted to know.

"Enough," he admitted, "but unless it gets a lot worse I have a chance. We've got to move out right away, though. We'll be a couple of hours late any-

111

way. If the plane does arrive, we'll have to hope it waits long enough."

They decided to leave by the rear of the butte, a shallower descent than if they had gone down the way they came in, and out of sight of the Rawter mansion and grounds. Neither Shelby nor Larch made any move to look over the rim at the front again, but Jode made one last check on the scene. "No one came out of the house to see what happened," he reported. "Maybe no one's home." He added mournfully, "I didn't see the cat around either. Do you think he was in that little house?"

"They're very cautious animals," Shelby comforted him. "I'll bet that cat shot right off into the forest at the first sound of the hopper, and won't come home till suppertime."

They descended from their promontory without trouble, Larch limping but making visible effort to move with his usual briskness. There was more brush, too, at the back of the butte, and the path they stumbled on to plunged from the brush immediately into forest again, so they wouldn't be totally exposed to view if the black hopper returned for a last look around.

At noon they rested briefly, traveled for another hour, rested again. The frequent stops were Shelby's idea, to save Larch from overdoing. Yet he, not Jode, was the one who chafed under the enforced halts, and spoke most often about the lateness of the hour.

"I'm tiring more rapidly, though," Shelby finally complained, half-truthfully.

"In that case, I apologize. You deserve every consideration. If my knee hadn't got busted, I would offer to carry you."

112

She smiled. "Thank you for the thought, anyway. I'm feeling better now. Let's go."

At about two in the afternoon they heard their first sound of mechanical origin since the Subcute experience. Where the path briefly paralleled a road or lane, a car roared past. The pines were thin enough at the spot that they could see a flash of red.

"Gasoline-powered," Larch mused. "Not Medcops. They wouldn't have the imagination to use an unmarked conveyance, especially one so flashy."

They would have forgotten the event if the car had not stopped up the road, still within their hearing. There was a sound of lowered gears as it backed up, then a swift movement up the ladder back to the highest gear before the red car sped past again, going the other direction. By this time the three fugitives had melted from the path back into the trees on the side away from the road.

"What could it be this time?" Shelby wondered.

"We've been hunted for too long," Larch said. "Pursuit leads to a kind of egomania. I suggest that red car contains a doc who was sent by his wife to the store down by the train station. I suggest that he set out, and halfway along had clean forgot what he was being sent for. Like that hemotologist we didn't visit, they have no telephone, out of touch by preference, and the husband has obligingly returned to have his memory refreshed."

Larch might have been right. At least the car disappeared the second time and didn't return. But neither did the trekkers feel free to return to the trail until it had veered far from the road, and by then the current leg of their journey was nearly three-quarters complete, according to Larch's reckoning.

"That map in your head is pretty good," Jode complimented him. "We haven't got lost yet, and you memorized some useful things, like Cooper's Butte."

"Never know when a butte is going to come in useful," Larch agreed lightly.

But all afternoon Shelby had, with deepening concern, watched expressions of suppressed but plainly increasing pain cross Larch's face as they forced themselves onward. She suspected that only the nearness of their destination now made it possible for him to continue.

At the end of their next hour, when on their present schedule they would have stopped for yet another brief rest, he shook his head. "If you and Jode can go on, we'd better. I'm afraid that if I stop now, the knee will stiffen so much I won't be able to move again. It's not so far from here."

Only when they had at last reached the place where Larch decided they must begin again to be extra-cautious—they were on the final fringe of the covering forest before the airstrip itself began—did he agree to another stop.

It was a measure of his present agony, Shelby realized, that he also agreed to let her do the reconnoitering this time. He would stay with Jode while she walked on, getting close enough to the clearing to see if the plane was there.

Alone, Shelby felt her body flag for the first time. Her legs were numb, her whole torso was numb. Each step seemed like seven, and seven steps a half-kilometer. She told herself that it was not so much true weariness as fear and anticipation which caused the numbness, but believing it didn't help much.

Moreover, though she had said little about the Subcute incident at the time, she could not get the Subcutes themselves out of her mind. As she had looked down from the butte top, Shelby had thought of her father facing these faceless beings just before he died, then had as quickly closed the thought away. Only to have it return again and again to haunt her with vicarious horror.

Now she came to a stone revetment, first sign of man-made construction since they had left the road. It was old, crumbling, built probably to retain soil in the field ahead when it was first cleared by some farmer in these parts, long before it had been used as an airstrip. She dropped to her hands and knees and crawled along the wall until she came to a thin place in the growth of brush along its top, where she could see into the clearing.

She raised her head slowly and peered out. At the same time feeling returned to her body in the form of a whirling nausea. It was as if the ground had dropped away, sickeningly. They had missed the plane. At least no jet waited there for them. But it was a very long strip, the kind needed for such landings. Could it be at the far end, out of her sight? Or been camouflaged against detection by the Subcute hopper?

No. By raising her head still higher she had a clear view of the entire cleared area. There was neither plane nor any branch- or grass-covered bulk which might conceal anything that large. Just a wide, smooth field thickly covered with grass and weeds. It was even beautiful in its peace and isolation, bright dots of mustard and lupine sprinkled among the brilliant green of wild oats and orchard grass. A mild breeze danced over its silent surface.

What could they do? Even Larch, she was sure, would have run out of alternate plans when he was faced with this latest setback. Had the plane come, waited a reasonable interval, and given them up? Had the black hopper intercepted it on the way and disintegrated it in midair?

They might never find out. They were on their own, every underground contact already severed, cut off by circumstances or purposely abandoned in preparation for the trip abroad which would now never take place.

But there was nothing to be gained by delaying her return to the others. How would they take the news? Larch realistically, though he might cover his dismay with bravado, his own mild sort. And Jode belligerently, she was sure. He would be angry at the whole Iatrarchy for thwarting them, and even at his age would be aware of the seriousness of this new situation.

Larch, Jode, herself, and the baby. Four lives now lost, when there had been such hope they could make it to safety. Others had. A few. But not her father. And not Larch's Kira. Was there then some curse upon herself that spelled doom for those she held dear (even extending to those *they* held dear)?

But that's only maundering, she told herself. *I'm behaving like a pregnant female of the old style, when pregnant women were cosseted and nursed and watched and fed curious foods on demand. And prevented from making arduous tramps through the mountains in order to arrive exactly nowhere.*

To her surprise, tears spilled down her cheeks. She dried them energetically with the cuff of her mackinaw. She backed away from the fence, still crouching. Then she decided it was silly to be crawling around when there was absolutely no one to see her.

She was about to rise, taking one more cautious look across the clearing, when she discovered she might be wrong about that.

From an eye-corner she had caught a suggestion of movement in the border of trees which were the width of the field away, directly across from the stone abutment she had hidden behind.

In a time now long past such a flicker of changing shadow at the edge of a woods would have meant the presence of deer. Shelby had never seen a deer except in old films. A timorous doe, her pair of spindly fawns behind her, nosing cautiously into the cleared space, about to emerge and graze.

Not a real possibility now, only a remembered fantasy. Yet the movement seemed to be caused by a fairly large body. It would have to be a man. As she watched, the object shifted once more, finally presenting a continuing rhythm. Definitely someone walking, keeping out of sight, watching the field just as she was.

Her heart leaped. It had to be—*please* let it be—someone sent by the underground to tell them what had happened with the plane, to reassure them it had only been delayed, or to present them with some carefully worked out, safer alternative.

Rational reconsideration, however, warned her of the more likely chance that it was a Medcop stationed here to watch for their arrival. Or even a Subcute, though she had received an impression of

117

dark clothing rather than the gray armor of the elite corps. If so, they could not after all assume that the officials had called off the search, satisfied with the inconclusive report that the fugitives had been trapped in the summerhouse when it was destroyed.

How could she find out without revealing her own presence?

. . No possibility, she decided. She waited a moment longer, watching the place in the woods past which the unknown person had walked, but there was no further sign of a presence there.

She turned back from the field, knowing she should leave, yet reluctant. She was frightened, certainly. Frightened at both the discovery and its implications, yet compelled to wonder if she shouldn't look now for some message left for them here, some subtle code conveying some hint of what had happened to the plane. (Croatan, 15—.)

But even as she considered this she knew it was absurd. No Ab would be so foolish as to leave signals which might also be spotted by the authorities. Hence any sign she might find could be assumed to be spurious, a ploy of the enemy.

Slowly, she started back.

Larch, resting against a tree with his right leg stretched straight, received the news with no change of expression, no sign of dismay. Jode looked crestfallen but said nothing.

"We'll have to assume it was a Medcop you saw prowling," Larch said, "which means we can't stay here. If they're conducting a full-scale search, knowing we're somewhere around here looking for the plane, they could pop up any minute."

To Shelby's amazement, he was already off the ground, standing, testing his weight against the in-

118

jured leg. "Even if you can walk, it seems to me we have nowhere to walk *to* this time," said Shelby. "Have we?" She spoke in vexation, having deliberately chosen it over despair. That might come next, and her tears again, but she would stall it off as long as she could, just as Larch was stalling off the pain.

Incredibly, though, Larch seemed to be considering her question, weighing possibilities. Were there still possibilities for them? She doubted it. At last he said, "Yes, there's a place we could go, not far from here, and we might be reasonably safe. For how long, I don't know. But it would be shelter, and maybe even a chance to sleep, especially if we took turns at sentry."

Jode immediately took heart. "I hope it's a cave," he said. "I always wanted to explore a cave, or a mine."

"It's very like a cave," Larch promised. "And it's near enough that we could still hear the jet coming in if it makes it after all. We won't count on that part of it, though. We can only hope the pilot got warned off in plenty of time and didn't get atomized by Subcutes instead."

"Won't the Medcops know every feature of the landscape around here just as you do?" Shelby asked him.

"Maybe. But maybe not about this place because it's a secret. It wasn't even on that map I studied. I know about it only because Jeff Rawter told me about it some time ago when we were talking about the airstrip and its possible usefulness to us. He was in one of his talkative moods, and went on and on about it. Said I ought to visit it sometime as a curi-

119

osity, gave me explicit directions to find it, which I only hope I remember."

"All right, Larch, I'm convinced," Shelby said. "I don't care what it is, if you can move at all, let's go to it."

"I'll be first sentry," Jode offered.

During her absence, Shelby noticed now, Larch had used his knife to fashion a cane from a tree limb. (Did this mean he hadn't really expected her to find the plane waiting, had anticipated having to continue walking somewhere?)

He leaned on it heavily as they set out, going in a direction at an angle to the airstrip, but not back the way they had come. It was a steep climb that immediately grew steeper as they veered back into the mountains by way of a gully filled with many rocks.

"We can certainly be seen from the air here," Shelby said, after they had toiled upward for several more minutes. "We've run out of trees again, bushes too."

"But there's no other way up, and we're almost there. *If* this is the right gully."

"Where's the cave?" Jode demanded.

"It's not a natural cave, Jode. It's man-made, cut into this mountain in greatest secrecy back in the nineteen seventies or thereabouts for a purpose no longer considered valid by the now-prevailing medical mentality. Maybe they're right, at least about that, and maybe not. But that needn't concern us now."

"Are you purposely being mysterious?" Shelby demanded.

"I guess I am," Larch admitted. "It occurred to

me when I thought of it that occupying it might be kind of—well, depressing."

"You mean it's a tomb? Somebody's private catacombs?"

"In a way. Hey! We're here! I found the way the first time. Somebody should congratulate me."

"I congratulate you," Shelby said. "I only wish you'd explain as you go."

"I don't see anything at all," Jode said.

"That's because we haven't said 'Open Sesame' yet," Larch teased him. "When we do, the mountain will fold back. Like this, see?"

He brushed aside a growth of blackberry canes to disclose steps leading down. At the bottom was a solid steel door set into the living rock. It was secured by a hasp and padlock, but the lock looked small and not very forbidding, though it was obviously fairly new.

"We can smash that off with a rock, I hope," Larch said. He put down the cane and picked up a medium-sized boulder.

But Jode, who was already twisting the padlock, cried out, "But we don't need to. Look, it's open. It only seemed locked."

Larch limped down the steps and Shelby followed. "That's odd," he said, "but we won't argue with success. We may have to deal with a tighter security inside." With Jode's help, and a scream of gravel against the concrete threshold, he eased the door inward.

As she paused beside the narrow entrance, Shelby saw the sign, a lapidary plaque, well weathered, obviously very old: CALIFORNIA CRYONIC SOCIETY—TRESPASSERS WILL BE

PROSECUTED. "I understand now, but—should we be breaking in like this?"

"No one home any more. The vaults are empty. During the war there wasn't anyone available to maintain them, of course. The power source eventually broke down, the liquid nitrogen—or whatever they were using at the time—ran out and wasn't replenished."

Jode said, "This was for the frozen people? I know about that. Back in the twentieth century—"

"Yes, Jode," Shelby interrupted, "but what happened to *them*? Are the remains still—?"

"No, not now," Larch reassured her. "Jeff says that a long time afterward some surviving relative remembered the existence of the vaults and notified the Doctors. All the sleepers and their expensive Dewar flasks and the rest of the equipment were removed. If there were any human remains by that time, I suppose they were cremated, or atomized in the prescribed way."

"More plans that went wrong," Shelby mused.

"Actually, it might be looked at as a piece of luck. These people were terminally ill if not clinically dead at the time of processing. Can you imagine being revived from cryonic sleep under the Iatrarchy only to be told that by law, because of your medical condition, you faced immediate thanatization?" And Larch added, "I'm exaggerating, of course. They would never have been returned to consciousness."

They now stood in a small foyer, facing a second door, of regular size, with the decorative brass scrollwork on polished dark wood still in good condition, except for an overlay of verdigris. Here the lock situation was even more puzzling. Two stages

122

in the history of the door were evident. The original lock was centered in the portal, disguised as part of the decoration, but its brass dial, probably operating an electric motor, had obviously been deactivated long ago. A second lock, mechanical, of the kind once used on safes, had been attached later at the closure, and still later blasted loose with some explosive. It now hung askew, useless.

"Someone's been using the place," Larch commented. "I guess it isn't such a secret as Jeff imagined."

If Shelby had expected the room they now entered to be dank and crypt-like, she was pleasantly surprised. The salon carved out of rock was airy, well-ventilated, but dim, illumined only by some system of hidden skylights. Nor was there any feeling of being in a cave. The walls were a warm-colored neutral, hung with discreet tapestry here and there, suggesting the lobby of a hotel. Only the furnishings—lounges and deep chairs covered in crushed velvet of jewel-rich hues, gold, maroon, deep blue, and carpeting of a mottled gray—spoke faintly of the mortuary waiting room of historical fame. (No mortuaries for the Iatrarchy. If mourning is discouraged as detrimental to the psyche, so must be displays of remains, and funerals.) Of course everything was a little faded, more than a little dusty. Those who knew about this place and visited it for whatever reasons evidently did not come often. Nor houseclean.

The sudden brightness and noise startled them all, especially Jode, who—Shelby saw at once— had experimentally pressed a switch beside one of the tapestries, throwing the room into muted chaos. Glow of diffused electric orbs distributing their

123

light evenly, without shadows. The noise—or rather sound—was disturbing only because unexpected. Actually what came from the concealed speakers was soft, very circumspect, just short of solemn: Buxtehude's Prelude and Fugue in G Minor, for organ.

Jode expressed their common wonder. "How could the current be still working if the power plant is busted?"

"Whoever comes here must have installed another, or repaired the original," Shelby guessed.

"Handy for us," Jode said.

"Maybe not. Larch, can anyone hear the music from outside, do you think?"

"No way to know, unless one of us goes out to check. But surely the lights can't show and we could use them if we turned off the sound." Larch pressed the switch again. The lights went out but the sound continued. Once more and they had it the way they wanted. Lights without music. The switch had three positions.

"This is a crazy place to hide," Jode said. "But I like it okay. Why was a thing like this put up here in the mountains in the first place?"

"They wanted it kept secret then too," Larch explained. "Humankind went through two stages of thinking on death. The first, and longest, where everyone talked about death, but no one did anything about it. And the second, shorter and terminated like a lot of other projects by the war, where everyone who could afford it did something about death, but no one talked about it."

"This is nonsense," Shelby scolded, "for us to stand around talking when we could be resting. You especially, Larch, should lie on one of these lounges with your leg as comfortable as you can get it." She moved around the room, using a scarf from her pocket to remove the worst of the dust from three of the sofas. In an enclosed niche at the end of the long room she found a small lavatory whose taps still gushed water. Encouraging, since they had long since run out of the imitation milk. There were even disposable cups in a dispenser. Again she took packets of food from their dwindling supply and passed them around.

"Where's that big door lead to?" Jode asked.

"Don't talk with your mouth full," his sister admonished. "I suppose it leads to the vaults, or the corridors where the vaults once were. But don't ask to explore them, please. There's nothing in there we need."

"In fact there's probably nothing at all in there," Larch agreed.

Jode's disappointment showed in his downcast expression. Only his evident weariness kept him from arguing, Shelby was aware.

But now their exhaustion, a burden before, would serve them well. Surely they could sleep here as they could not in the woods, with less fear of discovery. Did the Medcops know of the vaults? Shelby decided it was safe to assume not. Probably only a few Doctors knew, and Doctors were notorious for keeping information among their own. Except for Jeff Rawter, who talked a lot.

"What about the lookout?" Jode said sleepily. "I was going to be first."

"On second thought, let's take the chance of not posting a lookout," Larch suggested. "If either of you hears the plane coming in, wake me instantly. If I hear it first, I'll wake you."

"Do you really still expect the plane?" Shelby asked him. "In three hours it'll be dark."

"They may have decided darkness would be better for arriving here, especially if they got the word the Subcutes had been called into the area. Now that I think of it, that could explain everything. The jet was messaged to hold off till the Medcops—if there really were Medcops up here today—got tired and gave up, and until it got dark."

"Do you really believe that, Larch?" she said.

"I'd like to. I don't know what to believe. None of us does at this point."

Just before Shelby fell asleep, there was another twinge, like those of before, except fainter, less decisive. If it was followed by another, she wasn't aware of it. She drifted into unconsciuosness immediately.

Her dreams were unpleasant, mostly inchoate, a prolonged struggle against palpable shadows and disembodied wills. There were barren landscapes from which all living and constructed matter had been removed by atomizing weapons, and over which she was forced to tramp in ever-widening circles, seeking but never finding some sign which would tell her which direction to take, where to go.

They had begun their evening-into-night of rest on separate couches, Shelby concerned that Larch be as comfortable as possible on account of the injury. But at some point he had risen and come to lie beside her, his arms around her, two bodies crowded but amiable on the narrow lounge. She was aware of his presence and yet remained uncomforted in her mind. The dreams went on.

Once she saw her father, a big, highly noticeable

man, with a wide, wrinkled forehead under a roach of graying hair, and quizzical, dubious, green eyes that could change instantly from brooding to humor. In the dream he confronted her, but seemed not really to see her, the green eyes fixed on something past her in the distance, something she was faced the wrong direction to see. Finally he turned away and, still not attending her frantic exhortations, walked from her side toward the summerhouse, which he finally entered, dropping down the straw screen behind him so that he was invisible to her.

The summerhouse disappeared.

She screamed again and again, but soundlessly, so that no pursuer would overhear.

Once she thought she heard the plane coming, jets howling down the night to their rescue. But when she half woke, her hand already on Larch's shoulder to wake him too, there was no sound after all. The room was breathlessly still around her, as still as the night beyond the iron door. Larch and Jode slept on, Jode the more peacefully, since at least twice in the night she was sure she had heard Larch moan in pain.

At what her watch told her was five in the morning, she could sleep no more. This time there was no denying the message from her body. A cramp of a magnitude to make her gasp seized her, wrung her, and after a long moment spent itself, leaving her trembling.

She made herself lie absolutely still (the remedy which had worked so well before), willing relaxation upon every muscle. She refused to let herself think beyond the point of: *if it is only another false labor, it will pass away; if it is not...*

At ten minutes after five a pain of approximately the same magnitude pressed in. Pressed and pressed, and then respectfully withdrew. A third occurred at the same interval.

Half an hour later, Larch woke. He bent over her and kissed her cheek, apparently noticing nothing amiss. He immediately rolled off the lounge to an upright posture and began testing his weight on the right leg. "Where are you going?" she said.

"Out to take a look around, then down to see if anything's happened at the field. Obviously we can't stay here much longer."

"Your knee—?"

"Much better. Practically well. Probably the night's rest was all it needed to start mending. Last night I loosened the bandage you put on. I'll tighten it again now." But Shelby noticed he limped as much as ever as he started for the door.

He was about to open it, cautiously, when she called out, "Larch—?"

He misinterpreted her concern. "You and Jode will be as safe here as anywhere, probably safer than most of the places we could possibly be right now. I'll be back in just minutes."

She decided to put off telling him. There was still the hope it would fade into nothing, as before. The last contraction five minutes ago, for instance, had been noticeably milder than the others.

And if Larch didn't return? Impatiently, she shut the possibility away with the other terrible unanswered questions that haunted her. She would keep them all suppressed. She had never been a worrier; no point in starting now.

Another half hour crept by. The contractions recurred regularly but neither increased their force nor decreased the interval. It was after six now, there would be full daylight outside. Larch had not come back, though he had promised it would be "minutes."

Choosing her time carefully, immediately after one cramp completed itself with nine or so minutes before she need brace herself for the next, she rose to her feet and walked around the room. It did indeed look like a funeral parlor to her now. On his own sofa, Jode sprawled on his stomach, one arm trailing the carpet, still sleeping heavily.

In the tiny lavatory she examined her face in the dust film. She told herself she actually felt fine despite all, rested even though she had endured the dreams, able to accomplish whatever the day might demand of her. But her eyes seemed larger and a darker green than usual, with faint circles beneath, lips and cheeks pale. She rinsed her face in cold water and scrubbed it ambitiously with her handkerchief. She carefully combed her dark hair. There was nothing to be done about her clothing. She felt gritty and ill at ease in the jeans and shirt she had slept in, that she had not removed since she put them on in such haste at Galentry.

Nearly fifty minutes now since Larch had left. With an eye on her watch, Shelby crept back to her sofa and lay down again. The pain swept over her right on schedule.

How could she find out what had happened to him? Wake Jode and send him out to see? Certainly not! A boy of ten? At least not yet. . .

The rhythm changed with no warning at all. Hystera performing like a great bellows, squeezing powerfully, and not nearly so much time elapsing between seizures. How much? Seven minutes? Five

minutes? She had no sooner decided it was approximately five minutes than another sweep of the pain
pendulum showed her that it was only three.

"Larch! Oh, Larch!" she called foolishly into the
silent room. And immediately scolded herself for
almost waking Jode.

Childbirth is only a natural function, she reminded herself severely, calling for no histrionics, no
special sympathy. (And in the case of her
mother—?)

It might prove a serious misfortune that she had
not been able to carry this child full term. She must
be prepared for that. If it was alive, there might
still be many problems. For all her prior thought
about this possibility, she had still gone on planning
to give birth *after* they got to England, in ease and
freedom, under the care of an obstetrician. Even after the first false labors she had gone on planning,
knowing so little time would have to pass before
they were really there. If things went all right. But
they had not gone all right.

Now she supposed they would never get to England. It was the first time she had allowed herself
to be quite so pessimistic about their chances. Even
after the terrible thing at the summerhouse yesterday, the incident which more than any other had
spelled out the seriousness of their plight, she recalled that she had been able to allow herself to go
on hoping. Fatuously hoping.

And now . . . now she didn't even know if Larch
would ever. . .

The outer door crunched shut, the inner one
clicked, and he was beside her. He was out of
breath, rumpled-looking, his face again showing
him to be in severe pain.

130

"Shel, I—"

"What is it?"

"In a word—trouble. The place is jumping with Medcops. They're all around the landing strip, staked out through the woods. There was one cooling his heels even at the foot of the gap that leads up here. That's what took me so long. I couldn't come in through the ravine. I had to invent a new way to get here."

"And do you think you were seen?"

"I think not. I hope not. And the fact that the Medcop was just waiting there in the foot of the ravine might mean this place is still a secret. Otherwise he'd have been on his way up here."

"Subcutes too?"

"Just Medcops. So far. We must have been downgraded again after yesterday." He was looking at her closely now. "Shel—? What's wrong?"

She told him. Speaking simply. Trying to maintain a sensible position midway between de-emphasizing the situation and causing him unnecessary alarm.

What happened immediately after this made her believe that she must have fallen into another dream. Larch simply disappeared again. This time it seemed he went—though she knew better—through the inner door leading back to the vaults deep under the mountain. But, sunk in pain, she must surely have imagined it.

He returned an indeterminate time later bearing with him a pile of crisp, laundered linen, white as that from a facility, sealed in transparent wrappings.

Working quickly, he broke open package after package and spread sheets on the sofa opposite

131

where she lay. Gently, he removed the clothing that had felt so gritty and stiff, and covered her with a soft, clean gown. Then she felt herself being lifted into the made-up bed.

She *must* know how the miracle had been wrought, meant to demand that he tell her at once, but was swept under the new relentless wave and could only cling to him and listen to her own breath being emitted in ragged sobs.

Amniotic fluid bathed her. Sweat stung her eyelids. Momentary blackness wiped out still more pain, but the baby was born neatly and swiftly, slipping from one world into another as easily as a puck over smooth ice.

Then a different kind of crisis as she saw that Larch had turned his attention from her to work over the baby. He lowered his mouth over the tiny face in the traditional gesture of resuscitation. Shelby held her own breath. She prayed. She closed her eyes and waited to hear some sound from the child, but none came. None at all.

Eyes still closed, she came to the stunning moment of hearing him give up the respiratory effort and turn to other tasks.

The baby had been born too soon then, just as she feared. Larch was evidently cutting the cord with his knife, tying knots, wrapping the tiny body in more linen. These movements were felt by her rather than seen. She determined not to open her eyes until she could control the tears that threatened her with a fit of wildest hysteria. She must not alarm Jode, nor make needless trouble for Larch.

Instead of immediately bearing away the bundle containing the body of their child, however, he placed it beside her. She understood. *He thinks I'll want to hold it just once before he carries it off to some secret grave.*

Obediently, only to please him for she was beyond this now, she allowed her arm to close around the tiny parcel. A body so slight it weighed nothing. *No wonder it was incapable of existence.*

But the parcel moved.

"Very small," Larch reported quietly, "but she *looks* all right." He laughed ironically. "I mean, to my non-medical eye she looks all right. I'm no doctor."

Shelby opened her eyes and looked at the baby through tears of surprise and relief, "I heard no cry, no breathing. I thought the worst."

"No, she hasn't cried. But her breathing's fine since I helped her get started. Maybe she's keeping quiet because she senses our situation. Good to know she's on our side."

With the baby safe, it was possible to think of herself again. No pain now. She felt tired, but almost as well as she had earlier, looking at herself in the lavatory mirror. And though nothing about their situation had changed (except for the worse; since there were four of them now, they were that much more vulnerable), her depression over their chances had lifted. Unreasonably, it seemed possible after all that they might get to England. They had one more reason to *have* to break free.

"She won't have a passport," Shelby reminded Larch, "but she can travel on mine. Also she'll need a name. If you agree, I should like to call her Kira."

Larch remained silent for so long that Shelby decided he wasn't going to answer. They should have

133

talked it over. She had thought there would be plenty of time for that, before the baby came. But now she must have hurt him, even angered him by imagining he might want his daughter to bear the name of the lost girl he had once loved, and loved still in memory.

But he roused himself from reverie to say, "An admirable choice, a hopeful link from past to future. Kira it must be."

In response Kira opened her delicate mouth and gave an interrogatory sort of cry, a sound too thin to have carried outside their sanctuary, but strong enough to convey the stirring of hunger.

Jode, who had slept through it all, sat up and stared in concern at his increased family. "Hey, what's going on?" he demanded.

Shelby rested luxuriously. Later in the morning Larch went out again and returned to report that the problem remained much the same, Medcops still around the field, though not so many either there or in the fringes of the wood. And none in the ravine. They might be gradually cutting back their forces. It was too soon to tell. But once they had satisfied themselves that the fugitives were no longer expecting the plane, they might all be ordered away. No Subcutes had joined them.

She now remembered the mysterious appearance of the immaculate linen and asked about it. "A miracle, all right, and a mystery," she was told. "After you fell asleep yesterday evening, I did some exploring, like Jode wanted to. He was right that we should have gone in. The inner door to the vaults doesn't even have a lock.

"And in there, it turns out, it's more like a medical facility than anything else I can think of. Cabinets and cabinets full of pharmaceuticals, surgical equipment, linen supplies—from which I 'borrowed' what we needed—a nurses' lounge with a coffeemaker and supplies of tea and snacks all carefully wrapped and—uh—frozen. And farther back is the most curious development of all. There are people in there."

Shelby's eyes widened. "Then we're not alone?"

"We are not alone. But neither will our presence be challenged. Not by the residents here. Cryonics patients. Ten of them. It explains why the power is on, why we have light and water and all the comforts. I was going to surprise you with a cup of tea when you woke up, but I wasn't back in time. And then you beat me to the punch by asking about the linen."

"What do you suppose it means?"

"I've no idea. Jeff definitely said that all the patients who 'died' here when the power failed had been removed. But things have been repaired and these are obviously all new arrivals.

"As a wild guess, I'd say the medics have come across some cases they couldn't figure out a way to save at this stage of their research, but these people were too valuable to them to give up on and thanatize. Doctors themselves, undoubtedly. So they violated their own laws and clandestinely re-instituted the cryonics program."

"Does it also mean the vaults are included on some physician's regular rounds? I mean, these places have to have routine maintenance. Someone from the Iatrarchy might walk in any minute and find us here."

"Somehow I discount the notion that a
135

maintenance person coming here would be from the Iatrarchy. It's too—well—too ill-maintained out here in the lounge for it to have the stamp of officialdom. It's some secret business of an outfit of wheels within wheels, Doctors planning something without telling all. Interesting, to say the least. But the chance of someone coming here is very great, as you say. I do think that as soon as you and Kira are able to travel, we'd better get out of here."

"I think we could go any time. I feel so well. But—again I have to ask you, Larch—where do we go now? Surely even you are all out of ideas by this time. Or do you know something you haven't told me?"

"There's one possibility I didn't mention because I never thought we'd need it. It's risky, maybe more so than any chance we've taken up to now. Do you know a woman called Quistlethorp?"

Shelby smiled. "She sounds like someone in a book. But, yes, the name rings faintly. I believe I've met her at meetings."

"Christian Science practitioner. Real diehard for liberty of the individual and so on. So furious with the Iatrarchy and all it stands for that she makes some of the rest of us look like political dilettantes."

"Yes, of course. An elderly lady, kind of acerbic on first meeting, but warm and friendly after you've talked with her awhile. But what could knowing Mrs. Quistlethorp possibly do for us at this point?"

"Maybe very little, but I'm sure she'd help us if she could. Her brother, it seems, is a Doctor. He's not a member of HA and has no use for the Abs, but on the other hand, he's an anomaly among ranking Iatrarchists because he's never been able to bring himself to turn his sister in, apparently. He

136

does try to keep her hidden away, though, and one of the ways he's chosen to do that is to let her live in his summer place in the mountains."

"At Orthohaven?"

"Exactly. Out of sight, out of mind, he hopes. Only she remains very active in the movement despite him. The house is on the opposite side of the mountain from where we are now, unfortunately. Farther than the distance back to Jeff's, where we can't go anyway. Farther than back to Galentry, where ditto. What do you say?"

"Well, distance hasn't really hindered us so far."

"It's as much as twenty-five kilos, maybe more."

Shelby considered. The baby. Larch's injured knee. Jode. The mountains still full of Medcops. The Subcutes already alerted to their case, ready to return to duty the moment it could be shown that the fleeing Abs had definitely not been in the summerhouse. But she finally said to Larch, "Well, it's great weather. We can take food from here. Kira and I are ready any time. And if your knee is mending—though I'm not entirely convinced—then why not? Besides, do we have any other choices?"

"No."

"Then what are we waiting for? Maybe we can make it to Mrs. Quistlethorp's inside of a day, even with lots of rests."

"No, again. Let's risk one more night here. The Medcops have proved by now that they don't know about the vaults, and as long as they stay in the area, they'll be doing us the favor of keeping away anyone else who might be wanting to come here. And you've got to agree the people here, though they may be important Doctors, have been hospitable."

137

"Not inhospitable," she agreed.

Ponderously slow hours now began to pass. Kira slept and woke and fed and slept again. Larch made several more furtive trips to reconnoiter, reporting each time that, unless he was guilty of wishful thinking, the Medcops seemed to be gradually thinning ranks. The food taken from the nurses' lounge refrigerator was not bad, in fact a cut above the "nutritionally balanced" compounds.

Jode, of course, was restless. Precluded by Larch and Shelby from going outside, and forbidden the vaults except for one visit he made accompanied by Larch, he became bored even with the diversion of examining the remarkable miniature digits and features of his new niece, who slept most of the time anyway. He eventually discovered, stashed behind the long-unstaffed reception desk at the rear of the room, a pile of standard reading matter for waiting rooms in contemporary medical facilities. *Your Doctor Is Your Best Friend*, *Medical Marvels* (in comic strip format), *Wonder Tales of the War: How Physicians Saved the World for Freedom*, and so on.

To the boy, whose learning so far had been "limited" to the pre-war history and literature provided by the underground school, this kind of reading matter was all new. For a while he became absorbed in the feats of heroism performed by the Medarchy in exotic settings throughout the world (a Doctor Rex Morgan, rigid of facial expression but resplendent in Medburo *Haupt Chirurg* uniform, particularly took his fancy).

But all too soon he began complaining to Shelby that the stories were "all the same," and that, even though the tales were supposed to be about medicine, it wasn't possible to learn anything about medicine from them. Still, they served to remind him of something he had mentioned before. "When I grow up, I'm going to be a Doctor, like Dad. But not join the Iatrarchy, I'll have my own practice and start my own facility and not 'modify' or thanatize anybody."

This kind of announcement from Jode never failed to elicit a chill fear in Shelby, even as she encouraged her brother to hang onto his dream and try to make it real. For unless world affairs changed radically in the next few years, it might mean that Jode, having elected to study medicine under whatever alias, could eventually be drawn into the Iatrarchy (perhaps with every hope, at first, of being able to precipitate a change from within), or—like their father—be driven to speaking out against tyranny at the cost of his life.

When Jode brought up the subject again now, however, with Kira warm against her breast, and their prospects at least partially restored if only by her own state of euphoria, Shelby said, "I believe an American *could* become a Harley Street doctor, and have his own practice and make his own ethical decisions. As soon as we get to England, we shall investigate the possibility of your studying toward that end. You'd have to apply yourself to your books, though, study harder than you ever have. I believe you're mentally equipped for it. I think you might do it."

The boy glowed under the implied praise, for praise from his sister was rare enough. She had always been a demanding teacher, saving compliments only for worthy efforts.

In the morning, at first light, Larch again went

out to survey the activities and distribution of the Medcop forces. This time, as they had hoped, the news was good. "Not one of them in sight. I think they really have withdrawn."

Again they packed very lightly, taking only enough food from the nurses' stores to last through the day, leaving room for their only "extra" baggage, the several meters of gauze Larch had selected from the vault's hospital supplies to serve as diapers and clean wrappings for Kira.

Outside, the air was moist and cool, the sun invisible behind a high-riding fog. Good, brisk walking weather. Larch, ambulating now without the cane and hardly limping (unless he was again suppressing the limp to convince Shelby), insisted on carrying the baby, who was enveloped in one of her father's heavy shirts, her face covered against the damp air. Shelby suggested, however, that they must take turns with their newest burden. "She weighs nothing, not even as much as the things we have her bundled in."

"We'll see," said Larch, and led the procession still farther up the mountain that contained the secret vaults rather than down again near the airstrip, just in case he had missed seeing some lone remaining Medcop on patrol.

"Dumb Medcops," Jode said. "They never knew we were here, and they'll never know we've gone."

"Don't underestimate the Medcops, and don't ever underestimate the Subcutes," Larch warned. "As it happens the route we're taking will bring us into a place that's more thickly populated than the ones we've been in so far on this trip. We even have a highway to cross and very soon we can expect to meet someone from time to time on the trail."

"Who?" Jode inquired with interest.

"He doesn't mean meet someone we know, on purpose," Shelby explained. "We'll just have to hope that those we can't avoid meeting will be hikers like us, with no special interest in interrogating strangers."

"But Kira," Jode pointed out, "is too young to have learned to keep her mouth shut, like me."

"It's something we've thought of," Shelby agreed. "If she cries at the wrong time, it might be very bad for us. But we're taking a lot of chances anyway. One more won't make much difference."

Shelby fervently hoped she was right about this, while admitting its dubiousness, admitted to the madness of carrying a newborn infant into the kind of situation they might encounter any moment. *Why* had the baby come so soon? If the labor had only held off another twenty-four hours, it might have made all the difference in their chances.

But futile speculations were not to be made aloud. Kira was with them as she had been with them from the outset of the journey, only in a different way. And in another sense, it was good to have the delivery behind her. She had not lied to Larch when she had declared herself able to travel. She really did feel fine, though she knew enough about the post-partum condition to expect to tire more easily than usual. And she knew she must make herself rest, eat, and relax, in order to keep the supply of milk steady and nourishing.

Surprisingly, after what Larch had said about meeting strangers, the first half of their day's hike passed without incident. They met no one, though the private estates of the Doctors soon began to seem more numerous, closer together. They passed

141

forbidding gatehouses and imposing driveways and place-name signs with words like "Rx," and "Healer's Hideout," and "Duncuttin," the last apparently the home of a retired surgeon with a lame sense of humor.

As usual they walked, rested, walked again, and had lunch in a secluded spot far off the trail. They were still in the pines, not yet down to redwood country, and the stands of trees were reassuringly thick. Jode ate in haste, then began exploring their surroundings, poking under rocks, climbing trees, still expending the energy suppressed in their enforced stay at the vaults.

Shelby knew better than to urge him to rest, but when she realized he had shinnied up a nearby pine, was in fact very high into the small limbs, which shook and swayed with his weight, she cried, "Jode, come down from there. If you break a leg we'll be in even worse trouble."

To her mild surprise, he made no demur; he didn't even answer her but obeyed instantly, hopping out of the tree almost at their feet, facing them white-faced and anxious.

"Is something wrong, Jody?"

"Medcops! When I was up in the tree I saw them. Coming along the trail fast. On foot, like us."

"How many?" Larch said. "And how far away?"

"Two. Or anyway I only saw two. They were just crossing the creek we crossed not very long before we got here."

"Half a kilometer, no more," Larch judged.

"You're sure they were Medcops?" said Shelby.

"Gotta be. They're in uniform."

Larch was already gathering up their belongings. He passed Shelby her pack and took Kira from her.

"A good thing we're already off the trail. We'll just keep going this direction, cross-country again. Back to the compass." Kira wailed thinly, as if to remind him. "And we mustn't make any noise we can possibly avoid. No calling out, not even any talking." As they set off, he remembered to add, "You're a good sentry, Jode. If it hadn't been for your good work, we could have been taken by surprise."

This time the presence of the Medcops had to be a random phenomenon, Shelby decided. In historical times, she knew, their situation would have been more predictable, perhaps. An old-fashioned posse, fanning out in every direction from the airstrip, or from the middle of Orthohaven (where Jeff's house was), could provide sufficient numbers to reduce the odds that any quarry could slip through the net. But so far as she knew, Medcops never recruited law-enforcement help from Patients. And there was only a specific number of Medcops for each job. They had raided the cottage, presumably, and patrolled the airstrip; now there were two in the woods nearby. It didn't make sense, but neither did it prove that the fugitives were being deliberately pursued this time. They still had a chance, a reasonably good chance, so long as they remained out of sight.

Or was this just part of her off-again-on-again optimism and nothing to do with reality? Obviously the number of Medcops and Subcutes allocated to Orthohaven was in direct ratio to how desperately they were wanted by the authorities. She tried not to fool herself about this. The children of Gerrod Harmon and—though it was not yet officially known—his grandchild, traveling in company of an arch-leader of the underground. Such a group could

143

not be allowed to escape the continent to cause further trouble from exile. A dynasty must be wiped out in its entirety.

Shelby thought about these things as she moved along silently and quickly behind Larch, who still carried the baby. At least the walking was not difficult now. The pines had at last given way to the redwoods. The trees were old and the trunks widely spaced; neither fire nor man had come ravaging through. The down-slope was gentle, the heavy leaf mold soft under their feet. The sun had emerged at last and, where the foliage was thin enough, formed little warm puddles of light edged with broken shade.

Had coming to Orthohaven—her idea, a decision made in haste and anxiety after Luke suggested the cottage—been their worst mistake then? Orthohaven, meaning "correct sanctuary," the right place. But one could so easily find oneself in the right place at the wrong time.

Surely the real mistake lay further in the past. Joining (in fact, being born into) an underground of faulty nexus, too loosely knit, too undisciplined, too idealistic in its rejection of violence to function well. Now, for instance, when they might need at any minute to defend themselves from attack, they were not even carrying weapons.

And the business of their betrayal, so hard to assimilate, so impossible to pinpoint, yet so difficult to ignore, was only another symptom of the faulty looseness of their organization. Betrayal was indecently easy, and ever immune from retribution because of the noncombative nature of the group.

Every man to his own conscience—that was the basic rationale of the underground. Objection to the Iatrarchy was the only real common denominator for members. A negative foundation might be no foundation. In turning away from Iatrarchy, one courted anarchy, even embraced it.

The World Medarchy, on the other hand, though flawed idealistically and fallen into obsession, was not only invincibly self-defended and highly organized, it served a fundamental human purpose, responded to a deep and positive need. No denying that the Doctors were in tune with the times. Most people shrank from freedom and the idea of freedom, learned a thousand devious tricks to avoid it. Frightening freedom, yawning pit of chaos, all certainties removed, the will left to its own. As in Greek democracy which was, of course, not democracy. And the Romans: senatus populusque: first the triumvirates, then Caesar Augustus, god-imperator.

Security. Civilization. Roads and communications. Caledonia to Parthia. The barbarians feared their own freedom so much they enslaved themselves to the strongest robbers, the most successful pirates. John and the Magna Carta, Charles I and the chopping block in the window at Whitehall. The Rights of Man, the Goddess of Reason, the Republic One and Indivisible giving way to the First Consul. Father, protect me. History is a helix. No wonder all calls for freedom are lost in a sea of incomprehension.

As for instance now. Very few Patients would ever defy the Iatrarchy or citizens elsewhere the World Medarchy. The Ama's authority rested on much more than sullen acquiescence. Most people accepted the press releases of the Authorized Public Enlightenment Service (familiarly reduced to

APES) as truth. Doctor knows best. In Doc we trust.

Only the one ray of hope now, that the whole wheel would begin to turn again. For was it believable, really, that the human spirit could be quelled once and for all time? Revolution might lead to reaction, but reaction surely bred revolution. It always had. One must never, her father had often quoted, come to look upon tyranny as a permanent condition.

Their silent defile among the redwoods continued. Occasionally they halted to listen for sounds. Once Jode was delegated to climb another tree and look in all directions. He reported no Medcops, but said they were in sight of one of the trails. And on that trail at quite a distance he could see five hikers swinging along, in step, performing some kind of cadence. All wore dark blue and had alpenstocks and funny-looking hats.

"Jode, *please*," Shelby scolded him. "This is no time for jokes. Are you making that up?"

"I swear it's true, Shel. But they're not coming this way. And they're all looking straight ahead anyway."

"It's the Medical Scouts, Shelby," Larch said. "Young people, adolescents. They march and sing and hike. You've heard of them."

"I guess I just never happened to see any. But it's good we didn't have to confront them. They'd be as eager as the Caduceus Church people to report something odd to the authorities. Like a baby wrapped in a shirt."

Though Larch hadn't said so yet, Shelby soon began to believe that they must have covered the twenty-five kilometers. Only a morning's walk for an able person. They had needed, planned, to take longer, but the day was going fast. She said nothing, however.

Already the character of the landscape had changed. The open spaces were growing bigger, and there were stands of yellowed grass, dotted with still-green weeds, and more lupine. And farther down, occasionally visible as the land unrolled before them, were gelatine-green pastures, cattle country, or what must have been cattle country in times past.

Kira had been quiet most of the way, apparently lulled by the rocking motion of her father's arms. The moment came, however, when Larch handed her to Shelby and again consulted his compass, though he had looked at it not five minutes before. "Odd," he said. "According to what I recall of the map, we should at least have come within sight of the Quistlethorp place by now. I know I'm not infallible, but—"

"Are we lost?" Jode asked, more in excitement than dismay.

"A little. But we can't be very far wrong. We've walked steadily southwest, downhill all the way. It's got to be around here somewhere."

"We never crossed that highway you said we would," Jode remembered.

"You're right, Jode. And on or off the trail, we should have come to the highway about an hour ago, that is, if we—"

How tired he looks, Shelby thought. And bewilderment was an emotion in Larch with which she was almost totally unfamiliar. They simply could not go on depending on him this way, day after day, twenty-four hours a day, all of them leaning

147

on his strength, feeding their hope from his ingenuity. They had to get out of Orthohaven somehow, since they were being—or had been—hunted at Orthohaven, but finding Mrs. Quistlethorp's place might take hours more. And even if found, there was no certainty she would or could take them in. She might not even be home.

"Let's rest for a few minutes, and then just keep going downhill till we come to the highway that runs past the ocean," Shelby said. "Maybe someone would give us a ride back into town. It'd almost be worth the risk. Then we could re-contact the group and find out what happened to the plane."

"I don't know, Shelby. You may be right, but I don't like the idea of re-opening contacts there, putting others in jeopardy when the Medcops and Subcutes seem to be after us with such a vengeance. And we couldn't go back to our own apartments, or contact anyone from the school—"

Characteristically, Jode had seized their momentary hesitation to run ahead, scouting, looking for some sign Larch might have missed that would show they were, after all, nearing Mrs. Quistlethorp's brother's property. Now the boy came bounding back, plainly proud of another of his discoveries. "Hey, there's a creek right ahead through those trees, and a trail that runs along it for a little bit and then crosses it."

She and Larch followed Jode through the trees to see, but the presence of the creek didn't seem to help Larch figure out where they were, or why they weren't where they should be. Actually what Jode had seen wasn't a trail. "It's a road," Larch said, "an old road."

"Not the road we're looking for, huh?"

"Can't be. It hasn't been used for years."

Shelby saw that the road was deeply leached where the ruts must have run at one time, and there were large chuckholes where the ground had given way beneath pools of water. A ford had been made where it crossed the creek, banks pressed down at that place to water level and the old ruts resuming on the far side.

"I bet it leads to an abandoned mine," Jode said. "We could go there and hide in the mine and if the Medcops or the Subcutes came, we could go down the shaft. There might be another way out and we could trick them. Or a landslide might happen behind us."

"Oh, Jode, please!" Shelby wasn't usually irritable, but the stress was building again. She was suddenly very tired after all, the baby stirred in her arms and whimpered.

"No, Shel, maybe he's right. I mean, not about the mine, necessarily, but the road must lead somewhere. If not to a mine, maybe to the main road. If we could find that, I'd know where we are."

So they plodded forward again, without having rested after all, Shelby half convinced they were getting more and more lost, headed, perhaps, to some abandoned and uninhabitable shack, perhaps a place where they could be easily trapped.

But in a quarter kilometer the old track did indeed angle into another road, just as Larch had hoped, one far better maintained and clearly used recently. There were fresh tire tracks, slightly muddy, as if a vehicle had parked off the shoulder, then pulled back onto the narrow pavement. Larch seemed more confident. "Still isn't the highway," he muttered, "but we're going the right direction. I hope those tracks don't mean the Medcops are lurking in this neighborhood too."

"Should we do our walking away from the road then?" Shelby said. "Across that field perhaps?"

Larch shook his head. "Nothing to hide behind or under. Let's follow this road for a while, listening for cars. If we hear someone coming, we'll have to dive for the weeds again, like we did that first night coming out of Galentry."

It was almost dusk again, and they had been on the way since dawn. When, Shelby wondered, does one simply give up? At what moment does a beleaguered human being decide that to keep struggling against the inevitable is futile? For them, it seemed now, the moment was surely at hand. Or perhaps had come and gone, none of them having recognized it, fools that they were. She felt that she could go on only a little farther before collapsing. She wondered if the others felt the same. Kira whimpered continuously now. Even Jode looked weary. He made no more forays ahead, no side trips to investigate things that interested him.

Trees appeared only in scattered clumps here, laurels and sycamores, a few birches. All during their journey through Orthohaven, Shelby was to think later, it had been trees that protected them from the sight of their pursuers, but in this case it was trees that did them in.

For ahead now was an unexpected curve in the road, obscured by a clump of trees. Rounding it, they found themselves within a few meters of a fallen dead trunk, stripped of its bark and many of its limbs by weather and decay. It blocked the road. Just beyond it was the nose of a red car, possibly the same red car they had seen earlier traveling back and forth on the other road.

The surprise of it brought them to a halt. Before they could rectify their mistake and try to run, or at least move away, it was already too late.

Someone was sitting in the driver's seat, a woman. This stranger first stared at them and then jumped out, an old-fashioned rifle in her hands. "Don't move," she ordered them. "Don't come any closer and don't try to get away."

She rested the riflestock under her arm, finger lying lightly against the trigger, muzzle unwaveringly pointed. With her free hand she tucked a lock of springy black hair back under the bright blue silk scarf bound tightly around her head.

The woman's overbearing air of authority made the gun almost superfluous, Shelby thought. She was as tall as Larch, perhaps in her late thirties or early forties, dressed in dark trousers that disappeared below the knee into smooth, fitted boots, and a loose, tweedish, parti-colored tunic, the blue in which matched the scarf.

"Are we trespassing on your property?" Larch inquired. "We thought this was a public road."

The stranger did not answer. She continued to stare at them, levelly, speculatively. The rudeness now seemed to Shelby almost as shocking as the pointed weapon.

"We are on a hike," Shelby explained, hoping her voice sounded normal, "headed toward the highway. Perhaps you could tell us how far it is?"

The gunwoman also ignored Shelby's question, but she said, disbelievingly, "A *hike*? Curious choice for diversion with your friend limping so badly. I watched you coming around the corner. I saw you before you saw me."

"I wish we'd never seen you at all," Jode declared. "We were minding our own business. You got no right to—"

"Jode, never mind," Shelby cautioned.

"I was limping because I stumbled over a rock," Larch said quite truthfully, and added, "I plan to see a Doctor about it as soon as we get to town."

Her sudden smile exposed excellent white teeth, slightly too large for her mouth, but strikingly set off by her high complexion. "What luck for you. *I'm* a Doctor. Dr. Dena Sublett."

Shelby's breath stuck in her chest. Less than an hour ago she had been sure they were at the end of the tether. But she had been wrong. *This* was the end. The only thing left to happen was for Kira to cry. Unable to stop herself, Shelby let her gaze move to the covered bundle on Larch's arm.

Kira made no sound, but at this subtle signal Dr. Sublett stepped toward them so that only the fallen tree separated them from her. Her broad smile broadened still more, became as threatening as the gun she still aimed at them. "You carry your luggage so tenderly one could almost believe you have a baby hidden in there. I suppose it is my public duty to ask to see your charts, but I've something else on my mind right now. Something more pressing; an illegal child can be dealt with any time, if it *be* illegal."

Shelby's blood turned icy. She had to force herself to stare back at the woman threatening them from only a log's width away. Crazily, perhaps because she had already recognized this moment as extremity, acknowledging that very likely nothing mattered any more anyway, she began a rather detailed appraisal of Dr. Sublett. In her terrible way, she was an impressive enemy. Attractive, masterful (there was no other word), courageous (of course *she* had the gun, they didn't), capable of irony ("curious choice for diversion"), even at home in the use of the subjunctive mode ("if it *be* illegal"), a refinement believed lost long ago in another century.

Preoccupied with her fear and her foolish rush of thoughts, Shelby almost missed what Dr. Sublett was saying to Larch. "—so that you and the boy can move that tree out of the way of my car. You look strong enough to manage. I have a rope in the trunk, but I was reluctant to try moving it that way, afraid I might damage the clutch. Then, fortunately, you came along."

"It seems we haven't much choice but to try, as long as you keep that gun on us." Larch handed Kira to Shelby. "Come on, Jode. And are you going to help too, Dr. Sublett?"

"I prefer not. This is an exchange of services, let's say. You move the tree so I can get the car through; I'll take a look at the injury which makes you limp, and—ah—whatever other medical problems you may have."

It was not a large tree. Shelby felt sure Larch, in good health, could have moved it easily. But now he was tired and in pain. And Jode, though strong for his age, wouldn't be much help. Should she offer to help too? But she was holding Kira, whom she was certainly not going to put on the ground or let Dr. Sublett hold, even if she would, even if she could, considering that the Doctor still cradled her rifle. She must be in some frantic hurry to get some-

153

where in that car, frantic enough to make her threaten passersby with a gun just to get a fallen tree moved. Why hadn't she just *asked* Larch to move it? He probably would have, or tried.

With concern Shelby watched him now. He looked the prospective job over, then seized the trunk high on the slender end, which lay off the road on the far side. He motioned Jode to a spot closer in. Then, using the root-end as a pivot, they heaved. The tree moved sluggishly upward, twisted on its axis. The jagged edge of a broken bough scooped at the ground. Larch and Jode walked, holding their burden at waist-level, turning it like a gigantic clock-hand, dropping it finally at a place enough out of the way to permit the car to pass.

(How had it happened to fall? Considering its condition, it must have fallen simply from age and decay since there had been no heavy wind. It wasn't reasonable to imagine it had lain there a long time, since the road was obviously used, probably regularly.)

Larch stepped away from the tree. "There you are, Doctor," he said with overtones that were only faintly caustic. "Call on us any time you want another tree moved. We're in the book. Now, if it's okay with you, we'll go on with our hike."

"It is not all right with me. All of you will please get into the car." Her expression, formerly so mock-cheerful, now told Shelby nothing.

"And if we refuse?"

"This is a lonely road and it *is* on my property. You were quite correct when you thought you might be trespassing. At Orthohaven, it's not unheard of for trespassers to be shot by property owners, especially if they happen to be fugitives

154

from the law. And *most* especially if they happen to be three—make that four—notorious Abnormals wanted for treatment."

Larch must have decided that any denial, any check of their forged charts, the names on which must also be widely known by now, would only anger Dr. Sublett. Instead he said, "How did you know?"

"The APES have gibbered of nothing else for several days now. The search for you is the most exciting thing that's happened around here since the Surgeon General moved the Summer Whitehouse to Orthohaven. But let's not waste time. It happens I'm in a great rush. You will get in the back seat with me, Mr. Rosst alias Mr. Koyne. And you, Miss Harmon—or if you prefer, Miss Mackin—will drive, while your brother sits beside you in front holding the baby—fancy there being a baby; the APES certainly missed a good angle there!—so that I can easily shoot anyone in the front if necessary. That should in turn keep you in line, Mr. Rosst." Again she smiled. Shelby shuddered inwardly.

There seemed nothing to be gained by not complying. Jode, taking his cue from Shelby, climbed into the car and allowed Kira to be placed on his lap. He held her gingerly, in a stiff-armed embrace. Dr. Sublett waited until Shelby was behind the wheel, then she motioned Larch in, taking her own place beside him. "Start the motor. Or are you going to stall by saying you don't know how to drive?"

"I'll drive." Reluctantly, Shelby started the red car's engine, shifted into first.

"No," their captor objected quickly. "I didn't tell you to do anything but *start* the car. Now back up.

There's a wide space behind us where you can turn around."

"But you were heading this way," Jode said. "You wanted the tree moved so you could get past."

"You talk entirely too much, child," the Doctor said. "You and your sister should be aware at all times that the rifle is aimed straight ahead. But since my business is of such interest to you, I'll tell you. I was on my way to town from home. Since I met you, I've been having some second thoughts."

The car moved uneasily backward, bumping over roughness as the back wheels left the pavement in the turn. "Not too fast, please. It would be a pity if you jolted the rifle and it went off and shot your brother, who talks too much. Or your baby, who may have to be exterminated anyway."

Shelby, controlling a rising fury, returned the car to the road and drove slowly, wondering if her anger would be greater than her fear, imagining that she could hear the thudding of her heart over the noise of the motor. Would Larch have some idea of trying to wrest the gun away? No, he wouldnt do anything foolish; it might go off in the struggle. If there was any chance for them to escape Sublett it lay in the future, not the present.

Now the cool, imperious voice cozied phonily, "You may be interested to know, Miss Harmon, that I hold the position your father once did before his curious defection from the ranks of orthodoxy: personal physician to the Surgeon General. Quite a responsible post, a position of honor and trust, not to say power. Hard to understand why he gave it up in exchange for living the life of a hunted Abnormal. But then, *'Chacun à son goût,'* eh, Miss Harmon?"

Shelby bit her lips hard. She must make no reply that might anger the woman with the gun. It occurred to her that Sublett might be insane. A strange notion in this context, one she had never really thought about in this way. When Patients were classified as abnormal, there was never any question of diagnosis, for Doctors made the decision. What happened when a Doctor lost his or her sanity? Who diagnosed? And was the measure of abnormality in a physician the same as that for a Patient? Someone ranking as high in the Iatrarchy as Sublett—if indeed she told the truth and wasn't just trying to needle Shelby—might well be immune to diagnosis altogether. So long as the Doctor held onto the job. Who could bell the cat?

They drove in silence for several kilometers. Once Shelby glanced over at the bundle Jode held. Kira lay perfectly still, but her petal-blue eyes were open, seeming to stare up into Jode's face. *Dear God, let nothing bad happen to Kira. Let nothing bad happen to Jode.*

"There's an unmarked intersection ahead," Sublett said at last. "Turn right and go up the hill." The new road, graveled instead of paved, wound steeply. Pines appeared again and through occasional breaks in their foliage, it was possible to see glimpses of the ocean, blue in the dusk and far away.

As the road ended at last in a loop, the bulk of a large, unlighted house appeared. "This is my own place," Sublett now explained, almost chattily. "When the SG is at Orthohaven, I'm on call, of course. But I find it more relaxing to have separate

157

quarters where I can do my own work, and not be pestered with the special Subcute guards that follow him everywhere."

At the mention of Subcutes, Shelby put down another shudder. But the fact that the house was dark was hopeful. It might mean Sublett lived here alone. (Her remark had seemed to mean that she was not personally protected by guards.) There were three active members of their own party, only one of her (perhaps). How long would she try to keep them here? Surely it wasn't reasonable to think she could hold the gun on all of them indefinitely?

She was holding it on all of them now, however. She hopped out of the car first, holding the rifle pointed as she waited for them to follow. "No, don't take the baby," she said sharply as Shelby was about to accept the bundle from Jode. "I want you to open the door." She tossed a nosegay of keys at Shelby's feet. "The red one. You unlock and I'll keep you all in sight as you enter."

There was no feeling of the relaxed rusticity of an Orthohaven cottage-in-the-woods about the room they now entered. Creamy, molded-plaster walls rose to a lofty ceiling. Opposite the entrance hall a row of undraped, gothic-shaped french doors gave on a vista of garden, the verdancy of which was now deepening in fading twilight. Furnishings were predominantly Empire: elegant, with much pale silk upholstery and delicately carved and polished wood in evidence. Of course, being a Doctor, and an important one, Sublett could exercise her own tastes, but the interior did seem to present an anomaly in a utilitarian world.

Shelby was still absorbed in the room when Dr.

158

Sublett barked another of her orders. "This way, quickly." She gestured with the gun barrel toward a closed door.

Jode passed the baby back to his sister and they filed down a spare, unfurnished corridor, the Doctor in the rear. At its end was another door, wide and seemingly heavy, perhaps made of painted solid metal, like a fire-stop panel. This time Sublett passed her ring of keys to Larch, indicating which to use.

As had the first, this second chamber contained surprises, but of a different nature. This time no windows at all, only austere, white walls against which were arranged many cabinets and a variety of large surgical equipment: cautery machine, cardiac monitor, suction equipment, several kinds of scanners, various pumps, power units for surgical tools, and a number of other pieces whose use Shelby could not guess. Even the ceiling was encrusted. A battery of lights. Gleaming gadgets engineered to descend and retract.

But the most arresting sight occupied centerstage: a fully draped operating table, shimmering whitely, seeming to emit a light of its own much brighter than the rest of the illumination in the room.

The table was occupied by a supine, bulky body completely obscured—even the hair, the top of the head—by the blanched, surgical linen.

Surely I'm dreaming again, Shelby told herself.

Dr. Sublett faced them across the OR table much as she had faced them across the fallen tree at their first meeting. Just as she had then, she kept the rifle leveled.

"Now listen carefully. What I'm about to say is

159

of utmost importance and time is running out. I have a proposition for you, Mr. Rosst, that would be most foolish of you to try to turn down. While I keep your family hostage here, I shall send you on a mission. If you fulfill it—and with your reputation for cleverness I believe you won't fail—I shall in return provide you all with impeccable documents of identification and insure your safe passage to England immediately afterward. I believe England is where you want to go?"

A tense silence ticked along. Then Larch said, "What sort of mission?"

"Not a simple one, but this is no longer a simple world. I want you to kill Jacot Mosk."

"Mosk? The chief assistant Surgeon General?"

"The same. He's not here, he's in Capital City during the Surgeon General's vacation at Orthohaven. I'll provide you with air transportation there and back, tell you exactly how he can be found and how to get in to him undetected by anyone, including his bodyguards, and furnish you with an infallible weapon which cannot be traced to you or me. The whole project can be accomplished in something less than eight hours."

Again the ticking tension. Shelby felt, rather than heard, Larch swallow slowly, with effort. Sublett turned slightly so that the rifle was trained precisely at the baby. "I frankly don't see that you have a choice." She barked out her cynical laugh. "And anyway, isn't Mosk one of your own arch-enemies? Wouldn't all you Abs like to see him dead?"

This time Larch answered immediately. "I am not a killer, Dr. Sublett."

Sublett looked faintly surprised, but she said only, "Interesting. Interesting. But perhaps I'm pressing you too hard? Under other circumstances I could allow you time to think it over. In this case, though, as I've already taken care to warn you, time is running thin."

Shelby's thoughts reeled, but then quickly meshed with memory and things began clicking into place. Could this be—? Certainly it must be. The crumbling at the top of the heap that Gerrod Harmon had predicted. Not a wishful prediction, but one based on facts he had accumulated when he was in a position to have an insider's view.

Later, when after several years no such crumbling had taken place, other members of the underground had given up the notion, decided her father must have been wrong.

Not that a coup by one entrenched faction over another in the Iatrarchy could directly benefit the Ab cause. None of them had been so ingenuous as to believe that, especially when the unrest would be occurring in only one of the four continental governments.

But wasn't any break in the dike better than no break? If it eventually led to the flood, all the better. The Abs would be ready. Have patience, said the old proverb, and you will witness your enemy's funeral procession.

But *witness* was the word, not *kill* in order to precipitate the funeral itself. By denying he was a killer, Larch was only presenting to Dr. Sublett, whether she was aware of it or not, the official Ab position on the issue.

The development proved exciting, then, theoretically. But personally they remained in the same position as before. Their only hope still lay in somehow, together or singly, being able to outwit and outflank the mad Doctor, and soon, before she gave up in disgust at trying to persuade Larch into her scheme, and either disposed of them all outright (with the rifle or perhaps by some less noisy, less archaic, and neater means), or took them back to town and turned them over to the Medcops.

She was still waiting, weapon raised, smiling her bemusement at Larch, who stared unfalteringly back at her without speaking. It was as if they were still measuring each other, enemy to enemy, both having discounted for the moment Sublett's tactical superiority.

Somehow the last thing Shelby expected to hear at this moment was the sound of a car approaching. But there it was, the whirr of a powerful drive, something unidentifiable but plainly superior to any ordinary gasoline or diesel engine, speeding up the last, steep leg of the incline to the house. Behind the closed door of the surgery, the noise was muted but unmistakable.

It was Jode who said, half triumphantly, half fearfully, "Someone's coming."

"I can hear," Dena Sublett snapped. "I'm not expecting anyone, but I may have to answer. After all, my car's in the drive. Whoever it is will know I'm at home."

Her gaze remained on Larch, but less penetratingly, more absently, as she considered the new situation. "I believe the best thing to do is stay right where we are. All of you, of course, will do exactly as I tell you. You will make absolutely *no* sound."

Sublett's eyes flicked now to the baby in Shelby's arms. Kira was sleeping, the way very young children will when exposed to outdoor air for substantial periods, but Shelby knew it was past time for

162

her to wake and be hungry again. "So that there will be no awkwardness," Sublett went on, with great assurance now, "you, Miss Harmon, and your child will make yourselves as comfortable as possible in this autoclave." She swung a round door of very heavy metal out of the wall at the level of her waist. "Don't worry. It's very large, more than room enough, and there's plenty of air for the few minutes it'll take for me to get rid of the visitors."

The sound of the motor had stopped, replaced by a new sound of activity at the front door, a clatter, then heavy pounding. Once more Shelby saw no purpose in resisting. She climbed easily into the oven-like enclosure, holding Kira close. The door slammed behind them. There was a panicky moment of claustrophobia, quickly fought off. Sublett was right, there was plenty of room, room to sit, almost enough to stretch out. It wasn't even dark, only dim. An inset, transparent panel on the door emitted a filtered glow from the room. But the autoclave was not quite the soundproof enclosure Dena Sublett had evidently hoped it would be. Shelby could still hear everything that went on, not at normal volume, but very clearly.

The pounding at the door soon stopped, followed by a prolonged rattle at the lock, as if it were being forced with keys or other tools. Sublett began to swear softly.

Then more noises of entry, footsteps in the main room fading to silence as the visitors apparently went over the rest of the house. Finally the corridor leading to the surgery was invaded. Someone rapped impatiently on the OR door.

Sublett's voice, very angry: "Who is it?"

As soon as the answer came, Shelby experienced

the half-expected shock of recognition. The cool, impersonal, threat-laden voice, monotonal and uninflected, but this time she heard not just the sound of it but the words: "Captain Fifty-eight-dash-twenty-four and Lieutenant Seven-ought-dash-six of the Surgical Bacterial Custodial Technicians, Dr. Sublett. Open up."

Simple anger was instantly enhanced to complex fury: "You two borgies get away from that door. At once! No one comes into this surgery while I'm operating. If you don't leave this second, I'll have you busted to the lowest echelon of the Medcops."

In spite of her terror, Shelby was impressed again with Sublett's flair for sheer audacity and ingenuity. And the outburst began to have results. There was a momentary pause of uncertainty, then a hint of request in what had been the voice of demand. "We were not told you have an operation going on. But it is absolutely necessary that we speak with you. There's been a top-priority emergency."

At this Sublett seemed to turn down her own burners a bit in compliance. "If you insist on any speaking, it will have to be through that door."

"That would be against the rules."

"Then get lost. Those are my terms and my patience is running out. You're interrupting me at a crucial time."

Another hesitation; then, "Are you operating alone in there, Doctor? And is your Patient under total anesthesia?"

"I'm alone, using an automatic nurse."

"*What* kind of nurse?"

"Automatic, you fools! Just like yourselves only much more useful to society. A computerized device that controls the administering of anesthetic, monitors vital signs, hands me what I need, sponges up the blood. . ."

"Very well, Dr. Sublett, here is the message. The Surgeon General has disappeared."

"What?!"

"He was last seen two hours ago in his study at the Summer Whitehouse. It is thought he may have been kidnaped—"

"You're crazy!"

"—by Abnormals. There have been three politically deviant Abnormals at large at Orthohaven for several days. It is believed they may be the kidnapers. You are wanted for questioning at the Summer Whitehouse immediately."

"Me? I have nothing to do with this. I haven't seen the SG since three days ago when I gave him his regular checkup."

"Nevertheless, everyone on his immediate staff has to be questioned."

"Preposterous! I shall be tied up here at least four more hours."

"You must finish what you're doing in less time."

"We'll see. Now, is there anything else? I'd like to get back to business."

"There is one other message. A guard is being left here at your house."

"Certainly not. What kind of guard?"

"Two Surgical Bacterial Custodial Technicians from the Whitehouse specialized forces. In fact, we are your guard. You admit you are alone here except for your Patient. You must be careful with those Abnormals around."

"Ridiculous. You'll need all the guards you have

at Orthohaven to find the kidnapers. I refuse to let any of you Subcutes stay here."

"Orders, Doctor."

A real scream of outrage met this, louder and fiercer than any of the other imprecations produced by Sublett during the curious conversation. "You damned mechanical idiots! *I'm* the Doctor. *I* give the orders."

Climbing out of the autoclave when the door was opened a few minutes later, Shelby stretched and breathed deeply. Kira slept peacefully now. Everything seemed the same as before. Larch, Jode, and Sublett were even standing in approximately the same positions. Shelby looked again at the figure on the table, confirming what she had half-noticed earlier. There was no movement, no rise-fall of the drape to indicate breathing.

Dr. Sublett still held her rifle, but now she was laughing. It was the first time Shelby had seen her express real mirth. "A great performance, didn't you think?"

No one answered her obvious bid for a personal compliment, but she seemed not to notice the slight. In fact she said, "I don't mean my own performance, though it had its moments. I mean theirs. Did you notice that they didn't have the wit to ask the key question? How could they possibly have forgotten to ask who it was I'm supposed to be operating on? That little omission right there points up the whole weakness in the present miserable handling of the security forces in this society."

Larch now spoke as if he were only continuing another, interrupted conversation, which—in a way—he was. "But why Mosk? Have you already got Carvey then? Is that what the kidnaping means?"

"Your job, Mr. Rosst, is not to ask questions but to perform a function. However, you're already in this thing up to your occiput, and either you'll keep your mouth shut so your family won't be destroyed, or you'll decide not to cooperate and you'll all be destroyed anyway. So I might as well fill you in. Owen Carvey is already dead."

"How do you know?"

She flashed the broad smile that best displayed her splendid dental arch. "Because I thanatized him myself." There was no mistaking the ring of pride in her words. "About an hour ago." For the first time she lowered the rifle and removed her eyes from her captives to the figure under the surgical drape. "Right here, on my operating table."

Abnormals

His knee. The world could be collapsing around him. Life in peril several different ways. Shelby threatened. His only child's chances of survival reduced to almost nothing. Jode. The cause to which he had devoted himself hanging in uncertainty. And yet his overriding concern centered on his ailing body. His knee.

Over the past forty-eight hours the injury had progressed through a number of vicissitudes. Shattering pain alternating with an ominous numbness, the agony of putting damaged tissue to prolonged active use, the steady swelling, the real or imagined flutter—accompanied by the most intense pain of all—of shifting cartilage, fragments of bone. A relentless overall stiffening and weakening that it would soon be impossible to resist. Noticeably rising fever that he feared might soon lead to collapse and delirium.

Still, the dilemma managed to touch his still-working sense of the ridiculous. So did their adventure with Dena Sublett, or at least the long view of it did. From the moment of their abrupt meeting with the Mad Doctor of Orthohaven, he had known her to be more dangerous than any Medcop, or even Subcute, for their actions were more often than not predictable or inefficient or both, as Sublett herself had pointed out. Who knew what whim might take Sublett as she moved from one manifestation of lunacy to the next?

At first he had only half believed her announcement that she was personal physician to Carvey. The deluded are endlessly inventive; case histories abound in imaginary roles of megalomaniac proportions. However, though the staff surrounding Carvey was not discussed by the APES for security reasons, Larch had heard that the spot once held by Gerrod was now occupied by a formidable woman who, some said, was feared and respected by many, including the SG himself. And though the precise location of the Summer Whitehouse had not been on the map of Orthohaven he had memorized (nor any other map), it was known to be in the neighborhood.

Having granted her that much, then, he was presented with the next demand upon credulity: that she had assassinated Carvey, and was eager to annihilate Mosk in the same purge. But there was still no hint of whether she was acting alone in monumental egocentricity, or was backed by an or-

172

ganization. Curious, if the latter were true, that she should be so eager to embroil him in the plot. Surely such an organization, carefully planning a coup d'etat, would have better and more trustworthy people for the job than an Ab stranger picked up on the road.

On the other hand, that might be precisely the point. When Dena Sublett met them, she immediately saw the opportunity to employ a known Ab with the idea of being able later to blame Mosk's death as well as Carvey's on the politically restive Abnormals.

But all this, confounding as it might be, important to the whole world and especially to the Ab movement as it might prove, did nothing to help the roiling pain in his leg. For him, it came down to that.

What he really wanted to keep his mind on, however, was the possibility of separating Sublett from her weapon. That shouldn't be impossible. It wasn't as if the gun were one of those he'd heard of with a power unit so miniaturized it could be palmed, even worn under a fingernail. (Or inset into the body of a Subcute.) It was only a rifle. (*Only* a rifle?) A rifle with a jutting barrel which could so easily be deflected by one hand of an attacker as he unbalanced his opponent and grabbed the butt with the other.

But the moment for this had not yet come. Not on the road, not in the car, certainly not since they had been held in Dena Sublett's home.

And she *had* saved them from the Subcutes. Why argue with that, even if her reasons for doing so were misbegotten? And in saving them had saved herself, for she could hardly have opened the door of the surgery with the dead body of Owen Carvey (or at least a body said by her to be Carvey) on the operating table.

As the sounds made by the departing Subcutes faded, the whine of their official vehicle ebbing down the mountain, he had listened with mixed feelings to Sublett's announcement of Carvey's murder and then made his decision. Hardly a decision, really, since only one course seemed possible.

"All right, Dr. Sublett, I'm impressed by the seriousness of your efforts so far, and terrified of the threatened retribution against my family. I agree to whatever you want, in exchange for what you promise us."

"Well, now." The smile broadened. Every tooth was perfect, premolars, molars. "That's much better, Mr. Rosst. Of course, I knew you'd agree."

"The difficulty is, how am I to believe you'll see to our safe passage out of the country in return for the death of Dr. Mosk? The last time we entered into an exchange-of-services compact, you forgot your part of it."

She looked genuinely puzzled.

"You promised that if Jode and I moved the tree out of the way of your car, you'd provide medical treatment for my injured knee."

She laughed easily. "Why, so I did. How thoughtless of me to have forgotten so quickly. But other emergencies did arise, you know. I shall make it up to you by treating not only your injury, but examining the new mother and her child, if Miss Harmon agrees."

Larch exchanged a quick glance with Shelby, saw a flinching-away expression in the green eyes. "I don't mean to seem entirely selfish, but if your

174

time is so limited, perhaps the one errand of mercy will be enough."

"As you say." She backed away, still holding the weapon, but it was lowered now. Was this the time to lunge for it? But no, let her render her medical services first. The time would come. And surely he needed her services as much as she needed his.

Both her quick, harsh smile and her imperiousness had evaporated, in favor of a polished, professional attempt at kindness. "Please come this way," she invited. "The boy too. I have my office here, and a small examination cubicle."

In her office she unlocked a cabinet and, without comment, placed the rifle carefully on an empty shelf. She relocked the cabinet. From another cabinet she drew out a clean white jacket, which she pulled on over the tweed tunic. The sudden whiteness against her rosy olive skin highlighted her handsomeness in a way not so noticeable before. She seemed younger, magnificent in a (strangely) womanly way. Obviously, she was in her element.

Larch noticed that, after locking the gun away, she had kept the ring of keys in her palm until she had adjusted the jacket over her well-proportioned torso. Then she casually dropped the ring into the jacket pocket.

"Into the examination room now, Mr. Rosst. Your family will wait here."

In the cubicle she ordered Larch to lie down on a narrow examination table. With the image of the man in the other room fresh in mind, he did so, gingerly.

In her no-nonsense way, Sublett seized something sharp which she kept at hand—knife? razorblade? scalpel?—and slit the leg of his jeans from hip to ankle. A little more gently she also slit the clumsy binding over the injury so that the cloth fell away at once in a compact piece. "You should *never* have applied a bandage to an injury like this!" she scolded him. Her gentleness at an end, she palpated the knee as Larch gritted his teeth. "Effusion," she recited. "Hematoma. Possible patellar fragmentation. But I shall need to look inside." She swung a scanning eye into position and flipped several switches, one of which lighted a screen which they both could see. The light and shadow moving over the panel meant nothing to Larch, but Dr. Sublett clucked and murmured. "How you could possibly have been ambulatory with this is more than I can understand. Just as I feared, you have extensive patellar fragmentation as well as a lateral torn meniscus. What you need," she concluded ominously, "is immediate surgery, probably a total replacement."

Before Larch could protest, she intervened, "But as we both know, there isn't time. I shall simply have to do a stopgap job, but you must promise to see an osteopathic surgeon as soon as it's feasible."

When the pain ebbed, almost abruptly, Larch realized she must have injected procaine or some other anesthetic. She bustled about, selecting medications. To his unsurprise, a thermometer was thrust under his tongue. "An amazing case," she complimented him, still busy among her equipment. "You have a great deal of stamina. That may come in handy when you perform my errand for me."

So he had become a "case" and not a person, Larch mused. Oldest defense of the medical mind. If one were human, one might be in line for sympathy from a fellow human, even a Doctor. But a case was only a case and could never be anything else. No wonder the Medarchy could turn lives on or off as they saw fit. Depersonalization must be the key. The corpse in the adjacent room—he was just a case too, a terminated one, though he had been a man whose good health had been entrusted to Dena Sublett by the "republic." Carvey might even have regarded her as a friend, and almost certainly as a fellow professional.

Sublett, obviously one of those thinkers who gained confidence by talking to herself, was going on, "Perhaps, after all, the best thing for me to do with you is—"

Since she left the sentence unfinished, Larch was obliged to supply his own conclusion. Amputate? Thanatize? Nothing under the Iatrarchy surprised him any more. Nothing ever could again. Lucky for him that Sublett had already decided he was useful to her, or he might never get out of this cubicle alive. Of course he was exaggerating. Or was he?

He had to admit the pain was gone, perhaps temporarily, but any relief was welcome. She seemed to be making conclusive motions, turning off her machines, putting things away. "You must put no weight on that leg," she said solemnly. "No weight at all. I shall supply you with the necessary pair of crutches."

Crutches? A bad blow. How does a man on crutches manage to grab a rifle away from a powerful woman in obviously perfect health? Or, as matters stood now, wrestle her to the floor in order to extract keys from the pocket of her jacket?

No answer presented itself. She helped him to a sitting position on the table. Then she fell into a chatty mood. "You're so fortunate in having run into me. Most Doctors specialize in the way they have for centuries. All branches of medicine interested me equally, so I specialized in—everything. A general practitioner in the new sense. I'm an excellent surgeon, a splendid pathologist and diagnostician. But if I had to be classified as a true specialist, it would be in the field of holistic medicine. Emphasizing the preventive side, you see. I can deal in bio-rhythms, dietary considerations, measuring and managing all kinds of stress on the human organism so that illness can be circumvented. I can keep a Patient in perfect physical and psychological condition. He has only to follow my orders. It certainly helped when it came to acquiring my present position."

Present position! Larch marveled. He had recognized madness and obsession in this woman, but obviously not the depths to which it had penetrated. Had she forgotten that she had failed to keep the SG in perfect health? Had in fact just murdered her employer and ordered the murder of his successor? Or did she mean that she herself had already, in all but name, acceded to the office of Surgeon General, a promotion made possible in part by her having had the wit to be a general practitioner with a knowledge of surgery and the perspicacity to place herself in the right place at the right time?

Sublett disappeared behind a curtain and came back with the promised pair of aluminum crutches. "Here they are. Try them. And I can furnish another pair of trousers. You will have to be dressed quite differently anyway to go on the mission I expect of you."

Swinging onto the crutches, he discovered that

178

for the first time in many hours he could move around with some relief.

The Doctor now said a remarkable thing. "If your party is hungry, I can find some food for them before we leave."

"I thought this mission of yours was very urgent."

She shrugged it off. "That was part of the rhetoric I used to persuade you, Mr. Rosst. It's true we don't have much time before you must start, but we do have a little."

He *was* hungry, Larch suddenly realized. And so must Shelby and Jode be hungry. Their food had run out hours ago. Sublett's talk of leaving must have to do with his departure for Capital City as an assassin. Her next words confirmed it. "The crutches will be helpful not only for your injury but in the disguise. So far as I've heard, none of the reports on you has mentioned a leg injury. You'll be traveling as a special correspondent for APES, carrying only a small attache case. A man on crutches should find that no encumbrance. We shall pick up your identification papers and medchart and the special passes you'll need to get into the center of Capital City as soon as we get to town. We'll also get the proper clothing there, along with your detailed orders."

His mind swung back from the theory of the lone megalomaniac which Dena Sublett might be, to the notion of a tightly organized and even militarized junto, poised on the eve of a well-planned overthrow of government. For surely such documents and arrangements as she mentioned couldn't be improvised in a last-minute effort. (Perhaps some special correspondent for APES had already been

179

conveniently thanatized, his papers and clothing seized.)

In the office Sublett, while failing to press Shelby into an examination, lightly broached the subject of Kira's development. She glanced at the baby casually and said, "She seems remarkably vigorous. Have there been any problems?"

"It was a seven-month pregnancy," Shelby admitted.

"Mmmm. But having been carried into the third trimester, she may have been ready. The rate of growth of a fetus cannot be generalized about. The individual case can show considerable variation."

An argument against conformity, Larch thought. But not of much use to them now.

Dena Sublett, perhaps to her credit, did not remove the rifle from the locked cabinet when she invited them back into the elegant main part of her house. She even performed another of her lightning changes of role: concerned physician to perfect hostess. She invited them to freshen up in a large, immaculate bathroom, opening off one of the corridors. She had removed the white jacket to receive them a few minutes later in the Empire drawing room and inform them that food was being prepared by automatic means and would be ready shortly.

Larch was surprised, however, when she returned to the guarded subject of the murder. "I know you think me heartless, Mr. Rosst, in terminating the Surgeon General in the manner I did. But since you know altogether too much already, you might as well be told still more. Owen Carvey was suffering from an incurable multiple myeloma. This may sound inconceivable in a time when almost any

180

cancer can be either prevented or immediately cured. I might add that the condition leading to the illness was already entrenched before I took over as his personal physician. Be that as it may, the diagnosis was incontrovertible. I had the best oncologist in the land as consultant. Had Owen's illness become known to the general public, the Mercifuls would almost certainly have tried to assassinate him anyway. I had a perfectly legal right to do what I did, and also a humane one. If you are familiar with the symptoms of myeloma, you will understand what I mean."

Larch tried neither to show his amazement nor to catch Shelby's eye as she sat on a sofa across the room from him, placidly feeding Kira, Jode at her side. "Then why not start a rumor that Mosk has the same disease?" he suggested recklessly. "Circulate such a rumor among the Mercifuls and let them perform your task for you."

Sublett tossed her head, from which she had removed the blue scarf. The springy black hair, cut short and smoothly waved, bounced in irritation. "Don't be absurd."

. . He had gone too far. If he'd kept his mouth shut, she might have gone even further in her ramblings, maybe into the actual plans for the coup. He and Shelby would have had more information, in case they ever found themselves in a position to report to the underground. In an attempt to sooth their hostess, repair some of the damage, perhaps even get her back on the track, he said, "Are the Mercifuls that powerful then? I was under the impression they're only a fringe outfit, roving bands of renegades, widely scattered.

"They *were*. But thanks to the fantastic ineffi-

181

ciency of the law enforcement under Carvey's government, the latest reports from Medical Intelligence show them thickening their ranks faster than the Subcutes can thin them out. It's just terrible, Mr. Rosst, the things they do. They kill people. Quite arbitrarily. Let some Patient with his chart perfectly in order, who's being legally treated for a simple fracture, say, appear in some lonely spot with his arm in a cast and a Merciful may shoot him from ambush. There's even a rumor of a band of Mercifuls in these very mountains, at Orthohaven. I understand the same Subcutes sent here to track you down have orders to be also on the lookout for Mercifuls."

"Interesting," Larch said. "Interesting." He had found a second pair of jeans, approximately his size, thoughtfully provided for him in the bathroom, to replace those the Doctor had ripped at the examination. She was a strange woman, no doubt about it, cruel and considerate at once. She had even offered a choice of whiskey or sherry before the meal.

And the meal itself was served in a beautifully appointed breakfast room at the rear of the house, overlooking the now softly lighted garden. It was almost as exotic as their hostess.

Cornish game hen with a raisin sauce containing mysterious and delicious ingredients, buttered asparagus, salted almonds and strong black coffee. Even Jode abandoned his uncustomary and long-imposed silence: "Real food!" he exulted. "I've never eaten anything like this before."

"All imported. Frozen. Brought back to palatability by sophisticated kitchen equipment," Dr. Sublett explained. "Overseas, especially in Africa, the Medarchy is encouraging the raising of certain strains of fowl that survived the bacteria. In this country too, certain things are being done to promote the cultivation of fowl and other livestock again. Diet is important to morale. Doctors should be the first to realize that. It's not a matter of nutrition, since the packaged foods are perfectly balanced and carefully regulated. But it's time for a change, a change that could only be possible under a Medarchy."

"Then why," Larch inquired, "are you doing all you can to cripple such a government?"

This time Shelby shot him a nervous look, but their hostess remained unruffled. "It's a matter of capabilities," she explained primly. "Even among Doctors, some are more capable than others. The more capable must obviously take the reins when the less capable falter."

Something occurred to Larch. A bolt from the blue, a shot in the dark. He only wondered why he hadn't thought of it before. "Are you one of the CGP, Dr. Sublett?"

She smiled again, her high color increasing markedly. "How very discerning of you, Mr. Rosst. Yes, I am a clone. I am perfect, mentally and physically. Only such Doctors, already perfect, and also highly intelligent and excellent at their work, were eligible to be cloned at the outset."

This experience was like peering into a whirling kaleidoscope, but gradually the motion was slowing and he was able to see patterns. "And Owen Carvey was not a CGP member? Neither is the about-to-be-unlucky Jacot Mosk?"

"You are very clever, Mr. Rosst. Too bad we shall be unable to use your services after this one job. But the rules among us are not negotiable; in the new government we will include no outsiders. Fortunately much of the Ama is salvable since many of them are CGPs who stand ready to assist us in the quick purge of those who are not."

And the sleepers in the new cryonics tanks they had seen in the vaults? Those must also be CGPs, Larch decided. Since clones of this special, postwar generation had aged to the point where some of them could expect to die or fall into moribund condition, this must indeed have happened to CGPs who would be considered indispensable after the takeover. Their numbers were too difficult to replace; none could be allowed to desert the cause, even in death.

Preservation of the elite. No new idea since before King Tut, but one of the important notions on which the Iatrarchy had fed itself. That Patients were superior to Abs; that checking nurses were superior to Patients; that Medcops were superior to Checking Nurses; that Subcutes were superior to Medcops; that Doctors were superior to Subcutes; that CGPs were superior to ordinary Doctors. A pyramid-shaped nightmare.

He knew that Shelby, during this strange evening, had arrived at the same assumption as he, had long since recalled her father's prediction of the coup, now almost a fact. He wondered if she also shared his pessimism. For an all-CGP government would advance no cause of liberalism, restore no human rights, fight no battles for the Abs. If anything, it would set these hopes back with crushing force. Unless some use might be made of the fact that dearth of numbers among CGPs and their determination to trust no one but themselves might make them more vulnerable than the government they were trying to replace.

Dena Sublett had risen from the table. "I hope you've enjoyed the meal. But we must make ready to leave now."

"Are we all going with Larch?" Jode said.

"I shall drive Mr. Rosst down to the city to prepare him for his journey. You and your sister and the baby will come with us, since I can't afford the risk of losing my hostages by leaving you here unguarded."

She left the room briefly and returned before Larch could even begin to think of any way to use her absence with a view to escape. She wore a black suede coat and the blue scarf again bound her hair. Also, she carried the rifle.

They took their positions in the car, the same as before, Shelby behind the wheel, Jode beside her with Kira. Larch swung in, arranging the crutches beside him. The time to act was surely behind them now; *why* had he not moved to overpower Sublett when she was unarmed? What a fool! From now on they would either be confined in the red car or in the city, where any chance they might have would be even slimmer. They might even be guarded there by CGP friends of Sublett's until the moment he was forced to board the plane.

The car purred smoothly down the hill. At the foot of the mountain, well off the road in one of the fields, a black hopper crouched, its outline and color visible intermittently in the flash of a revolving searchlight set up nearby. Perhaps the same hopper that had come to the golf course. So the Subcutes had yielded to Dr. Sublett's order to post no guard at her house, but were watching the neighborhood closely all the same. Would they stop the red car, or recognize it as belonging to Whitehouse staff and ignore it?

The light dipped low, tilted to another axis and swept the car once, twice. Shelby maintained the same moderate speed. It seemed they were all holding their breaths, even Sublett. Larch caught sight, in one of the sweeps of illumination, of her strong, long-fingered hands gripping the rifle fiercely. Then the light swung away, over the fields again but in a higher arc, the car evidently recognized and cleared. The Subcutes would perhaps have decided that the Doctor was now on her way to the Summer Whitehouse as ordered. That there were others in the car with her was going to be overlooked. No more incredible than the other lapses in reasoning by Subcutes. As had been made clear earlier, *she* was the Doctor, her affairs above and beyond suspicion.

After another few kilometers Kira began crying, fretfully, piercingly. Jode turned nervously to Shelby. "What'll I do with her?"

"Lay her on her belly over your knees. She probably has a bubble of air in her stomach from the feeding."

As Jode awkwardly shifted his niece on his lap, Sublett in turn shifted the rifle slightly so that it was aimed once more directly at the children. Perverse bitch, Larch thought. She'd fire it, too, he was surer of that than ever. A woman who could casually murder her own patient on an operating table— never mind that he was their own top-ranking enemy—would think nothing of murdering any number of Abs even if they were children.

186

He tried to recall all he had ever heard about clones. They replicated every characteristic of the donor down to details of cell structure, hence perpetuated tendencies and characteristics. Only environmental influences could change them into different people from the originals. And the Iatrarchy had been careful to mold their precious generation of laboratory-bred Doctors by closely adjusted environment into precisely what was needed: brilliant, cold-eyed, unemotional automatons. As machine-like as the cyborg Subcutes and, like the Subcutes, functional only for their specialized purpose: leadership in medicine and government.

So far as he knew, however, clones could not reproduce in the human way. He wondered if this fact might provide Dena Sublett, a woman in all other respects, with a deep-seated and perhaps unconscious special hatred for children born in the natural way.

The red car rolled on through the night. The baby grew calm and apparently slept again. They met no one else. Their captor gave several directions to Shelby about turns at intersections and they pulled at last out onto a real highway, perhaps the "lost" highway of their hike, when his knee had been agonizing and his fever had raged so that he could not think, could not recall the memorized map, had gotten them lost. If only that part of it hadn't happened. If they had been able to reach Mrs. Quistlethorp's . . .

But futile regret was a time-waster, taking up energy better spent on some plan for the here-and-now. He remembered that the one sure way he had discovered to divert Sublett at least slightly was with conversation.

"Perhaps you're right, Dr. Sublett, that I shouldn't be too reluctant to have a hand in wiping out Mosk. It's true he's no more palatable to our movement than Carvey himself was."

"Ah, I was sure it would have a side-effect of satisfaction for you, even if you wouldn't admit it at first. There is some adage I once ran across, familiar in historical times, about politics making strange bedfellows."

"A truism that has proved not untrue," Larch agreed.

"But you can't ingratiate yourself with me, Mr. Rosst, if that's what you have in mind by announcing your new state of mellowness. I've already made it quite clear that we CGPs are for ourselves alone. I want you and all the Harmons out of the country as passionately as you want the same."

He did not believe this. What would happen, if matters got to that point, would be that as soon as Mosk's murder was confirmed, Sublett would see that he, Shelby, Jode, and Kira were destroyed without more delay. Things could not be allowed to reach that point, of course. "I have no more addiction to ulterior motives than the next man. Perhaps you've misunderstood my meaning. I only meant to point out that there is a common goal, which you know. Both our group and your own feel they could do a better job running things than the present regime."

He caught a glimpse of her smile in the dimness of the car. "But with a vast difference in basic ideology. We offer our services for the good of humanity. You Abs think only of yourselves. Elevation of the individual. Every man a king, or some such rot. Therein lies your sickness and that is why you are called Abs. But few sicknesses remain for which no cure has been discovered. And when we take over, you will all be cured, I promise you. So will the Mercifuls and any other deviates threatening Public Health. It's one of the most flagrant signs of the inefficiency of the Carvey government that you've all been allowed to run around wreaking havoc for so many years."

"A society made up of all shades of opinion is *healthier* than one in which everyone thinks and acts alike, Doctor."

"Dissent is only a failure of comprehension, Mr. Rosst. Can there be diversity of opinion on whether the earth is round, the square root of minus-two? Can you choose whether or not to believe in inherited characteristics and the germ theory of disease? Can you vote on the valence of alcohol, the composition of phenol?"

"As a Doctor you speak only of measurable quantities. How about art? Just for a start, shouldn't one be allowed wide latitude in honoring one's own tastes here? Yet the Iatrarchy bans non-representational art of all kinds, atonal music, experimental fiction and poetry, abstract sculpture, and so on."

"You are wrong, Mr. Rosst, in imagining these things aren't also in the realm of the measurable quantity. Mental aberration shows itself in certain forms. But anyone is free to prefer one type of art over another so long as the selections are made within certain reasonable limits."

189

"I can choose any color I like as long as I choose black?"

"As long as you choose reasonably, Mr. Rosst. Not only is the painter of an outrageous painting likely to be dangerously unstable, the painting itself if exhibited may endanger the stability of those who see it by confirming a similar but latent instability."

"How about religion, Dr. Sublett? Shouldn't a citizen be allowed some latitude there?"

"All societies have discouraged the more primitive religions and encouraged the more rational."

"Like the Church of the Caduceus?"

"Only one of Carvey's many recent mistakes. If he had—ah—gone on as SG, he would have paid dearly for allowing it to be established. Mysticism is dangerous. Humankind has had too many gods that failed."

"A narrow choice in anything isn't exactly what is usually meant by freedom, however, Doctor."

"We didn't narrow the choice, Mr. Rosst. Science simply excluded the absolutely inconsiderable from the permissible judged in terms of Public Health. One cannot allow children to play with bombs, nor neurotics to indulge delusions. If the Doctors had only taken over sooner, we could have averted all wars, even the very early ones. I could give you a long list of famous men who ought to have been hospitalized for obvious symptoms. Instead they were allowed to lead whole nations into disasters time and again, for centuries: Alexander, Tamerlane, Napoleon, Hitler, Nixon, Amin . . ."

"FDR? Lincoln? Jefferson?"

"Roosevelt certainly. The mind is affected always by malfunction of the body. Lincoln had what in his day was called melancholia, actually a form of paranoia. As for Jefferson, he had a rudimentary scientific orientation, but was victim of grossly unscientific superstitions. Definitely eccentric, possibly an advanced neurotic. We would probably have excluded him from public life as a precautionary measure."

"You have a point, Doctor. For every Ghandi lost under your system, you'd be excluding a dozen Stalins, a dozen Goebbelses—"

At this point the emergency happened.

The motor of the red car, running like a watch, suddenly hacked, guttered like a waning candle, chugged so violently that they swayed in their seats, and then quit.

Shelby allowed the forward motion to take them to the side of the highway, where she braked to a stop.

Sublett's familiar fury was like a palpable force. "What did you do to the car, Miss Harmon? Start it again at once."

Obediently, Shelby touched the starter. There was a querulous whine trailing to silence. Kira began to cry again.

"Start it! Or I'll shoot."

His thorough conviction that Sublett was mad again assailed Larch. Actually it had never left him, but it took these examples of how she habitually met crisis to remind him how dangerous she was. The starter again whirred ineffectually. Kira wailed.

"Can't that child be silenced?" Sublett demanded.

No one moved or spoke. Kira went on wailing thinly. Sublett did not shoot. Instead she turned to

Larch. "Have you any talent at auto mechanics, Mr. Rosst?"

He did not, but at least it would get him out of the car, possibly into some position that might suggest some further move. He clambered stiffly out, rattling the crutches, onto the shoulder of the road. Shelby released the bonnet latch and the red hood popped open as he arrived in front of the motor.

He was now invisible to Sublett in the back seat, it occurred to him.

Apparently it had also occurred to her. Her solution was to order them all out of the car.

"I'll need a light," he told her. "I can't see into the motor from the headlamps."

Sublett ordered Jode to get a battery lantern from the dash compartment. Jode handed the baby to Shelby while he complied.

But curiously, Larch noticed, Shelby passed the bundle back to her brother as soon as his hands were again free.

By the light of the lantern perched on a fender, Larch surveyed the inscrutable arrangement of steel castings, tubes, and wires under the hood. While the diesel engine, like the hopper, had remained virtually unchanged through the decades as inventors and theorists under the Iatrarchy lent their powers to better weaponry and medical equipment, that fact didn't help him much. Unlike Dena Sublett claimed to be, he was not a specialist in all things.

As he hovered over his assigned task, the Doctor kept the weapon directly on him, allowing Shelby and Jode to stand at her side. Stalling for time—though what good that would do, he wasn't sure; if another car came along now, it could only mean the end for themselves—Larch, leaning on the crutches, poked about in the engine, testing wires to discover if there were loose connections, peering into the battery to check the water level. It might soon turn out that Sublett herself knew all about engines as well as medicine and would spot his dallying, but as the minutes passed and she gave him no specific orders about what to do, this seemed less and less likely.

He was on the point of wondering how long he could, or should, keep his act going when the surrounding night exploded in his ears.

A simultaneous crash and flash as the rifle discharged, followed by sounds of scuffling behind him. A scream. Another lesser crash as the weapon fell hard against the front of a fender, shattering a headlight lens, coming to rest on the ground.

He cast the crutches away and grabbed the rifle in the same movement. Then turned to find Shelby and Sublett standing in the same place they had been when Shelby had struck the Doctor's forearm, deflecting her aim, hard enough to make her lose her hold on the gun. With her uninjured arm, Sublett had reached out and grabbed Shelby by her long dark hair, which she now twisted savagely, forcing Shelby to her knees.

But Sublett released Shelby as soon as she saw the rifle aimed at her own chest. And she said a curious thing, speaking less out of anger than a whining petulance: "Fools! Fools! You're going to ruin *every*thing."

Shelby rose quickly and moved behind Larch, pulling Jode and the baby with her.

Reason told him: *Kill her. Kill her now, swiftly*

and cleanly. There is no way to let her live and have any kind of chance yourselves.

Even Shelby must be expecting him to fire, as she waited there in the dark beside the red car.

Surely Sublett herself did. Her high color had drained away in the glow of the headlights and the lantern. Amazingly, even shockingly in view of her behavior up to now, she slowly crumpled from the waist and sank to the ground, lying motionless on her side, moaning slightly.

Larch heard his own voice speaking in a deceptively calm tone. "I'm not going to shoot you, Dr. Sublett." He turned to Shelby. "I can't do it."

"I never expected you to, Larch. But we'll somehow have to incapacitate her for a few hours till we can get far enough away from here not to be connected with her in any way."

"And how do you suggest we do that?"

"Tie her up, I suppose. But her in the backseat of her car and push the car out of sight behind those rocks just ahead. I remember she said she has some rope in the trunk that she thought of trying to move that tree with."

Remarkable, resourceful Shelby. "But I'm afraid this is the highway I was talking about earlier. Not a lot of traffic, but we can expect someone to come along any minute. Medcops, Subcutes, other Doctors."

"Then we'll have to do it fast. Someone from the Whitehouse is sure to be looking for her soon anyhow. If you don't think they'll find her by themselves, we can tip them off as soon as we get the chance. Jode, put Kira down carefully on the front seat, get the keys from the ignition, and find that rope in the trunk."

Somewhere along the line, Larch realized, they had exchanged roles. Shelby was now the pathfinder, the planner, the intriguer. She was doing well, better than he. *He* hadn't been able in all this time to get the gun safely away from the Doctor.

Jode came back with the rope. "I'll help," he offered. "I never did like this lady very much, even though she fed us and fixed Larch's knee."

"I know, Jody," Shelby said. "Evidently even special care in selection of donors doesn't always screen out insanity in clones. But we have to understand that she was doing what she thought she must do, according to the way she thought. And that's just what we're doing ourselves, isn't it?"

Now Shelby held the rifle while Larch and Jode bent over the limp Dr. Sublett, working swiftly. If someone came down the road, they'd have to muddle their way through an encounter, perhaps using the threat of the rifle. If it were Subcutes, however, the rifle would mean nothing against their mysterious invincibility.

With their captor-turned-captive now firmly bound around her ankles and wrists, and the wrists behind her back in a position Shelby said she hoped wouldn't be too uncomfortable for a few hours, Larch and Jode swung their burden into the back seat as easily as they had moved the tree.

Shelby handed back the rifle, slammed down the engine cover and hopped behind the wheel. "Wait for me. I'll get her out of the way."

"Have you forgotten, Shel? The car is busted," Jode said.

But Larch had already guessed. Beloved, endlessly inventive, clever Shelby. He had thought he

195

could never underestimate her. Yet he had done just that.

"When we were traveling at a good speed with the motor all warmed up and Larch had the monster-woman diverted with his inimitable conversation and irresistible charm, I just pulled the choke out all the way. Flooded. It should have cooled off enough now, I think."

She started the car easily and rolled up the road, pulled off the pavement again about twenty meters from where he and Jode waited, and disappeared behind a large rock outcrop which also offered the shelter of a few trees.

Then she returned and took the sleeping baby from Jode. "I never meant to break you in as a nursemaid, Jode. Don't worry, when we get to England, you'll never have to babysit unless you want to."

"It's okay. I *like* Kira. She's awfully cute. If only she'd keep her mouth shut at the right times—"

"We'd better get off the road," Larch said. "We've been very lucky so far that no one's come past."

They moved into a field, walking quickly until they judged they were out of range of car lights.

"Wow! You were great, Shel," Jode said. "The way you knocked that gun away from her. Almost as good as Larch getting me sprung from that Facility."

"I'd say a good bit better," Larch said. "I'm really proud of her, but then I always was."

"Thank you both. When the appropriate time and place coincide, I shall take a deep bow. But right now we have to decide where we're going, don't we?"

"I've been wondering about that myself," Larch said. "Do you have any idea what we should do, Shel?"

"How far do you suppose we are now from the place we were when we got stopped?"

"Hard to say. I'm not sure how many kilos we came down the highway. But it shouldn't be too formidable. Are you thinking we should try again to get to Mrs. Quistlethorp's?"

"I think under the circumstances it's a better idea than the one I had before, of going on into town," Shelby said. "There'd be too many unknowns there, I think. And only one at Quistlethorp's, whether she's home or not."

"Well, walking's no problem to me now, thanks to the excellent medical services of Dena Sublett."

"We mustn't forget that somehow we'll have to notify someone how to find her. That may take some ingenuity too."

"We'll do it. It seems we can do anything." Larch dug into a pocket. "I even remembered to bring the compass from the discarded jeans, but we'll have to move fast again. We'll be very visible in these fields when the moon comes up, or if the Subcutes decide to make a few sweeps this way with the black hopper."

"They can't find _anybody_," Jode said with assurance. "They couldn't even figure out the SG was on that operating table."

"They may yet, Jode," Larch said. "They just need a little time." He consulted the compass, squinting, finally lighting a match. "Okay. Let's head toward that line of trees, back into the mountains, or at least the foothills. It'll give us some cover until we can cut northwest, toward where we were before. If we hear cars on the way to the trees, we can lie flat for a few minutes, in case it's Medcops with a moving searchlight."

And they did twice resort to this tactic on their walk from the highway, once when lights appeared and a farm truck chugged past, and again, farther along, when a vehicle similar in shape and size to those used by the Medcops appeared, going at a much faster speed. But there was no searchlight; even no sign of the usual lighted, writhing caduceus on top.

"With the SG missing, Orthohaven will be thicker than ever with all kinds of cops and special investigators," Larch reminded them. "But if we're suspected of the kidnaping and they find us without him, at least they'll take us for interrogation rather than shoot us outright, if that's any comfort. We mustn't let them do either, of course."

"We'll just have to be quieter, and more cautious, and faster-moving than we've been before," Shelby said.

"Meanwhile, several other things might happen. The Subcutes might discover Sublett and her car by accident, and they might get suspicious when she doesn't turn up at the Summer Whitehouse and break into her house and find the body."

"They'd know who killed him then, all right," Jode said. "They'd find her and arrest her."

"It might depend on how the government struggle goes," Shelby said. "If Carvey's group manages to put down the insurrection right away, I suppose they would. But if the CGPs win, I have a strong hunch I know who's going to be the new Surgeon General."

"Who?" Jode said.

"Dena Sublett, M. D."

"She'd be awful," was Jode's opinion. "Worse than old Carvey. We should have wiped her out when we had the chance. Why didn't you shoot her, Larch?"

"Don't talk that way, Jode," Shelby admonished him. "Don't even think that way. If our side resorted to violence, we'd stand for nothing; we'd be no better than they are."

"As for clobbering Dangerous Dena, though, Jode," Larch added, "I have to admit that the idea did cross my mind."

The tree cover along the foothills was far thinner than the forests of the mountains. At just past midnight the moon was up, so they kept to the shadows. Larch seemed to know about where they were now. He estimated that another five hours would bring them back into the Quistlethorp neighborhood at just about dawn. He recommended that they stick to their usual mode of approach: get fairly close and then reconnoiter. It might even be a sound idea to delay the actual visit to the elderly undergrounder until broad day, so as not to provide her with a night-time alarm.

As he swung along on the crutches, Larch wondered about the effect of the past hours on Jode. He had seemed to take the whole adventure almost casually, but who knew what the real impressions of a child are?

Jode had been reared to a doctrine of quintessential pacifism, yet exposed constantly in his practical existence to its opposite. Kill, kill. Kill or be killed. Just like many another young person who has heard lip service from adults to one point of view and observed the working out of another, mightn't he merely become an early cynic, a doubter of all codes of behavior, throwing away the "right" with the wrong, the "true" with the false?

At every turn of Jode's thoughts toward violence from themselves in retribution, Shelby instructed him again in the way of nonaggression, Larch noticed. Yet he had spent the evening as a target in the sights of a known murderess, and seen the same weapon in the hands of both Shelby and himself. How long before Jode became inured? (If he were not already?) Protecting him from reality wouldn't be the answer even if it were possible.

Nor was the dilemma at an end. Now, for the first time ever, they were armed. Without discussion, or even comment, they had simply brought Sublett's rifle along. He would be carrying it now, except for the crutches. So Jode was being treated to the dismaying spectacle of his adored sister carrying a baby on one arm and a rifle under the other. Larch supposed Shelby might have turned the gun over to her brother to carry if she weren't having some of these same thoughts about Jode herself.

At least the ground wasn't rough now, and they had found a trail leading in the right direction. It must have occurred to all of them how much preferable it was to be in the open and moving under their own volition again than to be coerced in Sublett's house or car.

Twice in a three-hour stretch they heard the hopper, presumably the black Subcute vehicle. But both times it seemed to be searching lower down, near the highway and the shore, searchlight pointed groundward, sweeping like a pendulum.

The ultimate weariness struck them at about dawn.

One minute they were moving along almost as briskly as in the beginning. The next Kira was crying fretfully and Shelby was saying, "She's hungry again. And I can't go another step anyway. Please, Larch, we'll have to rest."

Of course they would. As if in sympathy, Larch's own terrible tiredness descended upon him. Only a very mild pain had recurred in his knee; the worst strain was in auxiliary parts, arms and shoulders. Unused to the crutches, he was paying with new pain for the amelioration of the old. And he was drowsing on his feet, had been, he realized, for the past hour. Jode, at the news that a rest stop had been ordered, had already dropped onto the springy, rough grass of a rolling hillside intersected by the path they had been following.

There was no really obscuring vegetation here, under or behind which they would be invisible. On the other hand, they had put considerable distance between themselves and the areas of Orthohaven where the search now seemed centered, judging by their last sight of the Medcop car and the two sweeps of the black hopper. It was four in the morning. They should be within two hours of their goal.

"Do you think it's relatively safe?" Shelby asked, reading his thought.

Larch scanned the hillside. They were on the side away from the highway. Jode seemed already asleep. Shelby had settled herself to feed the baby. Larch sank down, letting the crutches clatter. "Okay. Why not?"

After all their caution of the previous days, this

201

spot did seem rather open. But he would see that they didn't remain long. An hour at most.

Shelby passed him the rifle as she settled in the moonlight, cuddling Kira. Larch placed the weapon at his side, his right hand over the stock. He planned to rest, but remain awake. The fact that he had done this many times before and gotten away with it, been able to jump to his feet at the slightest noise, assured him he could do it again.

This time, however, he failed, fell into deep slumber. He must have remained thoroughly unconscious, not even dreaming, for hours.

Slowly, he came back into a vague awareness that the sky had lightened, not only lightened but the sun had moved into midmorning. The feeling that something strange had happened pulled him abruptly back to reality.

He smelled wood smoke.

There were voices, but not Jode's, not Shelby's. He remembered the rifle and felt for it, but it was not where he had so carefully left it. Instantly he sat up and looked around.

Into the faces of five strangers.

The rifle was nowhere in sight.

All five were staring fixedly at him. Three men, two women. One of the men was scarcely more than a youth, eighteen or so and of slight build. All of them presented an appearance of shabby genteelness, of respectability trying with difficulty not to go downhill.

Shelby and Jode woke now, almost simultaneously, and joined his own puzzlement as they stared at the semi-circle of faces.

Larch was the first to find his voice. "What do you want? We're carrying no large amount of money and no valuable property." (This was a lie. In Shelby's pack, along with the passports, was enough money for their passage to England. In his own pack, along with the microfilm, was a substantial cash reserve for living expenses until they could become settled overseas. In recent days, he hadn't given the money much thought.)

The older of the women said, "Now don't you worry. We wouldn't dream of taking your money."

She was somewhere in her late fifties, Larch guessed, and a bit overweight but not much. Her hair, chopped off straight around her neck, had grayed but her plump cheeks were pink and her skin smooth. Her dark blue trousers and matching sweater looked old, but well taken care of.

"What Mom says is right," the oldest of the men joined in. "We're here to help you and you must let us do it without causing any fuss." The second speaker was garbed in threadbare suntans, both shirt and trouser cuffs frayed. He was a little older than the woman, and grayer, and somehow conveyed the identity of a secondhand dealer, or a waiter in a down-at-heel restaurant.

Irritation with their senseless announcements seized Larch. "Who *are* you anyway?"

The woman smiled warmly. "Well, this is Daddy, who just spoke to you. And our boys, Conrad and Johnnie Lee, and Johnnie Lee's wife Susie."

Heads bobbed politely. Johnnie Lee and Susie were big-bodied, tall. Conrad was the teenager. "What have you done with our rifle?"

"Mom took it," the man called Johnnie Lee said. "You won't be needing it, and it's bad to have a gun around if you don't need it."

Susie, thirtyish, with a chipped upper incisor

203

which showed when she smiled, said, "We came up over the hill while ago to build a fire and cook some lunch. Our camping outfit is parked over yonder." She nodded in the direction Larch had figured the highway lay, but he had had no idea it was close. "Now how would you folks like some coffee? I've already got the pot on and it's about ready."

Larch suddenly felt the nerves under his skin begin to crawl, as unease and puzzlement turned to alarm. "Thanks anyway, but we won't be staying for coffee. We're leaving right away. Come on, Shelby, Jode."

Larch started to rise, reaching for the crutches, and then discovered that they, too, had been moved.

"Not *right* away," Mom insisted. "We already told you we'd help you. But there's no real hurry."

"Help us how?" Shelby demanded, and Larch knew that she'd been struck with the same alarm as he.

"Hey! You're Mercifuls, aren't you?" said Jode.

For some reason they all laughed at this, especially Conrad, who had not yet spoken to them. Susie, who seemed to be in charge of the campfire, moved over to where the thin stream of smoke rose in the morning air. There was a crackling sound as she added dry branches under the coffeepot, which dangled from a metal tripod.

When the mirth had died, Daddy said, "Why don't *you* tell them, Mom. You're the best talker in the family."

"All right," Mom agreed, "but I want us all to sit down and be comfortable. There's altogether too much rush-rush these days. It only leads to accidents and suffering and that's a fact."

As if to set an example, she settled herself on the grass, legs tucked primly beneath her.

"Now wait a minute, Mom," Johnnie Lee said. "You're making the same mistake we made last time. All this talk doesn't do a thing but *prolong* the suffering. When there's a job to be done, I say get it over with and talk afterward."

"You sit down and be quiet, Johnnie Lee. You were always an impetuous boy," Mom said mildly. "And Susie, you come back here so we can all be together."

The big man grumbled but he did as he was told. So did Susie. Now they were all sitting except the father, who hunkered in the background, looking nervously over a shoulder from time to time. The fire began to burn more briskly.

Mom included Larch, Shelby and Jode in her kindly glance and said, "It's true what your boy said. We're Mercifuls, just one small family out of a much larger group but we try to do our part wherever we are. We devote our lives to eliminating pain, and we discipline ourselves so as to be ready whenever we might be needed. We don't drink or smoke or take any drug that might cloud our senses. We don't dance or go to entertainments because there is no room in our lives for frivolity. We dress sensibly and keep ourselves neat and clean to set a good example. We risk our lives constantly to help others.

"And what is our reward? Misunderstanding from everyone. Even hatred and slander. We're hunted by Medcops and even Subcutes, and subjected to all sorts of indignities. We are martyred for a cause that—"

205

"That's all very well for you I'm sure," Shelby cut in angrily, "but what has it to do with us?"

Mom only enhanced her kindly beaming smile. "Why, I thought we told you. We've decided to help you to eliminate your suffering. When we came up the hill and found you all here asleep, we looked you over and we understood. We even had a little meeting and discussed it. All homeless wanderers you are, without a place to lay your heads. That poor baby, too tiny ever to get a grip on life." Here Mom looked benignly at Kira, who seemed to stare back but made no sound. "And the poor mother, who'll only grieve herself to death when the baby is taken. And you—" She turned to Larch. "—have surely met with some serious accident which will prevent you from ever being able to walk again."

"You mean you're going to *kill* us?" Jode demanded, more in outrage than in fear.

"Of course they're not, Jode," Shelby said.

"Now see what you've done, Mom?" Johnnie Lee said, rising to his feet. "You've got them all worried, just making them suffer more. *I* say—"

"Don't be rude to your mother," Daddy put in. "You know very well she wouldn't hurt a fly. Unless it was suffering."

"And I wouldn't *hurt* it even then," Mom corrected him. "Just put it out of its misery. Conrad, honey, go fetch the coffee. I'm sure it's ready, isn't it Susie?"

"I think you people all should consider something very seriously," Larch said, speaking suddenly and with such authority that everyone looked at him expectantly. "You speak of persecution by Subcutes and Medcops, and yet you come up to this

206

hillside and start a campfire that can be seen for maybe fifteen kilometers in every direction."

"Oh, bless your heart for thinking of us," Mom said, "but those terrible people don't ever make trouble for us around here. That's why we come here to camp. This place is called Orthohaven and only the Doctors—"

"That may have been true," Larch said, "until about three days ago. But now the place is literally hopping with cops. We've seen them," he added ominously, "several times."

"But why would that be?" said Daddy curiously.

"For one thing there's been a kidnaping at the Summer Whitehouse," Larch explained.

There was a small quietness while the Mercifuls apparently considered this. Then Conrad, the younger son, advised them: "Don't listen to him. He's just trying to make us nervous."

"Believe me," Larch said honestly, "I don't want any of you to get any more nervous than you already are. But I would advise you to put out that fire before it gets too noticeable."

"It wouldn't matter one way or the other," Johnnie Lee argued, "if we'd just finish our business and leave."

"All right, Johnnie, maybe you're right. Why don't you just go get ready while I talk a little more with these poor folks?" Mom was on her knees now, bending over Shelby and Kira. "Let me hold the poor little thing," she begged in a crooning voice. "So tiny. Too tiny for any use, isn't she? Born before her time, didn't I guess it?"

Shelby turned ungraciously away as she calmly put Kira to her breast. "Please, just let us alone."

Undaunted, Mom turned to Jode, "How old are you, sonny? Do you go to school?"

Jode squirmed out of reach of the plump hand Mom put out to him. "My, you're not very friendly, are you? I always tell my own boys, 'Be friendly with everybody, and always respect your elders.'"

"What about the fire?" Susie called from where she bent over the bubbling pot. "Should we put it out or not?"

Mom chewed her lip thoughtfully. "What do you think, Daddy?"

"I guess we'd better pour the coffee over it," Daddy allowed. "It's a waste, but there's no use taking chances on cops when we don't know for sure."

Johnnie Lee, who had been turned away, working busily at something he held in his palm, now re-entered the family circle. His attitude seemed changed, friendlier to both his own family and to Larch. Apparently now that he was being allowed his own way, he was responding with a certain mellowness.

In his right hand was a pistol, very old, probably older than Sublett's rifle, obviously lovingly cared-for. It looked oily around the hammer, the metal carefully blued along the short barrel. "My Colt Woodsman," he explained to Larch. "Used to be Daddy's. They don't make them any more. You ever seen one before, mister?"

Johnnie Lee had not once pointed the thing in their direction. It was more as if Larch were a fellow member of some target club on an innocent outing to fire at a few clay pigeons. (Here, pal, try my gun, you'll get a bang out of it.) Only Johnnie Lee didn't carry his act to the point of handing the weapon over. "I'm interested only in the return of the rifle," Larch told him coldly.

Johnnie Lee shrugged, plainly a little hurt. "Don't worry that this is the only gun we have, only a twenty-two. Daddy's got another one. Even Conrad's got his own gun, haven't you, Conrad?"

Conrad nodded solemnly.

"We're all going to help you," Johnnie Lee promised, "when the time comes. Okay, Mom, give the cripple back his crutches and we'll just stroll over toward those bushes. I'll take him first, then Con and Daddy can bring the others."

So far Larch had found the scene before him so improbable as to suggest bad theater. Even his contribution to the conversation and his fear—he realized now—had in them an element of spectatorship, a fascination as with something watched upon a stage.

At the word "cripple" applied to himself, however, personal involvement was no longer avoidable. He looked around frantically for Sublett's rifle. Their own luggage, the backpacks, remained undisturbed beside them. The traps carried by the Merciful family seemed equally light. A wicker basket, far too small to accommodate the rifle's length, and a paper shopping bag on the far side of the fire, which was now only a puddle of wet embers. They must have thrown the gun into the weeds, or buried it in a place they might or might not return to.

It seemed, then, that he was left with the same impossible challenge as he had been with Dena Sublett. He must somehow separate the historic Colt Woodsman from the man who held it so casually. Only this time the situation was far more hopeless at the outset. There were five in the Merciful family, all reasonably strong adults. And, if he could believe Johnnie Lee, all the men were armed. Only two adults on his own side, one crippled, one just delivered of a child, and two children, one an infant. It would be no surprise, either, to discover that Mom and Susie also packed weapons, perhaps concealed in the picnic basket and shopping bag.

No, his only hope this time was only hopelessness. Shelby had bailed them out before. Now she was as helpless as he, as Kira herself.

Mom was still going on in her encouraging, kindly way. "I told you all about it. We talked it over while you were asleep. There's only one answer for all of you. The young boy would only grieve himself too, with you all gone, he'd only suffer with no one to look after him. So we just decided, Why not help them all? We wouldn't be doing our duty any other way. There's so much pain, so much suffering in the world."

"You're even crazier than the Doctors," Jode burst out.

"Now, sonny, don't you bother your head about all this," Susie comforted him. "This is for the adults to figure out. Mom knows best."

At first Larch thought the low, humming sound was in his own head, a symptom of the awesome tension. When it continued and began to grow louder, he managed to exchange a glance with Shelby, who signaled that she heard it too.

None of the Mercifuls seemed to be paying attention to anything but their arrangements for the errand they felt duty-bound to carry out. "I must tell you what a pleasure it's been for us to meet you all," Mom was saying brightly. "I do believe, though, that Johnnie Lee has it backward. The mother and child have the first right to be helped, I should think. The cripple is suffering a lot, but it would be only chivalrous of him to wait his turn."

"The way we do it," Susie chimed in, "is we all wait here and maybe sing a song or two while the others are gone. Conrad, where's your banjo? Did you leave it in the camper?"

There was no mistaking the rhythmic droning now, and no mistaking its source. A hopper had appeared over the rim of the mountain range and was approaching fast. Because of the brightness of the sun, it was difficult to see what color it was.

Someone had seen the smoke, Larch thought. Undoubtedly the Subcutes.

Johnnie Lee was the first of the Mercifuls to look skyward. "Wait a minute, Mom. We got to hold off on this. Maybe you'll listen to me next time, not dawdle around so long."

"No, son, it's our duty," Mom argued, but already she was gathering up the basket, the shopping bag, and following Daddy, who had already set out at a run for the faraway trees. Susie and Johnnie Lee followed, with Conrad at their heels.

Larch, Jode, and Shelby holding Kira gathered their packs and streaked in the opposite direction. No trees, but a sparse fringe of chaparral into which they pitched headlong and rolled, Shelby protecting Kira's head with both hands. It wasn't much of a hiding place. Wisps of steam and smoke still rose fitfully from the charred circle where the fire had been. But if those in the hopper weren't, by some miracle, actually scanning the ground humanly or electronically, if no one was actually looking at this particular spot in the meadow . . .

Someone was, though. The hopper zoomed out

211

of the sun directly toward the field and hovered there, just over the dying fire.

There was only one tiny item in their favor. It was definitely not a black hopper, though it might be Medcops in an unmarked vehicle. Or a private party.

Perhaps, faced by the desperate need for numerous forces to scour the area for the missing SG and his "kidnapers," the authorities had adopted a posse system after all, Larch thought. Or commandeered the private hoppers of resident Doctors. For this one was white, the kind Doctors used for travel from Orthohaven back and forth to the facilities where they were assigned.

In any case, things looked bad. The fire had been seen and its remnants were obviously being inspected. They themselves might already have been seen, running for the brush. Or they might yet be seen lying in the low vegetation.

For a long moment the hopper continued to hover, like a bird that can't make up its mind whether to land or fly on. It actually had begun to rise a few meters and swing southward over the field when evidently the operator had still another change of mind.

It returned, lowered its landing gear onto the meadow, and the rotor spun itself to a final stop.

"We'll simply have to stay where we are," Larch cautioned. "We've nowhere else to run. The Mercifuls took the only safe route."

There was a brief wait, and then the door cracked open and a rotund figure bounced to the ground. He was short, broad, close-cropped, bearded, blond and fuzzy as a new tennis ball. And he too was armed. With a scope-sighted carbine.

212

Not r... ...breathed Shelby.
been forced, breathed Shelby.
to place his name ...ed Larch, without thinking.
in the underground. ...e moment that they had
...le at Jeff's golf course,

But that was absurd, as the ...possible betrayers
proved. ...g seconds

Jeff whooped at the sound of Larch's voice. And
as they came straggling out of the brush Rawter
said, "By the shades of Maimonides! I never
thought I'd see you alive. Where have you been?!
I've been scouring these mountains for you for
three days."

"So have a lot of other people. That's why we've
tried to make ourselves hard to find," Larch told
him.

"You mean the Subcutes?"

"Someone tipped off the authorities that we were
at Galentry and going to your place," Shelby said.
"They sent Medcops to the cottage and Subcutes to
meet us at the golf course. We've been in and out of
trouble ever since."

Jeff's hesitation was so brief that Larch decided
probably he imagined it. Then Jeff did a double-
take, stuck the carbine behind him and said,
"Who's this? Somebody else joined your party?" He
fluttered the makeshift blanket away from Kira's
face.

Shelby and Larch, with assistance from Jode,
gave Jeff a capsule account of Larch's fall down the
rocks, Kira's birth, and their disappointment over
getting at last to the airstrip and not finding the jet.

"I can explain about the plane. But we shouldn't

...eads off.

be standing here in the op...la were assisted in
Get in the hopper." ...awkwardly, sparing his
Jode sprang in, S... neglected to return the
by Jeff, and Larc... Rawter started the machine, ad-
leg. The Me... ...ntrols, hovered a moment more over
crutches a... ...dow, then wheeled off toward the ocean. "I
justed ... was just going home, giving up on finding you for
the ...
what I told myself would have to be the last time,
when I saw smoke in the distance."

"Not our fire," Shelby said.

"I didn't really think you'd be crazy enough to
start a blaze like that. But we're always worried
about forest fires at Orthohaven, so I thought I'd
check it out. When I got directly overhead, I saw
it had just been put out so I knew someone was
nearby."

Shelby told Jeff about their visit with the Mercifuls.

He arched his fuzzy, light eyebrows. "But you
weren't hurt?"

"Would have been if you hadn't come," Jode af-
firmed. "They were going to help us out by killing
us dead."

"It's been an eventful day all around," Jeff said.
"Since you haven't been near a teleron I suppose
you don't know the big news from last night?"

"Perhaps not," Shelby said.

"Well, brace yourselves for the shock of the century. Old Owen Carvey's been carved up. Dead as a
nail. You'll never guess where they found his
body."

"At—" Jode began, but Shelby and Larch both
said at once: "Where, Jeff?"

"In Dena Sublett's private surgery. First our good Top Doc was missing. Then Sublett was missing. Then some really brilliant investigator finally summoned the wit to look at the SG's appointment calendar and discovered Owen was to meet Dena for a medical checkup yesterday afternoon. It was the last appointment he kept that day. Last one he ever kept, come to think of it. So they all hotfooted to Dena's place. Everything locked tight there so they busted in. And found him. Not her, though, she's still missing. She was overdue at the Whitehouse, had promised earlier in the evening she'd come over and then didn't. Do you know what all this means?"

That we'll have to somehow phone an anonymous clue about where to find Sublett to the Medpolice, Larch thought.

"What does it mean?" he said.

"A definite breakthrough for the Abs," Jeff said confidently. "Mosk'll be SG now, already is in fact, whether he's been informed of it or not. Compared to Carvey he's a raving liberal. Only by comparison, though, as I say. Hasn't had a chance to show his real nature yet because of having to run on the ticket with Carvey. But I've known him for years. Wait and see."

Wait and see, Larch mused. *What the underground has been doing for too long.* And Jeff's information, rather than clearing things up, worse confounded matters in Larch's opinion. It had been fairly well established, to Larch's own satisfaction at least, that Dena Sublett wasn't acting alone on the plan to assassinate Mosk. When she didn't show up at the proper place and time with her selection of a man for the job (himself), someone else in her

215

organization would presumably step in and provide another hit man.

So what was *their* responsibility in all this, Larch wondered. To expose the plot and try to save Mosk's life (if there was still time) on grounds he'd be "better" for the Ab cause? (The lesser of two evils is still an evil.) Or try to save Mosk's life on humane grounds?

He admitted that his thinking was fuzzy at the moment. He couldn't explain, even to himself, why he had been reluctant to expose their adventure with Sublett to Jeff. It was an intuitive thing. He had headed off mention of it and Shelby had backed him up. Why? Everything was happening too fast. They—he, Shelby, Jode, and Kira—were too vulnerable on all sides. He still didn't know who had set the Medcops and Subcutes on them, and when it had been mentioned to Jeff, he didn't have an answer either. Actually he still wouldn't know that it had *not* been Jeff if not for the fact that Jeff was rescuing them now.

The hopper skated gracefully out over the sea in the rich suffusion of midday light, making a wide circle so they were looking back at the steep green carpet of Orthohaven, ending at the beach in magnificent fringed scallops as the series of ravines and ridges met a lacework of surf. It finally occurred to Larch to ask: "Where are you taking us?"

"Right now I'm embarked on a circuitous and devious route to confuse whoever might have been watching us since we took off from the meadow," Jeff explained. "After fifteen or twenty minutes we'll double back and come in from the north to Orthohaven."

"Not back to your place," Larch objected.

"We've run enough risks to last a lifetime. All we want to do is find the missing plane, and see if we still have a chance to use it to get from here to International Airport."

Jeff cleared his throat apologetically. "The plane is out. I called it off myself when the Subcutes began to get so thick at Orthohaven. Medcops too. Talk about risk—"

Though he knew it was the height of unreason, given the circumstances, Larch reacted angrily. "How could you do a thing like that? If we'd been there on time, and the plane had been, we could have gotten away before the cops and the cutes ever thought of looking in that neighborhood."

That was unfair. Too many if's. Was he even right about that? Right now he wasn't sure. Fatigue was again playing him tricks, even after the unfortunate four hours of sleep that had resulted in their brush with the Mercifuls. No, it must be that Jeff was right. A jet aircraft was far too valuable to take chances with in any case. Jeff had done everything humanly possible for them. Arranged for the new medcharts (which had not come, but that was hardly Jeff's fault), arranged for the plane (ditto), and had just spent hours, even days, searching (according to him) for them.

Larch shook his head, trying to clear his thoughts. Actually, he didn't know what to think about any of it, but there was no point in being small-minded. "I'm sorry, Jeff. Didn't mean to sound off. It's just that we're all ground down to a pulp and I'm irritable as hell."

"No apology necessary, no offense taken," Rawter said easily. He wheeled the craft into a new arc that took them far to the north. The sea, not visibly

217

in motion viewed from this height, produced a static brightness below, reflecting the glittering sky above.

With his thought processes this much slowed, it took Larch several additional minutes to realize that Rawter had still not answered his question about where they were being taken.

Once more it was Shelby who put things right. She had her way of cutting through nonessentials to practical considerations. "I don't see how all this darting and cavorting we're doing will help throw the Subcutes off, Jeff. Don't they have tracking devices for hoppers? Radar, sonar—whatever it is now?"

Rawter put the hopper into another sharp tilt. "Not this low over the water, and probably not this far from shore. They do have a lot of sophisticated stuff but they're famous for fouling up in application. Otherwise you never would have been able to evade them as long as you have."

"Then let's take a chance on their screwing up again," she suggested firmly. "If you don't stop swinging this machine around, I'm going to be airsick."

"Me too," Jode put in.

"Sorry. I'll do my amateur best. I'm not a pilot, you know. I'm a gastro-enterologist."

Once a Doctor, always a Doctor, Larch thought. *And they never let you forget it.* Then he again castigated himself for cynicism and impatience. There had been no better physician than Gerrod Harmon, who became a freedom fighter without peer.

"And you still haven't told us where we're bound," Shelby insisted.

218

"To a meeting."

"What kind of meeting?"

"Of the underground, of course. Everybody in this part of the district. Your own group and a few interested others. This thing about Carvey has blown things wide open. We'll have to evaluate the situation as it is now, and you and Larch being there will help immensely."

With each word Jeff spoke, Larch's glumness increased. Rawter's political ingenuousness and his habit of talking up a storm of half-truth and wishful thought were hardly a surprise, since Rawter had long been known for this kind of thing. The underground could not afford to be exclusive like the CGP; it had to accept help from whatever quarter it was offered. It was simply that Larch found Jeff more difficult to endure at certain times than at other times. This was one of the difficult times.

Calling a large meeting of Abs under the circumstances, with substantial numbers of Subcutes on the alert, seemed extraordinarily foolish to Larch. On the other hand, surely someone in the Ab organization would be more broadly informed on the true meaning of the schism that had developed between the CGP and the rest of the government. And the information would be valuable.

Meanwhile, he might as well go along with Jeff's easy assumption that this was a clear case of a hard-line Surgeon General being replaced by his successor, who *might* be (according to Jeff *was*) more easygoing. A softening of the tissue, not a breakthrough. Larch had certainly heard often enough that Mosk secretly favored abolishment of the rigid governmental control over marriage and eligibility for parenthood. But in whose court was the word "rigid" to be defined? Certainly not in that of the Abs. One could not discount, either, the old problem that politicians tend to prove themselves far more reactionary in office than on the election platform, or, as in this case, in talks with their known-to-be-liberal friends.

And though this seemed to be no time for personal considerations, Larch could not avoid wondering what would happen now to their plan to leave for England. Jeff had implied that it might have to be jettisoned. Cancellation of their transportation to the airport. Change in all thinking. An immediate better chance for them here with the change in government, possibly a hiatus in stringent treatment of Abs while new policies were formulated. This might be all very well for Jeff to think, but it would certainly leave themselves extremely vulnerable during the waiting period. What if they were captured and thanatized before any new government remembered to give the order to the Subcutes to desist?

Finally, there was one other item Larch could not eliminate from the outside fringe of his thought even though such a development seemed even less likely now than when Jeff had first appeared as their rescuer. How did they know at this moment, and beyond all doubt, that there really had been a meeting called, or that they were being taken to it? They had only Jeff Rawter's word. Wasn't it still within the realm of possibility that they were, even now, being flown directly into the arms of the Iatrarchy to be turned over to the Subcutes?

Such thoughts proved only, Larch realized, that for the moment, anyway, it was better not to think. The alternative, of course, was to go on listening to

Jeff, who seemed to grow increasingly euphoric as the hopper made a final wide sweep of the water and then started back toward the tree-covered coast.

"I've always thought, though I never wanted to say so to the Abs, that they've tended to put too much blame on the Iatrarchy," Rawter said. "Up to now, the government had been in the experimental stage and running scared. That's why all the emphasis on control, conformity, a heavy police force, stamping out the seeds of unrest before they can flower into rebellion. All this at the expense of letting the other things slide, technology, education, all kinds of arts and refinements.

"But now the change is upon us and, as always, the necessary leadership will surface to accommodate the change. Jacot Mosk is the logical man for this next step. He'll be lenient, but he won't go all the way all at once, throw the Patients into a panic. Good for the Abs, better than they'll realize themselves at first, because he won't be likely to let them have their way—entirely."

Larch said nothing, but he noticed that Jeff had again fallen into talking of the Abs as "they," rather than "we." This could not, however, be construed as a departure from the usual, he realized, since most HA Doctors offered only assistance to, not solidarity with, the Ab cause. Jeff had identified a little more closely with the underground in the past than most HA physicians. But he could surely not be criticized for changing his position a bit now, with so much uncertainty about the future. Certainly he must protect himself in any way he could.

"The Abs have never been able to see conformity

as a way of life," Jeff went on. "In a way, it's a deficiency in their thinking. In a civilized situation, the individual belongs to the group, never vice versa. Before the World Medarchy individuality was over-rated. Be different. Express your own personality. Stand on your own feet. Nonsense. Man is a colonizing animal, never meant to live alone."

Larch opened his mouth, then closed it again. He noted that Shelby hadn't been saying anything either.

"Now don't misunderstand. I am in deep sympathy with the organized Abs. They have some splendid leadership quite capable of assisting in, even forming, a government. Yourself for instance. But you'll have to admit that they also attract a lot of less stable people. I discovered that as soon as I began to attend the meetings. How could I feel easy with my personal security—my license to practice medicine—in the hands of some featherbrain who believes that research flies in the face of Providence, or that the way to cure the common cold is to pummel the spine, or that matter simply doesn't exist? What if someone is elected to office whose every action is based on a conviction that the Second Coming will occur next March 15 at precisely 2309 Greenwich, and it's therefore sacrilegious to bother with the ills of the flesh?"

"I can't see," Shelby remarked, "that it would be so much worse than what we have now, and if that person had been elected in a free system, he'd have majority support for his views."

"All right, perhaps I'm exaggerating, but a majority vote itself implies a certain conformity. And there's stability in conformity."

"Like the American Dream," she mused.

"There's always been an element of conformity there. For a few centuries the dream was Making It on Your Own, and now it's Giving Up and Letting Them Do the Worrying. If we're to be asked to conform to something, it seems to me the earlier version is the better."

"Constantinople wasn't built in a week," Jeff preached.

"And since you seem to know so much about it, Jeff, what will happen to Dena Sublett if and when they find her," Shelby asked carefully. "Will Mosk's administration—assuming Mosk remains Surgeon General—be obliged to—uh—thanatize her?"

"That may well be the only cure for her malady. Frankly I've been worried about her over the past several years. Her behavior has shown a marked lack of control and it seemed to be deteriorating. Even in public she often exhibited evidence of psychotic—"

"If she'd been a Patient instead of a Doctor," Shelby guessed, "then she'd have been thanatized long ago?"

"Oh, now, Shelby, that's hardly fair. You make everything sound so—so double-standard. Sure, I admit that if you're going to lose your mental grip, you have a better chance of hiding your condition in the higher echelons. But that's always been true. Madness at the top. Through history think how many kings, princes—and anyway, no one ever claimed Doctors can't get sick too. That was one of the difficult lessons I learned in medical school. As a student and even as an interne I used to think in terms of only two kinds of people: 'them' and 'us,' the first being of course the Patients, the sick ones, those individuals who had something wrong with

223

them and came to 'us,' the well ones, the know-all ones, to be cured.

"You'll find it's a common occupational hallucination of young doctors. My delusion lasted right up until the day the resident pathologist and I were sent to check out the symptoms of a man brought into the facility in terrible condition. I won't go into professional detail on the list of what was wrong with him, but he was moribund, we could see that without reading any gauges or looking at his chart. He hadn't got to the facility soon enough, you see. His circulatory system was involved, his respiration was already in Cheyne-Stokes. But the point is, do you know who he was?"

"A Doctor," Shelby said.

"Right. And not even an elderly one. He was about my own age at the time, an interne like me, assigned to a facility in the East, planning to go into gastro-enterology too. My double. He'd come west on a vacation and just popped off like that."

There was a sense of outrage in Jeff's tone that he seemed to be urging Shelby and Larch to share. the Doctors (sometimes) also die. Somehow this outrage wasn't quite appropriate, since Jeff's whole message was meant to be that he formerly, as a much younger man, had believed in a "them" and an "us," but believed it no longer.

Larch sighed. The contradictions in Rawter were inscrutable, and would probably remain so, since all his talk seemed never quite to clear anything up. "Tell me, Jeff," said Larch curiously, "if you really feel the way you do, whatever made you decide to help the underground?"

"I've asked myself that," he admitted. "I think it's because I have too much respect for the medical

224

profession to feel it ought to spread itself so thin, into areas better delegated to others."

"Hey!" Jode said, "we're back where we started from."

It was true. From the windows of the descending hopper were now visible the creek, the narrow abandoned road fording it and feeding into the better road on Dena Sublett's property. To one side of the pavement where it curved around a rock outcrop was the fallen tree, lying where Larch and Jode had left it after being ordered by Sublett at gunpoint to make a passage for her car.

"You here before?" Jeff said. "How you folks do get around. Well, your troubles are over. See that house over in that clump of gum trees?"

"Mrs. Quistlethorp's place," Larch said. "We were almost there. If only we'd turned left instead of right over the creek, if I'd remembered the map better—"

The hopper dipped until it was barely clearing the occasional clumps of liveoak, circled a field. "We're putting down," Rawter announced. "Hang on. It may be bumpy."

An understatement. The vehicle veered, thudded against the earth, bumped, twisted, rocked, bumped again, and became still. "I'll let you out and you can start for the house while I get this thing under cover."

They debarked to find themselves near a barnlike building which was apparently a hangar. Sitting inside, behind one of the wide doors, now open, was another hopper about the size of Rawter's and also painted a medical white. A young man in a mechanic's jumpsuit rode out from the building on a small electric tug-unit, to help Rawter tow his vehicle to shelter.

Very well to hide the hoppers, Larch thought, but no one seemed concerned about hiding cars. Three were visible around the driveway to a rambling, brown, shake-sided house, which they were now approaching from the rear.

From a design point of view the house was a disaster. Obviously built as a replica of a western ranch home (nostalgia for a time when cattle abounded, hence ranching was possible), it sprawled on a knoll like a brown lizard on a rock. The cedar shakes had perhaps been added as an afterthought, to hide differences in construction of the several extensive wings, built in different years. Other afterthoughts were even worse: false shutters, scalloped boards pretending to be cornices, and an obese, false cupola perched uncomfortably at the peak of a gable. Yet there was a livableness exuded by the place for all its incongruity. Someone had lived in and loved the house. An old-fashioned porch swing dangled in the backyard, hung from a strong limb of one of the gum trees, and the screened porch they entered was furnished with lounges and wicker deal tables.

From one of these lounges a figure rose as they appeared in the doorway. "Oh, my dears, what a surprise! Our faith has brought you through."

Mrs. Quistlethorp kissed each of them, including the baby. Including Jode, though he looked threatened and reluctant. For their hostess was, in some respects, a threatening figure. A gaunt, tall, white-haired, leather-skinned woman of queenly carriage and sharp features. Clusters of prismatically flashing gemstones emphasized the swollen veins of her thin hands. She was dressed in a loose, flowing garment of slate-gray satin, ambitiously but tastefully embroidered in scarlet.

Her house (or the house provided by her brother) might not be authentic, but Mrs. Quistlethorp herself certainly was.

"We thank you for receiving us, Mrs. Quistlethorp," Shelby said, passing Kira over to be held in the formidable arms. The baby, who had been restless since they left the hopper, immediately quieted, nestled on the bony, spare breast.

"You must call me Ralda," she ordered, "and be assured that I'm pleased to be able to do any small thing to help, for you are all the children of love." The Christian Science practitioner pulled the covering away from the tiny body and examined it fondly. "This baby will be all right," she at last pronounced unequivocally. "Error will not touch this child."

When Jeff Rawter arrived on the porch, Ralda greeted him too and explained, "It'll be several hours before everyone is gathered for the meeting. The decision to hold it was rather sudden and word is still being passed. But we'll all be safe here, and there'll be time for you to eat and rest. I must say the message screen of the teleron has been busy with news of you. There was a report yesterday that you'd been taken by the Subcutes, but I knew in my heart it couldn't be true."

"It'll be dangerous for you, having us all here," Larch warned. "The cars already gathering in your driveway could cause suspicion."

"Many cars come and go here," she assured him. "My brother often comes and brings large groups, so it should pass unnoticed. The neighbors will only

227

think it's another gathering of medical people on vacation. I see you put the hopper under cover, and that's wise, but probably unnecessary. Please don't think I'm being unrealistic. I know I have a reputation for seeing only the good, and it's true that any large, unauthorized gathering is a risk in these terrible times. Still, we shall be protected by His mercy."

Luncheon at Ralda Quistlethorp's, served from mid-afternoon on, was a triumph of ingenuity. Casseroles of fresh vegetables were arranged on two large buffets, along with spiced sauces and several varieties of something that looked and tasted very much like cheese.

"I raised the vegetables myself," Ralda admitted. "And the cheese is a soybean product from a formula I developed. I raised that too."

"We're having real food again!" Jode remarked. "How lucky can we get?" Then he asked Mrs. Quistlethorp, "Do you have a cat or a dog?"

"My brother brought me a kitten last year," Ralda said, "but error swept it away so I knew it was not meant that I should take care of animals. I love them, though. They're beautiful in their perfection."

They had joined several others who were also on hand early for the meeting. There was a poet named Mark, clean-shaven including his skull. He had enormous brown eyes and a gentle voice and wore a monk's robe of unbleached muslin tied at the waist with a sisal rope. While the others ate, he read some of his verse, making a good performance of it, Larch thought.

And there were Shavia, who said she was a white

228

witch; a sweet-faced lady herbalist called Dulce Nombre de Paz; Jorgan, who called himself an anti-structuralist but said he didn't want to talk about it because people were not yet ready to hear about it; a tidy middle-aged man who looked like a business executive and assured whoever would listen that they were seeing not him but his surrogate self, in accordance with a method he had worked out, and Vista, a young woman in scarlet shorts and matching cape, who had a rain of bright blonde hair. Vista said she was a saint.

"A Latter-Day Saint?" Larch guessed.

"No, just a saint." Vista explained that she had experienced several visions and had been tempted many times but had managed to resist.

As evening drew on, more people arrived and took their places in Ralda Quistlethorp's large, comfortable parlor until there were around forty, many of whom Larch recognized. Two nuns from an Ursaline Convent, the existence of which was tolerated but not condoned by the Iatrarchy, two osteopaths, a chiropractor, three polarity therapists, a renegade physician who had invented a life-ray treatment, a gestalt analyst, a committee of antivisectionists exercised over the Iatrarchy's use of animal matter in certain medical preparations when so few animal species had survived, a metabolic physiologist, a handful of Mrs. Quistlethorp's fellow Christian Scientists, some youthful political activists of both sexes, and others. The meeting had not yet formally begun.

General surprise greeted the appearance of Larch and the Harmons. As they moved through the room there was a flurry of handshakes, kisses, touches of reassurance.

Larch was surprised to see Strong Bayet, looking out of place in a corner, and moved over to speak to him. "Did you decide to join us after all?"

"It was the dirty Medcops that finally made up my mind, coming to the house after you that night. I don't know when you left or how you got away from them, but I thanked God you were gone when they got there."

Larch had not forgotten that Strong's son had been a Medcop, and knew what the decision must have cost.

"An unexpected pleasure to be back among Abs," he said to someone else.

A man Larch did not recognize, blunt-faced, blunt-fingered, tapped him on the forearm. "I object to our own use of that vulgar abbreviation. I particularly object to having it applied to myself or my patients. We are normal, sir, in every way. Perfect form means perfect function."

"I mean no offense," Larch apologized. "My own position is a little different. It's always given me a bit of pleasure to help turn a pejorative label into an honorable name. Much like the reaction of English settlers in New England to being called Yankees by the Colonial Dutch. I don't believe we've met, by the way."

"Freedom Rapt, DC," the man introduced himself. "I know who you are, and I'm pleased to meet you in person. I just wish I could persuade you that misuse of the word 'abnormal' is part of the intolerable conspiracy of the MDs to drive people deeper into ignorance and ill-health so they'll become more likely to be victimized by drugs and poisons which are unnatural and ineffective—abnormal, if you like."

230

"Drugs and poisons, that's the heart of it, Doctor." This from a youngish man in a black sweater who had thrust himself into the conversation. "But have you thought of it this way? Where chiropractic depends on manipulation and natural diet, osteopathy—"

"Ah, you're all talking about pain killers and that's right down my alley," interrupted another stranger to Larch. A hefty, moon-faced person, husky-voiced, of ambiguous age and sex. "The notion of being able to kill pain is fairly recent, as we all know, and perhaps a mistaken idea altogether. In the middle ages it was widely believed by the healers that if you killed the pain, you killed the patient. Like fever, pain has its uses, functioning as a signal of dis-ease, disharmony of the body. If you rid the patient of pain before you rid him of its cause, you introduce the hazard of destroying the wholeness of the individual. This wholeness can be restored only when the patient has *passed through* pain. Let me explain—"

"Please let us come to order," came the voice of Ralda, overriding the other voices. "Since I invited you all here, and since we're gathered at last, I suggest we waste no more time in electing a discussion leader and what not. I'm taking it on myself to start this meeting with some preliminary remarks. Then whoever else wants to speak may do so, taking turns, of course." She paused, and added, "Unless someone has a better plan?"

There was silence, indicating no other plan would be proposed. Those still standing found places in the deep, pillow-filled windowseats and on the chaises covered with faded *sarapes*.

"Our purpose," Ralda went on, "is to inform you of what has happened and then try to discover if from our point of view it serves any purpose."

"What *has* happened?" one of the Ursalines inquired. "We have no teleron at the convent."

With brevity and admirable organization of thought, Ralda described the disappearance of Owen Carvey and the descent of the Subcute forces upon Orthohaven in pursuit of Larch and the Harmons as the suspected kidnapers. Then she told of the "passing over" of Owen Carvey on Dena Sublett's operating table. "Early this morning," she went on, "Dena Sublett was discovered by the Subcutes tied up and left in her own car. She was arrested and was being held for interrogation. But meanwhile, in Capital City, someone assassinated Jacot Mosk and five key members of the Ama. The government is in chaos, even though the APES is still sending out soothing messages that everything is under control and all Patients are 'ordered' to remain calm."

There was much murmuring in the room. Then Jeff Rawter's voice, showing anger, demanded, "Who told you this about Mosk? That certainly wasn't on the teleron."

"I received that information privately."

Larch was still tangling with his guilty conscience. *We clean forgot to tell anyone about Sublett as soon as we got to Ralda's,* he thought. *She could be there still if the Subcutes hadn't for once been effective.* On the other hand, they still weren't off the hook. Any telephone message from the Quistlethorp residence might have put Ralda in jeopardy. *Just as well it happened this way.*

232

"So much for the exordium," said an impatient voice. "What about the loose ends? For instance, who tied up Sublett?"

"We did," Larch said, still wondering if he was wise to speak, but deciding to get it over with. "That is, Jode Harmon—" He nodded at Jode. "—and I did, Shelby having already performed the real heroics by depriving Sublett of the rifle she was holding on us." Jode beamed his pleasure at being included in Larch's report. Shelby, on the other hand, looked uneasy as Larch quickly skimmed over their meeting with Dr. Sublett, the visit of the Subcutes to the operating room, and their eventual escape. He added a few words about their brush with the Mercifuls and Jeff's timely rescue.

He then gave a more detailed account of what Sublett had told them of the coup which had been arranged by the CGP. "There's reason to believe that if the CGP now has the foothold it needs, Dena Sublett will soon be released by the Subcutes, may already have been. She'll be at the top of the pyramid of the Iatrarchy, one way or another, and she is dangerous. Abnormal, but in the sense that we here are not." Then he added, "That puts us in a very bad position personally, the Harmons and me; since we were the ones who detained her, she'll make every effort to have us found. And this may extend to the whole organization. There may be extra pressure against Abs now."

There was a renewed bluster of uncontrolled discussion enhanced by a buzz of consternation.

"There's something else you all should know," Jeff Rawter's voice boomed over the confusion. "Larch Rosst tells me there's an informer among us."

233

Shocked silence. "How else," Jeff said reasonably, "would the Medcops have known to come to Luke Algis's place to try to find Rosst and the Harmons? How would they have known to send Subcutes to the golf course at my place, and to leave a stake-out of Medcops at the airstrip?"

Well, it was out, and probably a good thing too, Larch thought. In his own ruminations lately, he had downgraded both Strong Bayet and his granddaughter on the list of suspects, since it was doubtful that either of them had known about the final destination in Orthohaven of the fugitives, the airstrip. Unless one of them had actually overheard his conversation with Jeff in the cottage at Galentry, which was entirely possible but not entirely likely. Downgraded them, but not removed them from the list, since eavesdropping outside a door was an ancient and often productive occupation of informers. That left Luke Algis, whose absence from this meeting meant nothing, since, unlike Jeff, Luke customarily steered clear of Ab organizational activity, and Jeff Rawter himself. And here was Rawter taking it upon himself to alert everyone of the stoolpigeon in their midst. That ought to remove suspicion from Rawter too, but did it really? Another traditional dodge in spy annals was pointing a finger at someone else before it could be aimed in the direction of the accuser. Rawter was pointing at everyone else. Or rather, *any*one else, but himself.

Larch suddenly felt more uneasy than he had at any time since entering the room. The newest announcement had again thrown the group into a buzz of conversation. Larch chose the moment to glance across the room at Bayet, whose ruddy, craggy face displayed an expression that could only be called grim, not guilty. And his big hands remained fisted on his denim knees, betraying no sign of nervousness. (Which also proved nothing, Larch admitted. A good informer is always the most relaxed-looking person in the room.)

Mutual suspicion is the cabin fever of the underground.

This time Ralda Quistlethorp pulled the meeting together by saying, loudly, until the din subsided, "Perhaps now would be an appropriate time, in view of Jeff's news, and before we go into discussion of matters which might be confidential, to ask the identities of the new people among us. I see two or three here, for instance, that I myself haven't met though I tried to greet everyone at the door. I presume they're sponsored by someone, or they wouldn't have known the location of the meeting."

Eyes swung now in several directions, most of them settling at the end of the long room nearest the door, where a slender young woman with shiny brown hair pulled into a low chignon perched on a settle, knees crossed, arms folded over her chest. She accepted Ralda's challenge of her presence at once. "My name is Joan Lambeth and I'm a nurse at Facility 167-3. I happened to be on duty when the Medcops brought that boy in." She paused here, to smile at Jode, who, after a moment of wonder, returned the smile, which broadened as he seemed to recognize her. "I'd seen a lot of things like that and it's been cumulative. Finally, when I saw them bringing in a Patient that young for interrogation, and knew what they planned to do to him, I knew

235

I'd had enough. My roommate's boyfriend is an Ab and I asked him how to get in touch with the organization. He told me he'd just heard about the meeting but wasn't able to come tonight. So I came anyway. His name is—is—is it all right to tell his name?"

"Yes, yes, of course," several voices encouraged her.

"Hal Marchant."

One of the youthful political activists, Larch thought, if he recalled correctly. He had met Marchant at some time in his association with local Abs. Still, it was a loose end for Joan Lambeth, being present at a first meeting without a sponsor.

As if she too realized this, the girl added, "I am not a spy."

The group seemed satisfied and turned to hear from Strong, who gave a brief account of himself, ending with the same thing he'd said to Larch earlier.

A third stranger to the group now said defensively, "I'm a Patient. Just a plain, goddamned Patient who got fed up."

"I invited him," one of the chiropractors put in quickly.

The new member was a deeply suntanned, handsome man of uncertain age, with creases of humor above a luxuriant dark beard, neatly trimmed. He wore canvas sandals and the uniform of the workingman under the Iatrarchy: tan canvas trousers and a blue cambric pullover shirt, open at the throat.

"You want to see my chart?" he challenged them. "It says I'm Tom Danns, qualified by proficiency on the Sapington Scores to be a technician in a medical laboratory. Which I am. Which I've been for too long, only it doesn't say *that*. It also says I'm to report next week to the facility for treatment 'to correct an abnormality.' What the chart does not say is what the abnormality is."

The group waited in sympathetic expectancy. All had heard Danns' story, with minor variations, dozens, perhaps hundreds, of times. It was, of course, their own story.

"My abnormality," he went on, "is that I had the presumption to apply for a change in occupational status. I have never liked being a lab technician, and I applied to become an artisan, a jeweler."

He had them all hanging now. This wasn't quite what was expected after all. Chiropractor, faith healer, waterwitch, gestaltist—perhaps. But somehow "jeweler" sounded too innocent, not something even the Iatrarchy would be likely to take a stand on.

Danns shot the left cuff of the cambric shirt to display a gleaming bracelet wrought of highly polished copper and brass. It was both massive and intricate, obviously the end product of hours of work and considerable originality of design. It drew appreciative "ah's" from the assembly before he went on:

"I've made things like this for years for my family and friends, and they've urged me to try to turn it into a kind of profession. But as soon as I sent in the application, a whole passel of investigators descended on me at the lab. They told me that any change in my status would not be 'compatible with the best interests of Public Health,' whatever the hell that means, and when I put up a fuss about it, I got the order to appear for examination and adjustment. So here I am. I'm willing to fight, if you can use me."

There were scattered cries of "bravo" and "good show," and "yes, yes, we can use you" and someone said, "You have to be a good enough fighter not to need weapons. We don't use weapons."

"I don't use weapons either. I plan to go up in the hills and build a little shack where I can work and not be disturbed."

"You'll need a bogus medchart," someone said.

"We'll help you get it," said someone else.

Ralda welcomed the three newcomers and said, "So far as I'm concerned, none of you is to be considered an informer. I'm only sorry I asked you to introduce yourselves under a cloud, but you'll understand how careful we have to be. Does anyone else have anything to say?"

Several did. Vista the saint, sitting in a wing chair much too large for her, said, "Why? Why does Tom need a phony chart and all of us have to hide and conspire and be secret? Why not let the Iatrarchy know everything? Our weapons are moral weapons, our force is not in numbers but ideas."

"You religious fanatics are all alike," complained an osteopath. "Scratch the surface and you turn out to be nothing but counter-revolutionary scabs."

"Now see here—!"

"The record of Jehovah's Witnesses speaks for itself," said a small, quiet young woman whom no one seemed to have noticed before. Without raising her voice, she continued: "We have not flinched before the cells of the former penitentiaries, the Nazi gas chambers, Soviet slave camps, or the operating tables of the World Medarchy."

"I don't mean to be offensive, but what good is martyrdom," said the surrogate-self man, "when what we need is a huge force of resolute people willing to agree on one single issue long enough to—"

"Religious nuts and HA members," said one of the chiropractors, "always wind up on the wrong side of the barricades because they're from the right side of the tracks."

"Barricades went out centuries ago," said one of the young political activists.

"I was speaking metaphorically," said the chiropractor huffily.

"Brothers and sisters," said Mark the poet, "you're right about God being on the side of the Abs—"

"No one has said any such thing. There is no God."

The nuns crossed themselves.

"God love you—if you want to call Him historical materialism, I doubt if He will mind. He has so many names a few more won't matter. You're right about His being on the side of the oppressed, but what other weapons dare the oppressed use? The Iatrarchy employs force. If we compete with them, then how are we different?"

"They use force to make us do things. If we *did* use it, it would be to avoid being compelled to do things against our conscience—a difference."

"You think now. But how long before we're using it for something else? Means and ends can't be put in different boxes."

"We aren't revolutionists yet anyway, only rebels. So long as Patients in large numbers don't feel oppressed, we're talking to incomprehension. When Marat exhorted, the sansculottes could see the gulf between the noblesse and themselves. When Lenin spoke, the workers and peasants had obvious reason to vote with their feet. But when we tell Patients the Iatrarchy robs them of every liberty but the right to die, they don't believe us."

"They can't do anything to me. I know that the flesh is unreal and so-called diseases an illusion."

"Please. Please! *Please!*" came the stern voice of Ralda. "It seems we have two factions here. Those who want to discuss theory and philosophy, and those who would like to get down to the business of analyzing what the governmental schism might mean to—"

"Two factions, hell!" cried a voice. "You count the number of people in this room and that's how many factions we got. That's always been the trouble with—"

"Exactly. If every Ab were 'modified' tomorrow by the Iatrarchy into perfectly adjusted individuals, there would be just as many more Abs the day after that. God loves difference; that's why no two blades of grass, no two grains of sand, are identical. But at least we can all agree on—"

With absolutely no warning, the door to the inner part of the house swung open and the large figure of Luke Algis filled its frame.

Before he could even comprehend Luke's sudden appearance in a logical way, Larch felt a visceral lurching, the sickness of certainty that this was some kind of ultimate moment. And then he knew what before he had almost refused to suspect: that Algis was, had to be, the informer. The least likely name on the list was the right one after all.

Behind him in the next instant would loom the Subcutes, brought to the meeting—and shown the way—by the arch-agent provocateur himself.

But between that moment of truth and the present was an instant of utter emptiness, when everyone in the room simply stared at Luke. He was a Doctor who really looked like a Doctor. Well above average height, thin lips, taut steel-smooth cheeks, antique eyeglasses instead of liquid contacts, well-brushed silvery hair, immaculate teeth and fingernails, a gaudy scarf wound high around his throat, its ends thrust with careful negligence into the collar of a pale, soft shirt.

And when he spoke it was with such authority that no one could think of questioning his words. "Whatever you're doing, drop it."

This seemed to confirm the worst, but Luke went on: "Prepare to hear bad news. In fifteen minutes a black hopper full of Subcutes will land on Mrs. Quistlethorp's field, ready to put the lot of you under arrest and annihilate all resisters.

"It's only because of a miscalculation and an incredibly arrogant overconfidence that there isn't a second force of them at this moment closing in on the house on foot."

"But why—? How—? Who—?"

The questions in many voices were respectfully treated as one question by Algis. "The man who tipped off the Subcutes about this meeting is the same one who notified the authorities that Larch Rosst and the Harmons were staying in a cottage at my place. I've just had a devil of a time convincing them that I had no knowledge of any Abs being there.

"The same informer gave word that Rosst was on his way to Rawter's golf course and then to the air strip. The only reason I can think of that he didn't inform on me too is—" Here Luke sighed and, surprisingly, produced a wry smile. "—he's got such a screwed-up sense of ethics that he wouldn't allow himself to discredit a fellow Doctor."

There was an explosion of glass at the far end of the room.

Larch looked from Luke toward the noise in time to see Jeff Rawter leaping through what had been a large view-window of the kind that does not open.

Chairs and small tables crashed to the floor as people in the room leaped to their feet. There was a rush toward the window, a secondary rush toward both doors in the room.

Then a very loud voice roared: "Let him go!"

Another took it up, then another. "Let him go. Let him go. We don't deal in retribution. That's for the Iatrarchy, not for us."

But the fact was, Larch realized, that Jeff didn't seem to be going anywhere. There had been the crash, and almost coinciding, a vast rattle of falling glass shards, but no sound of running steps.

He could not, however, be certain. Rawter might have gotten away, or simply passed out from the impact with the glass, or from the fall.

Meanwhile, everyone was running. Most of them plunged out through the doors. A few of the more confident paused first to gather belongings.

"Those who came in cars, please take someone with you," Luke's arresting voice boomed over the confusion. "You can make it out of here in plenty of time if you go down the back road and cut over to the highway at the bridge."

Seconds later came the sound of engines roaring in the driveway. Others were running off into the darkness.

The room was now nearly empty.

He was aware that Shelby stood close to his side, the baby pressed tightly to her, her other hand holding Jode's. She had not, of course, run out with the others, but was waiting for him, perhaps waiting for an answer to their mutual unspoken question: what do we do now?

But he had no answer. Somehow, he had hoped for a moment that Algis himself would give them some kind of help. But why should he? Because he had helped them before? Yet this was clearly an everyone-for-himself situation. They had no car. It would be foolhardy to try to commandeer Jeff's hopper from the hangar and go up just in time to meet the Subcutes coming down (even assuming either he or Shelby could fly the airhopper).

Should they start running then? *Again?* This time, however, it seemed impossible. Not again. Shelby with the baby. He without his crutches. And it was very dark outside now, well into the evening.

It occurred to him that if Luke weren't going to suggest what they should do, he could always ask Luke if he had any ideas. Perhaps somewhere nearby that they could hide without jeopardizing Ralda. But Luke had just disappeared out the window through the ragged frame made by the broken glass.

243

Larch and Ralda, with Shelby and Jode trailing, moved over to the window and looked outside.

On the ground beside the house, body crumpled, limbs splayed crazily, fuzzy blond beard streaked with bright blood, moaning faintly, was Jeff, with Luke bent over him, expertly investigating for breakage. Without looking up from his work, Luke called, "A bit of light out here, Ralda, please. Haven't you a floodlamp for the garden?"

Ralda went to the far side of the room and pressed a switch. The scene outside the window was drenched with light.

Luke drew a small black case out of a pocket and was removing from it a hypodermic syringe when Ralda returned to the window. "Wait, Luke, you know better than that," she scolded him. "I don't care how much pain that villain is suffering, there will be no medicines given or taken in my house. I will not be a party to the spread of error."

Luke paused with the instrument hovering over Jeff's bared forearm. When he looked up, Larch could see a quick flicker of amusement at this new contradiction from the remarkable Ralda. Pain, indeed. "Couldn't we work out some kind of compromise?" he begged her. "I of course apologize for even pointing this out, but technically we're not really in your house. And you can see that Jeff needs emergency attention."

After a second, Ralda seemed to relent. "As you say." She withdrew into the shadows of the room with a hand on which her rings flashed shading her handsome brow as if from sunlight. She seemed to be praying.

Luke, still busy, didn't seem to realize she had left the window. "I'll have him out of here in a few minutes. I can fly him to the nearest facility in his own hopper. If the Subcutes get here first, I'll explain to them there's been an accident and I have to get my patient some immediate help in an emergency room."

When he looked up again, the sight of Larch in the window reminded him of something else. "What are you standing there for? The keys are in the buggy I drove up here. Load in your crew, Larch, and take Ralda along. There's plenty of fuel to get all the way to International Airport, four or five hours' worth at least."

"Thanks, Luke, but what if the Subcutes stop us? What'll we say, among other things, about driving a stolen vehicle?"

"No chance. It's the one vehicle you can drive without fear of ever being stopped by anyone in the Iatrarchy. And you can speed all you like."

They hurried out to the driveway. The only car left was an ambulance, gleaming aseptically in the lights from Ralda's yard.

"Whoopee," Jode said, scrambling into the front seat.

"It belongs to the Facility," Luke called out to them. "Later—much later—I'll report it stolen so I won't be under any more suspicion than I am already. Whoever drives should put on one of those white jackets you'll find on the seat, and whoever else sits in front puts on the other. The rest can play Patient in the back till you get out of the city. Good luck."

245

Larch helped Jode open the sliding, transparent panel separating the driver's section from the rear of the ambulance and Jode burrowed like a mole into the rear of the conveyance, shouting out new discoveries as he went. He helped Shelby in and prepared to help Ralda. But Mrs. Quistlethorp said, "No. Thanks anyway. But I'm not going. I only came out to give you my best thoughts and hopes that you will always remain free of error."

She kissed the baby, lingering over Kira a moment. Then she told them again what she had said on their arrival: "Nothing can hurt the children of love."

"But you *must* come with us," Shelby objected. "Luke's a Doctor with an emergency case, but *you* can't be found here when the Subcutes come."

"Of course I can. I live here. There's no evidence now, with you all gone—and as soon as I do a bit of putting to rights in the parlor—that there was any meeting here tonight. And if they insist on taking me in, fools that they are, then I shall simply confront them with my faith and pray for them."

Larch and Shelby put on the white jackets quickly, and Larch passed the peacefully sleeping Kira back to Jode for safekeeping during the beginning of the journey.

As Larch started the powerful motor, there was Luke, still shouting directions at them from his place under the window, where he was now in the process of tenderly maneuvering the broken body of Jeff Rawter onto a shutter he had just ripped from Ralda's house. (*One of the phony shutters,* Larch thought. *Fancy their being functional after all!*)

"What did you say, Luke?" Shelby called back.

"I said: Don't forget to turn on the red flashers and the siren and keep them on all the way. Good-health! And good luck in England."

Free Flight

The ambulance screamed down the hill. At the foot of the twisting drive, a caducean car full of Medcops was just nosing across the right-of-way to form a roadblock.

Instantly, the Medcop vehicle was thrown into reverse, its rear tires jamming into a steep ditch at the roadside. As the ambulance whooshed past, Larch glimpsed a respectful half-salute from the Medcop driver. A narrow miss, but it brought a flood of confidence.

Real speed was impossible, of course, as long as the road remained tortuous. Every curve was approached with the certainty that on its blind side might lie trouble. Larch and Shelby scanned the blackness on both sides of the tunnel of light made by the headlamps, but saw nothing until just before they reached the highway.

Then a familiar figure loomed up in the lights to the left, walking along the shoulder of the road, not hurrying.

Larch braked to a full stop. "Get in. Quick. Keep your head down under the dashboard till we can get you into the back, with the others."

Strong Bayet waved the ambulance off. "Thanks but no thanks. I'll walk home. Angie will be wondering where I've been."

"You fool! We're not offering to take you home. Come with us. You're in danger of being picked up any minute."

Strong shrugged. "If they get me on the way, which they may, they'll only put me in the Age Adjustment Center, where maybe I belong anyhow."

"But you're one of *us* now."

Bayet grinned. "Never said I wasn't. Haven't you heard of sabotage? Infiltration from within? I'll go right on talking and converting and spreading unrest right up to the minute they stick in the needles. I'm too old to start a whole new life as a fugitive. Now you get out of here before I change my mind."

Shelby said, "We'll be thinking of you often, Strong. And when I say, 'goodhealth' I really mean it."

Gallantly, Bayet tipped a nonexistent hat. "Same to you, ma'am. And listen, Rosst, I take back what I said about the Abs being an abscess on the body politic."

Finally the turn onto the highway appeared. The ambulance took it with a squeal of tires and they were headed north, toward the city, traveling the ocean front. The moon had not yet risen, but they were strongly aware, even above the noise of the siren, of the waves rushing against the rocks to the left.

Jode rapped on the panel enclosing the rear of the ambulance and Shelby turned on the intercom. "Can we stop being Patients now? I want to come into the front and be a crew member."

"Is Kira crying?"

"No, still sleeping."

"Then maybe you could both wait till we get through town. Someone may look at us in the city. We don't want to take any chances. Maybe you could rest a while?"

"Rest? Who could rest with all the noise we're making?"

"Don't complain, Jode," Shelby said. "We're very lucky so far, to be riding instead of walking."

"Yeah," Jode agreed. "This sure beats hiking through the woods in the dark and bumping into trees."

"We'll let you know," she promised, "as soon as it's safe for you to come out."

Shelby turned to Larch. "If driving gives your knee too much strain, we could switch off and I'll drive through the city."

"I know it sounds crazy, Shel, but until you brought it up just now, I'd forgotten all about the knee injury."

"You mean it doesn't hurt at all?"

"My shoulders still ache, from walking with the crutches that the Mercifuls so obligingly took away. But there's no pain at all in the leg. I don't mind the driving."

"We'd better give Sublett credit. She must be a good physician at least."

"That I never doubted. Are *you* feeling okay?"

"It's odd, but I'm not even tired any more. The only thing I have to complain of is that this jacket is a terrible fit in the shoulders. Too big. I'm just hoping we won't have to convince anyone I'm an ambulance crew member."

"Perhaps you'll never again have to pretend to be anything you're not. Once we get on the plane to London, that is."

They followed the coast road until it was possible to cut inland onto an old but reasonably well maintained freeway. It was straight and monotonous, but better for speed. By now the ululation of the siren had become an accustomed noise to them, almost subliminal. They discussed whether they should turn it off going into town, where it might possibly be noticed that they would be neither coming from nor going toward the huge Facility that served the area (the one Jode had been rescued from), but had not yet made up their minds when they found themselves on the ramp that emptied traffic into one of the inhabited "pockets," or business centers of the city.

This routing was one of the expediencies imposed by the Iatrarchy upon a freeway system built a century before to move vehicles with great speed from one vast metropolitan center through many others with no need for slowing or stopping. This kind of thing was no longer considered desirable, for it would enable Patients to move vast distances with no interim checking to insure that someone with a not-yet-detected infectious condition, for instance, would not travel hundreds and

254

hundreds of kilometers and come to rest in a not-yet-infected part of the country, thereby spreading havoc.

Instead, at regular intervals, traffic was funneled past highway medcheck stations not unlike the old agriculture inspection stations, or border customs stops of a past era. For convenience, these were located in populous areas of the cities, or what had once been cities.

For with sixty percent of the urban population expunged, it had also become necessary to regroup the remaining urban dwellers in colonies spotted among the yawning, dead, vacant ruins of the no-longer-used parts of the metropolises.

The very fact that these "ruins" were not ruins in the true sense lent a special horror to their existence. Anyone who had driven about a city, past row upon row of abandoned, deteriorating living quarters once occupied, now no longer necessary, felt this horror keenly.

Time and again in the Ama sessions, it had been proposed that it would be better for morale if all the city houses no longer occupied or occupiable were destroyed and the space developed as green park land. There had been general agreement about this, but a serious lack of sufficient labor force to accomplish it.

The alternative arrangement of urban living was the island system, in which clusters of city residents accumulated around the necessary sources of goods and services. A city the size of the one the ambulance was now entering, for instance, would have as many as two hundred inhabited and functioning small centers of activity, with stores, gas stations, schools and medcheck points, these widely scattered over several hundred square kilometers of bleak and shabby ghost quarters. It amounted to a growth of villages in a wilderness. There were even Patients who had been born, grown to maturity and assigned a job in a single center and never left it. Never had any reason for leaving, never wanted to give up the security of being comfortably near reliable medical services in case something went wrong.

For the rumor had persisted—and even been augmented occasionally by the Iatrarchy—that it was still possible to encounter lingering spores of bacteria in the outlying sections. There was no truth to this, but it had been helpful in control of population distribution.

The deserted buildings had thus remained free of roving bands of brigands, black marketeers and other outlaws who might have set up business in them in other circumstances. Though Abs, acting both singly and as members of the underground, had hidden out there occasionally, only the Mercifuls regularly inhabited the uninhabitable sections; they were said to exist practically invisibly, deprived of all electricity and other services, using the abandoned houses as a base from which to make forays into the inhabited sections occasionally in performance of their "duty."

Shelby and Larch could now see the elongated and brilliantly lit medcheck station with its conveyor belt to one side. The few approaching cars were channeled onto the conveyor while their occupants got out with charts at the ready, to pass through the station with its battery of medical information-gathering devices. Those with papers in order who were running no fevers or generating no suspicions were allowed to rejoin their vehicles at the far end.

On the opposite side of the station was a lane marked, "Emergency Vehicles and Doctors." Larch took it and sped through. The checking nurse, whose white-capped head was plainly visible through the transparent walls of the station, did not even look up at the ambulance.

They were now in the business part of the first inhabited sector, where the atmosphere seemed much the same as in any near-midnight city of the previous century. Except that activity was minimal; no bars or nightclubs offered their entertainments. And an eleven o'clock curfew pared down the number of pedestrians to those few with special passes for late visits to friends or commutation to or from night jobs.

Street lighting in these island communities was excellent, rendering the broad streets as bright as they were at noon. The occasional Medcop patrol car purring quietly through seemed superfluous, for no irregularity ever occurred.

The ambulance screamed its way onward toward the perimeter, where light ended and darkness began. Here the city was in total blackness except for the hesitantly rising moon. Some of the blank-faced, silent town houses and apartments they passed were in perfect condition, suggesting there might even be sleeping inhabitants inside, due to emerge at first light to collect newspapers and milk deliveries left on doorsteps.

The truth, of course, was otherwise. Those who had once lived here, more than half a century ago, had either been victims of the *serratia marsencens*, or had long since fled as survivors, seeking as-

257

sistance and comfort among numbers, drifting into the newly formed centers.

The ambulance entered and left three more inhabited areas before finally connecting with the quickest route back to the freeway. Here there was another medcheck station, but they circumvented it in the same way as before.

Back on the freeway there was some night traffic, only a fraction of what might have been found in the same place a hundred years earlier, but some. And cruising among it was, now and then, a Medcop car with the lighted and perversely writhing caduceus. But with no indication that such cars were doing any heavier duty than traffic control.

Jode no longer rapped on the transparent divider when he wanted to speak to them. He had by now discovered how to activate the intercom from the other side. "Only trouble with the freeway," he said, "is that there aren't any more red lights. I sure like being able to zoom right through red lights."

"Jode, *please* try to rest. We've still a long way to go," Shelby exhorted.

"Can't rest. I keep thinking how great it is to get away from all that mess, not just the cops and the cutes, but everybody."

"I don't want to spoil your fun," Larch said, "but the fact is, we're not really 'getting away' from everybody. Or at least that's not the interpretation your sister and I put on it. In case we do get clear of this continent, we're going to go on working for the Abs just as hard as ever, even harder. Until 'all that mess' is cleared up, there'll be no real rest for people like us."

"And there are still a lot of loose ends it'll take us a long time to see tied up," Shelby mused. "For instance, I'm not at all sure what Jeff Rawter's motive was in turning traitor, informing on us."

"Power in the new government?" Larch guessed. "A slice of the pie when they get around to dividing it? If he had brought in a bunch of Abs the size of that meeting attendance, he could probably have written the specifications for whatever job he wanted."

"But Jeff seemed to be definite about Mosk being his man. With Mosk and all those others dead, what if the CGPs win?"

"Jeff might have had that figured out too. Anyone with scruples that weak might sell out to whichever team went to bat. Despite Sublett's ravings about the CGPs letting nobody play but themselves, the idea is unrealistic. There just aren't that many CGPs in the country. They'll have to let their select henchmen into certain top slots. Why not Jeff?"

"He sure did rescue us from those Mercifuls," Jode reminded them.

"If I explain to you why I think he did that, will you lie down as your sister suggests and pretend to be an unconscious ambulance patient?" Larch bargained.

"Okay. But it doesn't make sense, going to all the trouble to find us, and then turning us in to the cutes."

"It makes sense to him and to people like him. If Jeff wanted to impress the new government with bringing in a lot of Abs, then his track record would look that much better if three of them were the notorious political subversives wanted for treatment over a number of years because of their many crimes."

259

"What notorious subversives?"

"He means us, Jode," Shelby said.

"Oh. Are we notorious?"

"Jode, you promised Larch that if he explained—"

"Okay. How long do Kira and I have to keep on pretending to be ambulance patients? We really want to ride up front."

"About twenty minutes more," Larch said, "and we'll be on another long, straight, dull stretch of freeway where I believe we won't attract any attention. But you'll have to promise to duck you head if we meet any other traffic."

"Sure thing." Obediently, Jode turned off the intercom. Then he turned it on again and said, "Don't forget to call me when it's time."

They rode for a few kilometers in silence. The traffic was even thinner now.

Finally Shelby said, "I do hope Jeff will be all right. He looked so bad—all that blood, and the odd way he was lying."

"Lots of the blood probably came from surface lacerations when he struck the glass. As for the rest, we certainly left him in good hands. And he's too good a gastro-enterologist for them to thanatize for a couple of compound fractures. Luke isn't a Merciful, after all. What's more disturbing to me than his physical condition is the mental one that made him think he had to escape us when he was exposed. Did he really imagine we were going to hang him to one of the gum trees?"

"Another of his misconceptions, I suppose. He probably never did really trust us. As a Doctor, he probably never stopped believing the official cant that an Abnormal truly is abnormal."

"Attending all our meetings over the past several years wouldn't have done a thing to convince him otherwise," Larch said. "The one we just left, for instance, was the biggest gathering of nuts in central California since almond harvest. Admit it."

"Of course I admit it," Shelby told him. "Revolution is nearly always the same in the beginning. Nuts and oddballs and people with bolts a little loose get together and find out that none of them like the way things are. Dress them up in short haircuts and tall hats and they're Lollards or Levellers. Put them in kneebreeches and they're Sons of Liberty on one side of the ocean, believers in the Rights of Man on the other. Seventy-five years after that they've become Narodniks, city intellectuals convinced that salvation comes from the land and the grimy peasants who till it. We are no different, Larch, nor do we want to be."

"No, and my comment about the nuts was spoken in awe, not derision. I'm only sorry we broke contact with Jode before the history lesson. But you'll give many more. You'll be teaching in England, and lecturing, furthering the cause. And when we come back—"

"Do you think we ever can come back? Physically, in our lifetimes, I mean. Judging by that meeting, we're no further toward a real revolution than we ever were, no matter who ends up in the Surgeon General's office."

"On the contrary, Shel, the meeting at Ralda's showed we're further along than even the most realistic of us suspect. Think about the new members. Not so much Strong, who's been a fellow-traveler all along. Not so much Joan the nurse. Nurses have come to us before, and it's never a surprise. They're in a position to see the worst, forced to assist at all sorts of heinousness without any power to prevent it. But Tom Danns is an ordinary Patient, a very ordinary guy, with no pretensions, and no frustrations but the most grinding frustration of all: he just wants to live his own life and he's been suddenly confronted with the news that he's not going to be allowed to do it. By no stretch of the imagination can he be classified as a dingbat, a religious fanatic, a food freak, a non-medical medico, or anything else of the sort. How often has *that* happened in the past, that the movement just out of the blue attracted a totally ordinary citizen?"

"Exactly," Shelby argued. "How often does it happen? One swallow doesn't make a drunkard, as they used to say in the days when ordinary people had the option of becoming drunk if they had a mind to. But I do hope you're right and Tom's appearance means the dike's a lot nearer giving way than we've thought."

Entering another metropolitan pocket, the ambulance sailed past the guarding medcheck station using the same method as before.

"How long can we keep doing this?" Shelby wondered.

"Until Luke has to report the ambulance stolen, I suppose," Larch said. "He must have it checked out from the Facility overnight, and if he doesn't have to report it till morning, it'll give us plenty of time. This is the last stretch of city we have to travel anyway, till we get to the airport."

This time there were more lighted centers to pass through, linked by far larger areas of ghostly nonhabitations. In one of the latter sectors the head-

262

lights picked out a shadowy running figure traveling in the same direction as the ambulance. In the lights the figure speeded his already frantic pace for a moment, then disappeared into a dark doorway.

"A Merciful," Shelby decided.

The figure was the only sign of life they were to see in all the lifeless city blocks they passed through.

When they rejoined the freeway this time, Larch said, "A few more kilometers and we'll be on the loneliest stretch of road between here and our destination. I suggest we stop for a moment, let our other passengers up front, and jettison our obsolete medcharts before we have to go through the med-check at the airport."

"I'd forgotten about those," Shelby said. "And we don't have any to replace them. It's going to be awkward. We'll have to muddle through somehow with the passports alone. I wish Jeff hadn't let us down."

"And I wish that not producing the new charts was the *only* way Jeff had let us down. However, he did save our lives and that goes a long way toward smoothing things over."

Larch cut the red light and the siren, and pulled from the right lane into the emergency parking zone of the freeway. They would take a chance now that none of the few other vehicles sharing the free-way at this hour would be official.

Beyond the road, illumined in detail by the moon now, was a vista of gently rolling land covered with the yellow, dry meadow grass typical of California in midsummer, and studded at wide intervals with live oaks. Though this land might once have been a ranch, no houses were visible.

Jode, now much more confident in his handling of Kira, passed the bundled baby carefully out to Shelby and they all got out of the ambulance and walked several paces into the dry earth of the unfenced land.

"We could have tossed these documents out the window and been fairly certain no one would ever find them," Larch said. "But if we bury them here a few centimeters down, we'll be very certain."

Shelby turned over the medchart which recorded the statistics and personal history of Landra Mackin, and Larch produced the charts giving the same information for Fred Koyne and Jimmy Archer. He dug industriously for a moment with his pocketknife, placed them in the earth, and covered them.

"Ought to hold a funeral, like in historical times," Jode said.

"We're certainly burying three people whose identities served us well," Larch said. "But we may be pushing our luck again. Even when it's making no noise this ambulance could attract a lot of attention parked out here. Let's get back in and be on our way."

They were about to take their places again when Jode, who was dragging behind, called, "Wait! I think I hear something."

"What does it sound like?" Shelby asked.

"A whimpering. There's something crying right close to us. In those weeds, it sounds like."

"I don't hear anything. Don't delay us, Jody. We don't want any trouble now."

But Jode had already dived into the weeds.

"Be careful! Whatever it is might be—"

Then Shelby and Larch both stared at what Jode held in his arms.

"Put it down, Jode," Shelby said. "Don't even ask if you can bring it along. We have enough problems as it is."

"But it's a *puppy*," Jode said, awestruck. "And it's lost. Couldn't we——"

"No!"

"Something's wrong with it," Larch said, taking the limp animal from Jode. "It looks weak. Lack of food, I suppose. It's starving. Dogs are still too rare to think someone abandoned it. Probably it fell out of a car window or off a truck and wasn't noticed."

"Larch," Shelby warned, "you can't let him begin hoping to bring that animal along. We'll find some scrap for it to eat in the backpacks and then we'll have to leave it here and hope someone else will come along and——"

"It'll *die*," Jode cried. "No one will find it."

This did indeed seem likely. Even in the moonlight it was obvious that the black and white pup was undernourished and neglected. It whined pleadingly and wagged a limp tail. Larch passed it back to Jode. It seemed to be almost too young to have been weaned. It nuzzled weakly into Jode's palm, snuffling hopefully.

Shelby sighed. "What do you think we should do, Larch?"

"What are the regulations about dogs? Licensing, shots, that kind of thing?"

"I'm under the impression," Shelby said thoughtfully, "that there are too few pets nowadays to require a set of regulations. At least I've never heard of any. But that doesn't change the picture for us. We just can't risk the extra jeopardy."

265

"After I feed him, I'll put Luke in my backpack," Jode promised. "He'll just sleep a lot, like Kira, because he's a baby too. You won't hear a word out of him."

"Luke?" inquired Shelby.

"I'm naming him after Doc Algis. He was pretty good to us, letting us stay at his cabin, and warning us to get out of that meeting before the Subcutes came. Lent us this ambulance, too."

Larch exchanged a glance with Shelby and then said, "All right. *E*verybody in. This bus is taking off again immediately."

At the freeway turnoff to International Airport, a few kilometers short of the medcheck station leading into West Metropolis, they decided to do without the flashers and siren. In the sudden shock of silence the ambulance moved sedately down a long ramp, through a turnstile into a parking lot, and came to a halt.

Only a scattered few other cars were in the lot. In the terminal very few passengers waited.

Air travel under the Iatrarchy was coming back into its own, however. For years Patients were such xenophobes that no tourist business could exist, but the picture was gradually changing. Doctors set the example by traveling extensively, and gradually, cautiously, Patients had begun to move around the continent occasionally, accommodated by the Iatrarchy's single airline, National Med. At this predawn hour, however, with only the single flight to London scheduled, the huge terminal (built in pre-war times) was virtually deserted.

The most striking feature of the large interior

was, unsurprisingly, the brightly lighted medcheck station, which occupied a central spot.

No Patient was permitted to buy a ticket, check luggage, or board a plane before passing before the keen eye and alert instruments of the checking nurse. Or, as in this case, a pair of checking nurses, both of whom looked equally bored as the travelers approached, Larch moving slowly but without a limp.

The difficulty they had anticipated was now upon them, how to get through without charts. The passports, kept so carefully through all their adventures, were brought out by Shelby. They were in the name of Tolliver, Mr. and Mrs., traveling with their son Rufus, ten. The last thing Shelby had done before leaving the ambulance was to wind up her hair and arrange it in a heavy, dark bun on top of her head, the better to meet the requirement of Lillias Tolliver's age, which was thirty.

It was in their favor that they had arrived a scant thirty minutes before take-off, when checking officials would presumably be in a frame of mind to pass travelers through in a rush. And also in their favor that their citizenship had been thoughtfully—very thoughtfully—registered as "British."

Tourists returning to their English homeland from the American Iatrarchy were few (since so few came to visit in the first place), and could expect less pressure to be exerted upon them for conformity, since England had no ties with the World Medarchy. It couldn't matter less to the Iatrarchy if these visitors went home laden with cold germs, tubercle bacilli, staph infections and venereal disease, so long as they spread these maladies *there* and not *here*. Serve the British right for being so standoffish.

Of course this was all highly unofficial; no one, least of all a checking nurse, would admit to such a position. And there was still the consideration of National Medical disallowing any ill passengers on its planes on the chance they might endanger others.

Only one fellow passenger was in line ahead of them, a plump man whose electrocardiogram had evidently proved suspicious; he was being prepared for a rerun by one of the checking nurses.

The other nurse, attractively slender and prematurely gray, turned to the newcomers. "Goodhealth. I must see your medcharts. And hurry. You certainly haven't allowed yourselves—or me—much time. The morning plane leaves in eighteen minutes."

Shelby handed the baby to Larch and began rummaging frantically through her pack. "Medcharts. Medcharts. Oh, drat! I know I have them here somewhere. George, you saw me pack them, didn't you?"

Larch cleared his throat. "I'm not sure I did, my dear. Last time I saw them they were lying on the mantelpiece in the hostel."

"Oh, bother. Do you suppose I forgot to pick them up when we left?"

"I see you found your passports at least," the nurse said sourly. "Let me check those first, then, while you find the charts."

Shelby turned over the passports, which she had been holding in her teeth to free both hands for the search.

"Mmm," the nurse said. "British, are you?" She looked carefully at Shelby, Larch, and Jode in turn to assure herself that the pictures on the documents matched the faces before her. "And you have a baby, I see, Mrs. Tolliver, which isn't listed on your passport."

"Born on our three-week holiday here," Shelby mumbled, still bent over the bag, going on with the to-be-fruitless search. "She's listed on those charts if I can just put my hands on them. They said she wouldn't need a chart of her own since we were traveling home so soon."

"Really? Who told you that?"

"The Doctors at the Facility. Where she was born."

The nurse now began to look very impatient.

"Listen, miss," Larch suggested, "since we're running so short of time, do you suppose you could begin giving my son his medical check while my wife finds the documents? I assure you we're all perfectly healthy."

"Well, it's irregular, but maybe—"

"I'm afraid we just don't have them," Shelby wailed. "You see, we're not used to this sort of thing at home and—"

"How did you people get through the last med-check station that stopped you?"

"Oh, that was at Yosemite Park last evening, when we came in from hiking," Larch explained. "This morning we took the hopper taxi directly from the park to the airport."

The checking nurse looked them over again severely. "You are *required* by law to carry those charts on your person at all times," she scolded them. "You can get into serious trouble if you lose, or falsify or otherwise abuse medcharts. Of course, I understand that you're not American Patients. And you do want to leave the country . . ."

269

"Couldn't you just let us go? Our passports are in order," Shelby pleaded.

"Absolutely not. I'll at least have to examine you first. All of you." Her glance included Kira. "Well, each of you go into a cubicle and let's get it over with. If you miss that plane there'll just be more trouble issuing new temporary charts for visitors and I can't see what purpose that would serve."

Shelby and Larch exchanged a look of relief. It looked as if they were going to be processed.

"I shall have to call my superior," the checking nurse was saying ten minutes later. "Such a thing has never happened before in all my time at the station and I don't believe we have any regulations to cover it."

"But you found nothing wrong with any of us," Larch pointed out.

"That has nothing to do with it. This boy has an *animal* in his luggage. You people have already caused enough trouble—"

"All passengers on the flight for London will take their places," came a crisp voice over the speaker system.

"Could you at least let my husband buy our tickets while this is being straightened out?" Shelby said reasonably.

"No! Yes. I'm not sure about the rules in this case. That's why I have to talk to the supervisor. Oh, all right, get the tickets. But that doesn't mean you won't be held over for the next flight tomorrow morning."

Shelby exchanged a new distress signal with Larch. A holdover would bring real disaster. By that time the ambulance would have been searched

270

for, and undoubtedly discovered in the parking lot at International Airport.

As Larch hurried away to the ticket window, Jode spoke to the second checking nurse—the gray-haired one was now speaking on an intercom about their problem. "Couldn't you just check Luke over too? And if he doesn't have any germs let him go?"

"You mean the—the—*dog?*" The second nurse shuddered. "Certainly not."

The first nurse returned to her post at the same moment Larch hurried back with the tickets. He was now limping slightly but this passed unnoticed in the excitement over the dog.

Very angrily, their sentence was pronounced by the gray-haired nurse: "It's just as I feared. There is absolutely no regulation on the books that deals with transportng an animal on a public carrier since no Patient in the history of the present government has ever tried to do this before. So a special emergency regulation has had to be made up." She paused threateningly. Everyone waited expectantly, including a pair of uniformed clerks from the airlines and a maintenance worker who had wandered over with his electric dustmop. Luke, being held in Jode's arms, whimpered a little and licked Jode's hand. Kira woke and began to cry loudly.

"You will have to do one of two things: either leave the animal here where it will be disposed of at government expense, or take your places on the plane but in the quarantine section from which you will *not be released* until you reach your destination."

"Hoo-ray!" Jode yelled.

"At least they forgot all about the missing

charts," Shelby said as they hurried up the ramp into the plane.

"And they didn't get around to checking into anyone's luggage but Jode's," Larch said. "I had no idea Luke would bring us such good luck. Very shrewd of Jode to have found him."

Transoceanic passenger planes in 2055 were only about half the size of their huge counterparts of a century earlier. Even so, the one boarded by the fugitives was less than half occupied on the early-morning London run.

Cozily ensconced in the self-contained, transparent compartment at the rear of the plane, the fugitives could observe their fellow passengers but were not allowed to communicate with them. They could not have asked for a better arrangement than the quarantine section, provided by National Medical for just such exigencies as they had presented (but more often reserved for some infectious Patient who had to be shipped from one part of the continent to another for special medical attention).

Safe from prying questions, they looked out upon a small group clearly recognizable as Doctors, almost without exception. Doctors on their way to meetings of the Medarchy in Eurasia or Africa, or to consultations in Johannesburg or Cairo. They would deplane in London only to embark for these other locations.

Expensive tailoring, black attache cases or small black bags that were still a medical hallmark, pipes filled with special mixtures of the tobacco that was no longer available to Patients out of fear they would use it immoderately (as indeed they might,

272

and had in the past). And in the case of the women, cheroots or snuff.

Many of them, inevitably, knew one another and after the craft was in the air crossed and recrossed the aisles for greetings, exchange of information, small talk, jibes.

The party of ordinary Patients occupying the quarantine section elicited only brief attention as the story of why they were there was retailed. Then no on even glanced their direction any more.

They were, for all practical purposes, free.

For a long while, Shelby and Larch sat holding hands, not speaking. Jode curled with Luke on the seat opposite and actually began to catnap with no urging from his sister.

Then Larch said, "The first thing we'll do when we get there is find a vicar and get married."

She smiled and corrected him. "The *second* thing to do is find the vicar. The first thing we'll all do, including Luke, is see a good doctor."

"You may be right," said Larch.

The plane sped onward, into the dawn.

THE MANITOU

"Like some mind-gripping drug, it has the uncanny ability to seize you and hold you firmly in its clutches from the moment you begin until you drop the book from your trembling fingers after you have finally finished the last page."

—Bernhardt J. Hurwood

Misquamacus—An American Indian sorcerer. In the seventeenth century he had sworn to wreak a violent vengeance upon the callous, conquering White Man. This was just before he died, over four hundred years ago. Now he has found an abominable way to return, the perfect birth for his revenge.

Karen Tandy—A slim, delicate, auburn-haired girl with an impish face. She has a troublesome tumor on the back of her neck, a tumor that no doctor in New York City can explain. It seems to be moving, growing, developing—almost as if it were alive! She is the victim of

THE MANITOU
GRAHAM MASTERTON

A Pinnacle Book
P982 $1.75

If you can't find this book at your local bookstore, simply send the cover price, plus 25¢ for postage and handling to:

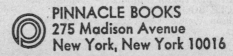

PINNACLE BOOKS
275 Madison Avenue
New York, New York 10016

A Question of Balance—
perhaps the most important question the United States will ever answer—perhaps the last.

?

Conflict between Russia and China is inevitable—
What does the United States do when *both* sides come for help?
This is

THE CHINESE ULTIMATUM

P974 $1.95

The year is 1977. Russia and China have assembled troops on the Mongolian border, and are fighting a "limited" war. A reunited Germany and a bellicose Japanese military state have joined the battle. The United States must step in, or be considered the enemies of both. The Chinese have said their last word on the subject—what will ours be?

"Absolutely gripping, I couldn't put it down."
—Rowland Evans, syndicated political columnist
"This novel is too incredibly real . . . and damnably possible!"
—an anonymous State Department official